Per

Philippa Gregory, w
history degree from
PhD in eighteent
University of Edinburgh. She is a fellow of Kingston
University. Philippa Gregory lives in Sussex with her
family.

PHILIPPA GREGORY

PERFECTLY CORRECT

HarperCollins*Publishers*

HarperCollins*Publishers*
77–85 Fulham Palace Road,
Hammersmith, London W6 8JB

This paperback edition 1997

1 3 5 7 9 8 6 4 2

First published in Great Britain by
HarperCollins*Publishers* 1996

Copyright © Philippa Gregory Ltd 1996

The Author asserts the moral right to
be identified as the author of this work

ISBN 0 00 649642 3

Set in Aldus

Printed and bound in Great Britain by
Caledonian International Book Manufacturing Ltd, Glasgow

This story is dedicated
to those of us who try to be correct
and fail to be perfect.

Wednesday

LOUISE CASE GLANCED UP from the screen of her word processor to her window, and beyond, to where the cameo-pink blossom of the apple orchard should have been visible, lilting in the wind. It was a familiar sight, which she had enjoyed many times this spring while working at her desk. She blinked. Her view of the apple blossom and the green hills beyond was completely obscured by the roof of a big blue van. A shiny steel chimney poked rakishly from one side, there were three long rusting scratches along the roof. Louise stared at it in incomprehension for long moments. Then, not taking her eyes from it, she reached out her hand to the telephone and dialled a number.

'Toby Summers please, Sociology department,' she said.

The big blue roof rocked slightly. For an instant she thought hopefully that the van might be about to move, to disappear as suddenly as it had arrived. But it was someone moving inside that made it rock. It remained, obstinately present, in her orchard, blocking her view of her apple blossom.

Toby's extension rang. Louise rose to her feet and could see more of the van. There was a small door cut in the side, which stood open. There was a stand of two steps leading up to it, planted firmly in the grass where last autumn

Louise had hopefully scattered mixed meadow flower seed. A large mongrel dog was tied on a long piece of string to a bracket beside the door. The inside of the van was in shadow. Louise could see nothing of the owner.

'Toby Summers.'

'It's me.' Louise had the right of the long-term lover to have her voice recognised at once.

'Hello,' Toby said.

'I've got the most extraordinary thing in my orchard. A big blue van. It must have just arrived. I was working in my study and I looked up and there it was.'

Toby chuckled. Since Louise's impulsive move to the country there had been a number of small crises. Toby preferred to take them as lightly as possible. If Louise was ever in real need both Toby and his wife Miriam would exercise their considerable powers to help her. But they had agreed that the move to the country was so eccentric – so unlike Louise, who had lived in Brighton since her first year at university, through MA and then PhD – that problems were inevitable.

'Very appropriate,' he said. 'Were you working on your Lawrence essay?'

Louise glanced at the screen, blank save for the heading 'D.H. Lawrence: *The Virgin and the Gypsy*'. 'Yes.'

'And now you have your very own gypsy to research,' Toby said, smiling. The graduate student in his room rose and moved towards the door. Toby shook his head and waved her back into her seat. His affair with Louise had been conducted so discreetly for so many years that it had attained the status of respectability.

'What should I do?' Louise asked. 'Someone can't just park in the middle of my orchard. It's private property. He's trespassing.'

Toby considered. 'Why don't you stroll out and ask him politely what he thinks he's doing? Maybe he's just pulled off the road for lunch.'

'He can't have lunch in my orchard!' Louise protested. She realised she sounded peevish and she lightened her tone to match Toby's detached urbanity. 'He *looks* rather settled. There's a dog tied up by the door, and he's put some steps out.'

'Ask him anyway,' Toby suggested. 'It's not as if you're an enclosing squire of the manor. Maybe he's looking for somewhere to stay. He could legally camp on the common, couldn't he? It's common land, isn't it?'

'I don't know. I suppose so. But not in my orchard.'

'Well, have a chat with him first, and then call me back. I'm here till three.'

'Is someone with you?'

Toby smiled again at the student who had turned in her chair and was ostentatiously examining the books in the bookcase behind her. 'Yes.'

Louise experienced a swift, illogical pang that someone else should be in Toby's intimate little office. She knew it was not jealousy. She and Toby had deliberately forged a completely open relationship, too mature to include archaic emotions such as jealousy. Over the nine years of their love affair he had started and ended other affairs, and so had she. They had made an agreement years ago that their relationship should be free from grasping possessiveness. Louise had watched his love for his wife, Miriam, evolve and change. She had seen him intrigued, passionately involved, and then bored by other women. She herself had experimented, rather callously, with other men. But no-one, it seemed, could quite take the place of Toby, and when he said there was a student in his room with him she felt a

3

strange breath pass through her nose to her chest, like a faint whiff of smelling salts, of sulphur.

'I'll make a survey from the upstairs window,' she said, making an amusing expedition of it. 'And then I'll just go down the garden and chat over the fence. After all, it *is* my orchard.'

'You *are* an enclosing squire of the manor.' Toby's telephone voice was warm and intimate. Louise felt stroked, desirable. The student, who feared Toby's intellect and disliked the aura of male sexuality which he deliberately radiated, slumped in her chair and pushed her glasses up her short nose. 'Talk to you later,' Toby promised and rang off.

Louise put down the phone and glanced again at the blank screen. The essay would not be started until she had resolved the issue of her own gypsy. She went out of her study and through the sitting room, up the little staircase and into her bedroom which looked out over Wistley Common.

The van was even bigger and bluer when viewed from above. It had entered the orchard through a break in the fence which had been made in the winter by Mr Miles skidding in his Land-Rover. He had promised faithfully to mend it and Louise – a newcomer in the village, and dependent on Mr Miles to clear the lane for her should the ice turn to snow – had not reminded him more than twice. His farm was further up the lane, his grazing land nibbled into the edges of the common. This cottage had belonged to his father, and was bought from him by Louise's aunt who had died and left it to Louise. Mr Miles regarded Louise's improvements to a cottage ready for demolition with an indulgent eye. He had been sorry to break her pretty new fence, and intended to mend it as soon as he had the time and could buy or borrow some fencing planks. But now,

4

the van had driven through the gap, down the grassy lane between the trees and parked, facing south to Wistley Common, with apple blossom petals showering gently around it and sticking, like damp confetti, to the battered blue roof.

The dog was lying by the steps, ears slack. Someone had placed a bowl of water beside it, and a small dustbin had silently appeared on the other side of the door. Louise watched for some minutes, but no-one came out of the van. If she wanted to see the gypsy she would have to go and tackle him direct.

She was not frightened. Years ago Louise and Miriam had attended women's defence classes, and assertiveness training. They had temporarily become women secure in their own worth, confident of their ability to deal with men and women. Since those easy undergraduate days Miriam had faced half a dozen violent men demanding to see their wives who were living in the refuge run by Miriam. Experience had taught Miriam that the hip-and-shoulder throw was of little use against a man twice her weight, fuelled with alcohol and anger, and with a knife in his pocket. But Louise's postgraduate life had been more select. She had never had to try the hip-and-throw technique on anyone more threatening than her instructor, and her confidence remained high. Besides, she would be on one side of her garden gate and the man would be on the other. If he were abusive she had only to walk half a dozen steps to the French windows in her study and pick up a telephone for the police and have him summarily evicted. She felt that it might be better as a police matter anyway. The man was trespassing, and would undoubtedly cause damage – breaking boughs and fouling the area. There would be litter and, if nothing worse, tyre marks in the grass. Louise had not owned a house before. She was rather fiercely proprietary about this one. Also, she believed that the countryside was an empty place, occupied only by small shy animals. That was how she liked it.

Still watching the window, she picked up the telephone by the bed and dialled Miriam's number at the women's refuge.

'Hello?' Miriam always sounded wary. For the past eight years she had been answering the telephone at the refuge and providing telephone counselling for the Rape Crisis Centre. It was very rare that she picked up the phone to hear pleasant news.

'It's me,' Louise said. 'I have the most extraordinary thing in my orchard.'

Miriam nodded at the woman sitting opposite her desk. She covered the mouthpiece with her hand. 'I'll just be a minute,' she said reassuringly. The woman in her early twenties looked resigned to waiting all day if need be. She did not respond to Miriam's smile.

'I have someone with me,' Miriam said suppressively.

'There's a van in my orchard. I think it must be a gypsy or a tinker or someone.'

'How did he get in?' Miriam's interest was sharpened at the first mention of a persecuted minority.

'Through the gap in my fence. It's still not mended. What should I do?'

'Is he doing any damage?'

'Apart from being parked where I planted my meadow flower mix and spoiling the view, no.'

Miriam held back a sigh. 'I don't think the view really matters, does it? Or the meadow flower mix?'

'Well, it *is* my orchard.'

'Then ask him to move on.'

'He can park anywhere on the common, or Mr Miles might let him rent a field.'

Miriam nodded, saying nothing.

'I'll suggest that to him.'

'Do,' Miriam agreed. 'Are you coming to the meeting tonight?'

Miriam and Louise worked on an ambitious adult education project with the aim of recruiting older, preferably abused, women into university degree courses.

'Yes. Seven o'clock, isn't it?'

'Yes. Come on to dinner. Toby's cooking.'

'Thanks,' Louise said. 'I will.'

She put down the phone, and went slowly down the stairs. She opened the French windows of her study and walked slowly down the garden towards the little gate which led into the orchard and from there to the common beyond. The garden was still very wild. It had been derelict when she had inherited the cottage. The little house had stood amid a sea of ferns. Heather and ling grew up to the very door, bracken made a waist-high jungle. The beloved flowers of cottage gardens, forget-me-nots, lupins, tall white iris, and blowsy tea roses sprawling into briars, extended from the cottage out into the common land until no-one could have said for certain where one began and the other ended.

In the long summer, while the builders worked slowly every week, laying a damp course, putting in drains, taking up floorboards and joyfully discovering dry rot, Toby and Louise had driven out at the weekend, with a picnic and a rug, and made love in the little wilderness which was her front garden. On those days Toby had laid his head in her lap and looked up at her face and sighed, 'This is perfect. I wish I could stay here forever,' which was a pleasingly

7

ambiguous way of telling his mistress that he preferred her to his wife, and also telling her that he would never act on this preference.

Louise's whole body, attuned to Toby over years of unequal loving, stirred at the thought of his happiness and, with the selective hearing of the long-term patient mistress, she heard his preference; but was deaf to his choice.

When the builders had finally finished in the autumn, Louise employed Mr Miles to enclose the whole plot, orchard, garden, house, with neat post-and-rail fencing which he put up, efficiently and cheaply, over four weeks, only to break it down one frosty night in the following winter when he drove home from the Holly Bush.

Louise reached her garden gate and paused. For a moment she thought of the Lawrence story which she was about to dissect in the most rigorous of terms.

The Virgin and the Gypsy was a story on the edge of pornography according to Louise's critical vision. It depicted an adolescent girl fascinated by a gypsy who was passing her home. There was a flood, and he galloped ahead of the rushing water (Louise was prepared to be very scathing about the libidinous image of both horse and flood waters) to save her. His solution was not to build a raft or bring a boat, but instead to mount the stairs to her bedroom and there deflower her until rescue arrived.

This was a deeply flawed story as far as Louise was concerned. It showed Lawrence's sentimentality for working people. It showed Lawrence's male fetish of virginity since the girl was young and innocent and the man older and sexually active. There was also the sexual double standard which was only to be expected from a man such as Lawrence. But it went further even than that. It gloried in the gypsy's mysterious maleness. Louise was prepared to be very sharp

with the notion of male mystery. It was generally acknowledged among her circle that it is female sexuality which is
the mystery. Male sexuality is all too transparent.

She was particularly tough on this little story, which she
intended to compare to the tremulous seducto-rape scenes
of so-called women's fiction because, while she had been
re-reading it last night with a pencil in her hand to make
sharp little deflating comments in the margin as if D.H.
Lawrence were one of her own, not very bright, students,
she had been surprised by the sudden rise of sexual desire.
Turning out the light, and sliding her hand down inside the
pyjamas which she was forced to wear for warmth in the
damp cottage, she found herself unexpectedly thinking of
Mr Miles crashing his Land-Rover through her fence and
how it would have been if he had been drunk with desire
and not with Theakston's Old Peculier. As she wriggled in
her bed in the dark room she found her unreliable imagination conjuring an image of herself as the girl, with the gypsy
galloping on his horse, with his awesome male potency, to
her alone.

That was why she was so particularly angry with D.H.
Lawrence in the morning. He had played, she thought, the
oldest cheapest trick of all – recycling outworn sexual clichés
which long years of consciousness training have not yet
wholly eliminated from the female erotic imagination. All
very well to say that women are fighting two thousand years
of patriarchal pornographic imagery and that they will make
their own fantasies anew when their imaginations are freed.
All very well to *say* that in meetings – a different matter
altogether at night when the smells of early summer wafted
through the bedroom window and the owls called passionately under flaming ochre stars, and Louise's wilful unreconstructed desires conjured the image of a man who would

9

push her roughly on the bed and take her urgently and breathlessly without a word being exchanged.

Louise hesitated at the garden gate. It was as if her fantasy had been made manifest, summoned by desire out of the dark scented night. What if a dark head brushed the top of the door frame, and warm brown eyes met hers? What if the gypsy himself had come for her; and nothing in her life – not her long sophisticated love-affair with Toby, not her pedantic work, not her affiliation to the Women's Movement – would ever be the same again?

For a moment she thought she would go back into the house, draw the curtains in all the windows that faced out over the common land tinged with early summer green, and wait for the gypsy to eat his lunch, and reverse – out of her orchard, through the break in the fence, into the lane and away. When she lingered at the gate, it was a succumbing to temptation akin to switching off the light and dropping the pencil on the floor. She was tempted to know who he was, this man who had driven without invitation into her orchard, into her morning, after her night filled with dreams of desire.

The van's interior was deep in gloomy darkness. 'Hello?' she called.

The mongrel dog lifted his pointy head and uttered one sharp bark and then wagged his tail as if to apologise for the noise. He sat up and vigorously shook his floppy ears. Nothing else moved.

'Hello?' Louise called again.

The dog and Louise regarded each other, unmoving. Louise was nervous of all animals. At Mr Miles's farm she shrank from the size and blundering folly of cows. She even feared sheep with their mad yellow eyes. This dog seemed particularly placid, but Louise dared not open the gate and approach him. The string tied to his collar was dangerously thin; it would snap if he lunged for her.

'Hello?' she called again.

The van rocked slightly as someone moved inside. Louise found that her breathing was shallow as if she were afraid or excited. 'Hel-lo-o!' she called. Whoever he was, he had heard her. Whoever he was, he was coming to the little door.

'Hello yourself,' came a sharp voice. 'Is it me you're wanting with your hello? hello? hello?'

'Yes.'

'Well, come in then.'

Louise hesitated. There was the garden gate, and the dog, and the dark mysterious interior of the van. 'I just wanted to know if you planned to stay here,' she said feebly, her voice high.

'I've got my steps down, haven't I?'

'It's my orchard,' Louise pointed out.

The van shook again as if with silent laughter and then rocked more violently. Someone was coming. The dog turned its head and raised its ears in greeting. An old woman stood in the doorway, dressed fantastically in red and orange and green. She wore a wide green skirt in some stiff shiny material, an orange dirty blouse and a red shawl flung round her shoulders. Her feet, gnarled and twisted as the trunks of Louise's old apple trees, were bare. From underneath a thatch of dirty white hair her dark blue eyes stared at Louise, unsmiling. 'And who are you?'

'I'm Louise Case.'

'Where's the old one?'

'The old one? Oh! my aunt. I'm afraid she died.'

The woman nodded at the information. 'And it was you put up the fence, did you? Who broke it?'

11

'Mr Miles skidded on the corner.'

'Drunk again?'

Louise had to stop herself agreeing.

'I'll thank you for some water,' the old woman said abruptly. She reached behind her and produced an enamelled and brightly painted jug. She held it out to Louise, not moving from her eminence at the top of the steps. Louise hesitated and then opened the gate, and walked towards the big dog. His ears dropped, his grin widened, his feathery tail stirred slightly in the grass. Louise stretched up to receive the jug; the old woman did not trouble herself to descend even one step.

Louise took it and went into the house, through the study into the kitchen. She ran water, and filled the jug. It was a beautiful example of folk art, painted in the bright garish colours beloved of gypsies, bargees, and all travelling people. There was a big surreal bunch of pink cabbage roses on one bright red side, and a sheaf of blue flowers like delphiniums on the other. Louise carried it back out into the sunshine.

The old woman was still at the head of her steps in the darkened doorway. Louise had to go through the gate again and closer still to the dog. As she handed up the jug, his breath stirred against her bare calf and she flinched. The old woman smiled at her discomfort.

'Thank you,' she said, and turned and went back inside the van again without another word.

Louise retreated behind the safety of the gate. 'I wanted to know . . .' she called. 'When you will be moving on?'

There was absolute silence from the inside of the van. It rocked slightly as if the old woman was about her private business with her fresh water and her brightly painted jug. The dog gazed at Louise.

'When *will* you be moving on? Actually?'

There was no answer. The dog settled back down and rested his chin on his silky front legs. Only his brown eyes and his mobile eyebrows followed Louise. Defeated, she went slowly back to the house. Out of habit she took her seat again before her word processor and looked at the blank screen. Beyond the screen, where there should have been the bobbing blossom of her apple orchard, the dented blue roof of the van loomed imperturbably solid.

Louise found she could not work at all and closed down the word processor and went to the kitchen which faced coldly north, over the lane, and made herself a cup of coffee. She thought she would go into town early, see Toby, and have a drink with him at the Suffix University post-graduate bar before the meeting with Miriam. There was no point in trying to work any more. Her concentration was gone for the afternoon.

Toby was in the bar, sitting at a table with half a dozen students. Louise felt the familiar tweak of desire when she looked around the crowded bar and was suddenly, once more, struck by the sight of him. She smiled and waved. Toby waved back but did not rise to greet her. Louise bought herself a drink and joined them. She knew all the students; one or two of them were writing MA theses under her supervision. They were laughing with Toby, there was a running joke about what sort of poetry a Conservative government would admire. Kipling was mentioned, and Wordsworth.

'But only if they didn't understand what he was saying.'

'Oh, but if we assume they don't understand we can give them anything. Shelley! Keats! Plath!'

Toby glanced at Louise and smiled. 'Did you expel your trespasser?' he asked.

The students, experts at interpreting when their time was up, moved discreetly to the far end of the table and exchanged gossip about external examiners.

'No.' Louise took a sip of wine and set herself to amuse him. 'I strode down to the end of the garden to assert my rights and found myself delivering fresh water. I shall be taking in her laundry next.'

'Her?'

'It's a woman. Eighty if she's a day. Dressed for a gypsy ball and with a huge silent dog. I don't know if she's travelling alone. I haven't seen anyone else. I was rather thrown by the whole thing. I came into town early and I've been working in the library. I can't write at home. Every time I glance out of the window all I can see is this most enormous van!'

Toby smiled. 'How wonderfully surreal! Did she say when she was moving on?'

'She said absolutely nothing. She asked me where my aunt was and I told her that she'd died. She asked me how the fence got broken and suggested that Mr Miles was drunk. She obviously knows her way around. Perhaps she's a regular visitor and I'm on her route.'

Toby rested his hand gently on hers as she held her glass. 'As long as she's no trouble, I suppose it doesn't matter?'

Louise let her hand rest passive under his touch even while she protested: 'Yes; but I don't want her there! I can't see out of my study window, I can't see out of the sitting-room window. When I look out of my bedroom window I look down on this enormous pantechnicon! What are her bathroom facilities? What if she starts burning my trees or my fence posts?'

Toby nodded. 'We'd better hope she moves on then,' he said. 'Or we'll have to do something about it.'

Louise was mollified at once by his use of the word 'we'.

'Are you coming back to dinner after the meeting?'

'Miriam asked me. She said you were cooking.'

Toby nodded. 'I thought I'd do lentil soufflé.'

'Lovely.'

'You could stay overnight. Perhaps your gypsy will be gone in the morning.'

It was not unusual for Louise to stay in Toby and Miriam's spare bedroom. Meetings often went on late or, enjoying their company, she drank more wine than was safe if she were to drive home. A new tenant now lived in their studio flat which had been Louise's home for six years. But she still felt a sense of ownership and comfort in the house. Although Louise and Toby never planned intercourse – they prided themselves on being spontaneous rather than calculating adulterers – Miriam always woke at seven and left the house at eight to be at her desk at eight thirty when the first bruised refugees from the night would start arriving. Toby and Louise never had to be at the university until ten. There was always time to make love, have a shower and eat a leisurely breakfast.

'I might stay,' Louise said unhelpfully.

One of the reasons behind her move to the country and a house of her own was a feeling that Toby's sexual convenience was too well served by an attractive wife in his bed, and an attractive mistress in his upstairs flat. The arrangement had been of Louise's own making – she had found them the house to buy and then suggested that she rent their studio flat – but after the illicit delight of the early months, she wondered if the chief beneficiary was Toby. His occasional affairs at the university, so prone to heartbreak and disaster, ceased. He no longer had to invent plausible late-night meetings to satisfy Miriam's polite inquiries.

15

He was no longer exposed to the risk of gossip among the undergraduates.

But his affair with Louise did not cramp his sexual style. If he was attracted to a woman at a conference they would sleep together, and he would tell Louise openly and frankly that he had done so. There was no reason for them to be monogamous lovers. It was only Louise who found that no-one pleased her as Toby did and that other encounters left her weepy and depressed. It was Louise, not Miriam, who dreaded Toby's weekend conferences on 'Vandalism and the Inner Cities' or 'Dependency Culture'. Miriam had the security of a contractual, property-sharing marriage. Louise sometimes feared that she was peripheral.

Even worse for Louise was that the chief beneficiaries of her arrangement were both Toby *and* Miriam. Louise did more than her share of housekeeping. She cooked meals for the three of them, she stayed at home to greet plumbers and electricians when Miriam had to be at work. When the married couple took their long summer holiday cycling in France, Louise maintained the house in their absence. Miriam's outpouring of energy and care to the poor, the dispossessed and the victims of sexual violence left a vacuum in her marriage which would inevitably have been filled by another woman. Any woman other than her best friend would have tried to break up the marriage. But Louise, loving Miriam and desiring Toby, was the only woman in the world who would satisfy Toby's errant sexuality without threatening Miriam's position.

And Miriam, sexually satisfied and overworked, trusted her husband and her best friend to be as honourable and as straightforward as herself.

At first Louise had thought herself lucky. Her luxuriously frequent sex with Toby was unshadowed by guilt and did not exclude other possible partners. Her constant and long affection for Miriam deepened and grew as the three settled comfortably into their house together. But slowly Louise began to resent Miriam's commitment to her causes and her absent-mindedness at home. Louise started to fear that at an unconscious level Miriam was glad to have Toby sexually served without threat to her marriage. This put an entirely different complexion on a love-affair which had been gloriously secret. If it were *not* clandestine, then it was not a hidden betrayal of Miriam but an open exploitation of Louise – and she hated the thought of that.

Then Louise's aunt died, she inherited the cottage and chose independence. Toby advised her to stay in town, and even took the trouble to take her to see attractive sea-front flats. Louise suspected him of wanting to set their affair on a permanent and unchanging footing – with a wife at home and a mistress in a pretty little flat. Miriam advised her to stay in town, citing the need of a peer group, of sisterhood, and intellectual neighbours. Louise suspected them both of wanting to keep the comfortable status quo forever. She feared a life of half-marriage, half-spinsterhood, forever waiting on Toby's free time, forever trying to please him, forever competing not only with Miriam but with younger and younger women. In the back of Louise's mind was the hardly glimpsed thought, that without her in the house Toby and Miriam's differences would surface and become insoluble. Their marriage, which from the start had been a three-legged stool, might topple and fall. Toby might leave Miriam for Louise; and the hidden issue of which woman was his favourite would be openly and finally resolved in her favour.

Toby tweaked a sleek lock of Louise's hair. 'Don't tease,' he said firmly. 'Say if you'll stay or not.'

Toby had lived with two feminists for all of his married life. He had never had to tolerate coquetry. He had never had to bear the uncertainty which most men learn to endure. 'Make your mind up now,' he insisted. 'I need to know whether or not to put sheets on the spare bed.'

Louise responded at once to the voice of bracing no-nonsense comradeship and wilfully cast aside the centuries-old tradition of female manipulative power. 'I'll stay.'

Toby finished his drink. 'I'll get home to my cooking then. I'll give you a lift. Are you meeting at the Women's Centre?'

Louise finished her wine. 'Thanks.'

They walked to the car park. In the shadowy interior of the car Toby reached for Louise and turned her face towards him. Her skin seemed very pale, almost translucent, her eyes a very dark brown, her hair silky and soft to the touch. Toby felt desire rise in him like a gourmet's saliva when he anticipates a meal. There was something so exquisitely lavish about having two women under the same roof. Louise, since her move, was more precious to him than she had been before. He had been starting to take her for granted after nine years of domestic adultery. But now, when she came into town there was a scent of strangeness about her; she was a different woman and the philanderer in Toby rose to the challenge of novelty.

Louise rested her head against his palm and let his fingers trace the line of her temple, of her cheekbone. She had slept with half a dozen men during the course of her affair with Toby but not one touched her as Toby could do. When they made love, though they never said, they both listened for Miriam's key in the lock, and feared her sudden unexpected return. It was a thought which would always bring them both to successful, mutual climax. It was a wholly secret

18

affair: rich, even rancid, with adultery. Nothing else for Louise could equal that sexy frisson of betrayal and guilt.

'You smell of outdoors,' Toby said.

Louise smiled.

'Let's go up to the Downs,' Toby suggested, cupping her face in his hand. 'You can be late, can't you?'

Miriam would never be late for a meeting. She allotted her time in tidy effective parcels.

Louise remembered this as she turned her lips to Toby's warm palm and let herself lick and then nip him. 'Yes,' she said.

Miriam was chairing the Fresh Start committee meeting. She glanced up with irritation when the door of the committee room opened and Louise came in late and slightly flushed. 'I'm so sorry,' she apologised. 'Car trouble.'

Miriam nodded. 'We were discussing the number of entrants to the science and industrial courses,' she said. 'They're not very satisfactory.'

Louise took her place between two women. On her left was a postgraduate student specialising in feminist studies, an earnest girl with cropped hair and deliberately plain glasses. On her right was Naomi Petersen, deputy head of the school of Sociology, elegantly dressed in a pale grey suit.

'Our own background is dominated by the humanities,' Naomi offered. 'We're probably not offering adequate models.'

Miriam nodded. 'We need more women who work in technology and industry on the committee and especially at the open day.'

'I suggested some months ago that we approach Sci/Ind

19

direct and tell them the problem,' Naomi said smoothly.

There was a visible stiffening around the table among the eight members. The engineering students were notorious for their hearty jovial behaviour. None of the women wished to seek help from that department believing that the professor, an industrial chemist of nearly sixty, was as likely to pinch their bottoms as his boyish undergraduates.

'They're not savages,' Naomi snapped irritably. 'They have a positive discrimination policy. Their problem is recruitment from the schools. Girls are discouraged from industry and engineering long before they consider their A levels.'

'Perhaps we should work with local schools,' Wendy Williams said softly from the end of the table. 'Go to the source of the problem.'

'But we want women undergraduates next year,' Naomi replied.

'And role models for open day,' Miriam reminded them.

'I don't think that Sci/Ind is a very empathetic place,' Josephine Fields remarked. Her enormous earrings clashed like temple gongs as she turned her head one way and then another. 'They're male dominated, their noticeboards are full of sexist jokes, in the workshops they have demeaning posters. I think we should campaign to change them, before we even consider encouraging women to attend. *They've* got to change. I don't see why we should ask them for help.'

'What exactly are these jokes and posters?' Naomi demanded.

'I've looked through the window,' Josephine insisted. 'They are offensive.'

Miriam glanced at the clock. 'We have to take a decision on this and move on. Is there any way we can recruit local trained women for our open day? It's very soon, remember.'

'I don't want this issue swept over,' Josephine said. She stared at Miriam challengingly. 'There's no point in us meeting as women if we're going to behave like men. I thought we were having a free discussion – not having to rush through a masculine-type agenda, in disciplined male-structured ways.'

'I suppose we don't want to be here all night,' Naomi murmured softly. 'Whatever gender the meeting is.'

Josephine rounded on her. 'I suppose we want to be here as long as it takes to reach a consensus,' she said. 'Till the problem is solved in a consensual agreeing way. It is men who suppress discussion by imposing unnatural structures and time limits. I thought we were sensitive to natural and organic rhythms, not patriarchal and capitalistic time-keeping.'

'I'm sorry,' Miriam said shortly. She did not sound particularly sorry, she sounded exhausted and irritable. 'I didn't mean to be heavy-handed. I didn't understand the complexity of this issue. I thought we were just trying to recruit more women scientists for the open day.'

'I think there's a wider issue about whether the Science department is *capable* of accommodating women students in large numbers,' Josephine declared, joyfully widening the issue yet further. 'I'm not happy about trying to recruit mature women students and sending them in there at all.'

'The alternative is that they don't go to university,' Naomi said rather sharply. 'Are we advising them to stay home and have children instead?'

Josephine flushed. 'How can we recommend them to attend a course at this university when we know that the course is sexist?'

Naomi smoothed her hair at the back where it was drawn up into an elegant roll. 'I don't think we exactly *know* that,

21

do we? We know that you've looked through the window and seen something you didn't like. But has anyone been round the department? Does anyone know any students or tutors there?'

The women shook their heads in unanimous disapproval.

'So what did you see that was so dreadful?' Naomi demanded.

'It was a very offensive calendar,' Josephine said. 'Advertising Unipart.'

Naomi gave an ill-concealed snort of laughter. 'And what did it show?'

'It was a picture of a half-naked woman astride a grossly enlarged spark plug,' Josephine said doggedly. 'Is anyone going to tell me that this committee believes that that is an acceptable image of women and technology?'

Naomi glanced at Miriam, inviting her to share the joke.

'Perhaps we could speak to the head of the department,' Miriam suggested wearily. 'But I really think that it is important to recruit mature women students into the department.'

'Into a place like that?' Josephine demanded.

Wendy nodded in agreement with her. 'They are openly showing pornography,' she said quietly. 'We know this encourages men to see women as sexual objects, and encourages violence against women. The statistics are very clear, Miriam. We can't send women in there, it's not safe.'

At the key words 'sexual objects' and 'safe' three other women nodded solemnly, their gigantic earrings clashing like cymbals. They had invoked a code as powerful as that of a Victorian drawing room where the word 'improper' once held the same power. No rational discussion could possibly follow the invoking of the word 'safe'. If a woman knew she was not safe, thought she was not safe, or even fancied on entirely mistaken evidence that she was not safe, then nothing could be said to dissuade her from her fear. It was a key taboo, and its invocation marked the complete end of all reasonable debate. Miriam threw a despairing look at Louise.

Louise responded. 'I'd be prepared to take a message to the head of Science/Industry from this committee, drawing the posters and noticeboards to his attention,' she said. 'If he's prepared to take them down then perhaps we could feature his department in our open day. It'd show he was open to education. There must be women working in the department who might be prepared to come and represent the department at the open day.'

'If there *are* women working in that environment then I think we should form a subgroup to discuss the issues with them,' Josephine persevered. 'They're being bombarded with male obscenity every day of their working lives. We should be working with them.'

'That's two motions,' Naomi observed, nodding at Miriam prompting her to move on.

Miriam shot her a look which was neither grateful nor sisterly.

'Can't we set up a women-only Science and Industry department?' Wendy asked. 'Housed in the same buildings but working alternate sessions. So that we train new women scientists and engineers by experienced women scientists and engineers in a safe and segregated environment.'

Naomi Petersen made a muffled exclamation. 'We haven't organised an open day yet, and we've been discussing it for twenty minutes! How the hell d'you think we're going to organise an entirely new university department?'

Josephine smiled at her. 'That's a very negative attitude

to Wendy's interesting suggestion, Naomi,' she said with slow triumph. 'And a very unsupportive tone of voice. A lot of women's groups have found that separate development solves many problems. I think we should consider Wendy's very imaginative idea.'

Miriam rubbed her face as if struggling to stay awake. 'Wendy, would you like to make a report on this, and bring it back to our next meeting, next Tuesday? And Louise, would you approach Sci/Ind and tell them our concern about their noticeboards? And Josephine, would you like to find out how many women are working at Sci/Ind already, staff and students, and we can then consider your idea for a subgroup at the next meeting?'

There was a rather disappointed consensus, but the most disaffected members had been skilfully lumbered with tasks and were reluctant to open their mouths for fear of incurring more chores. Miriam was no slouch in the chair. She glanced around the table. 'Does anyone want to say anything more about this item?' she invited. 'Absolutely sure? OK. Next item is crèche provision at the university. Susan has a comment.'

Louise and Miriam walked home from the meeting. Louise carried some of Miriam's box files. Both women were inwardly seething at the way the meeting had gone but neither could voice a personal attack against one of the sisterhood. It must be done; but it would have to be done in code.

'I'm very concerned about Josie,' Miriam began in a pleasant tone after they had walked for a while.

Louise glanced at her.

'She seems very stressed,' Miriam said. 'Stressed' was a

codeword for behaviour which in conventional society would be regarded as unreason verging on insanity.

'She is tense,' Louise agreed. 'Of course she has personal problems.' Josephine's long-term woman lover was a student in Naomi Petersen's department and had briefly enjoyed a staggeringly glamorous fling with her. The open nature of Josie's relationship and the general myth of feminist solidarity precluded any complaints when Naomi suddenly favoured the young woman, took her to London to see experimental theatre, kept her overnight at her Brighton flat, lent her books, cooked her meals, and then with equal suddenness sent her, reeling with delight and totally unmanageable, home to Josie.

Neither Louise nor Miriam would discuss other people's sexual affairs. They adhered to the belief that these matters were private and that any curiosity was vulgar and prurient. Even when they were longing to dissect a piece of rich gossip their conversation had to be conducted in a code as arcane as that of an Edwardian parlour, and always had to indicate first and foremost their concern for the people involved. 'Josie is bound to find it difficult to work with Naomi for a while,' Miriam said. 'Considering her relationship difficulties.'

Louise nodded. 'I understand that Josie and Viv are talking about a trial separation – ever since Viv spent time with Naomi.'

Miriam widened her eyes but was too restrained to demand details. 'That's unfortunate.'

'Viv seems to think that she may have a future with Naomi.'

'Oh,' Miriam said. 'I wouldn't have thought Naomi was ready for a commitment.'

'Viv is very determined. I think she went round to Naomi's flat and virtually camped on the doorstep.'

'It's good that she should ask for what she wants,' Miriam said doubtfully. 'But I don't know if Naomi is right for her?'

'And Naomi is going through a rather – er – unsettled phase,' Louise offered. Miriam nodded, understanding that Naomi's rampant promiscuity meant that no-one stayed more than a couple of nights in her elegant flat, and that Viv might force her way in, but would be swiftly bounced when the novelty wore off.

'She's rather brisk,' Louise said. 'I thought she wanted to chair the meeting instead of you.'

'She's welcome to it,' Miriam said. 'I have all the meetings I ever want. And things change so slowly!'

'You do wonderful work,' Louise said absent-mindedly. 'I couldn't do it.'

'Your contribution is theory,' Miriam reassured her. 'Have you finished that essay on Lawrence yet? Sarah told me she was waiting for it.'

Louise thought of the word processor screen still empty of anything but the little winking cursor, and the van in her orchard. 'How can I work? Every time I look out of the window I see this huge blue van and this mad woman in it with her horrible dog.'

Miriam glanced at her. The linked topics of madness and women were as taboo as the Unipart calendar. 'Do you mean she is ill?' she asked rather stiffly. 'Has she been released for care in the community? Is she alone and unsupported?'

'I didn't mean mad, I meant independent.' Louise retreated rapidly. 'She wears something like fancy dress. She seems to be alone. And I can't help but dislike the fact that she seems to know the neighbourhood and she has parked on my land without permission. There are plenty of other places she could go.'

'If she's not doing any damage . . .'

'She's invading my personal space.'

Miriam shot her a quick mocking smile. 'I didn't know your personal space went as far as several acres.'

Louise felt herself smiling guiltily in reply. 'Well, you wouldn't like it if it was your front garden,' she said.

Miriam sighed. 'It virtually is. The phone never stops ringing. I seem to be out every night at one meeting or another. If they all came and lived in a caravan in my garden it would be easier to manage.'

They turned in the gate of the tall terraced house. Miriam glanced up at the illuminated windows of the top flat. 'Oh, Hugh's in,' she said. 'He might eat with us.'

She opened the front door. A thin watery smell of cooking pulses greeted them. 'Lentils again,' Miriam remarked without pleasure. 'Toby has bought a New Age cookbook. We haven't had meat for weeks.'

Louise dumped Miriam's box files on the hall table and went through to the kitchen. Toby was stirring orange porridge in a casserole dish. Louise put her arms around him from behind and hugged him, resting her cheek against the smooth blade of his shoulder.

'I'm starving,' she said. 'It smells wonderful.'

Toby did not disengage himself as Miriam came into the kitchen. He smiled at her. 'Hello, darling, three phone messages for you.'

Miriam nodded and went out to the telephone in the hall. Toby heard her pick up the phone and dial a number. Only then did he turn to Louise and kiss her deeply on the mouth. While his left hand stirred the lentils his right hand smoothed down from her neck across her breast and down to her buttock.

'Lovely,' Toby said. With Miriam and Louise under his roof again he felt wealthy as a polygamous sheikh.

Hugh was not invited to join them for dinner. Toby said he had not made enough. Hugh stayed upstairs, eating baked beans with a spoon from the saucepan, tantalised by the smell of hot food and by the sound of popping corks and laughter. Hugh was Miriam's choice of lodger. She and Louise had together decided that another woman would not be suitable. Toby's faint, unexpressed hope, that a second woman lodger might invite him into her flat and into her bed in the morning and at weekends when Miriam was working, was disappointed before he had even acknowledged it to himself.

Hugh was researching into marine life and kept strict office hours at his studies. On Friday and Saturday nights he would go out to a modern jazz club with friends from work and get seriously but quietly drunk. Toby in his heart rather envied these bullish excursions. Toby had no friends. Colleagues at the university feared and envied the speedy progress of his career. Women tended to pass through his life, not stay. The Men's Consciousness group which he led on Thursday nights was an area of conscientious work rather than spontaneous pleasure. Too many of the men had sexual problems, too many of them would weep over their relationship with their father. Toby would facilitate their tears and their worries over the size of their genitals but he could not grieve with them.

He knew that Men's Consciousness groups were a pale shadow of the real thing. In this area the women had the edge. Female consciousness had the pulse of an authentic revolutionary movement. Women had so much more to say. They were angry with their mothers, with their fathers, with their kids. They had issues to challenge about social treatment. They had two thousand years of repression to cite. Every week, every day, almost every moment they suffered from inequality and had to evolve a revolutionary response. Male consciousness was nothing more than a bandwagon attempt by the left-out kids somehow to join in the game. All the unconvincing inventions of male bonding and tenderness could not conceal the fact that men were solitary, rather stupid individuals while women were spontaneously sensitive and collectively minded. Female sexuality was Toby's delight. Male sexuality held no interest for him whatsoever. Indeed he had to conceal distaste when his brothers wanted to hug him. Except for Miriam and Louise, Toby was a solitary man.

Miriam concluded the last of her telephone calls and came into the kitchen. The table was laid, Toby and Louise were drinking wine. A glass was standing ready for her at her place.

'Thanks,' she said, dropping into her chair. 'That was about the council again.'

The lease on the women's refuge was due to expire within six months and the council were reluctant to renew. Miriam had launched a lobby campaign on councillors but battered wives were not a priority in a tourist town where income depended largely on an atmosphere of carefree perfection.

'They're such bastards,' Miriam declared.

Toby and Louise nodded, looking suitably grave.

'Help me serve,' Toby said to Louise.

Together they arranged the soufflé on the plates and took them to the table. There was a green salad with Toby's special salad dressing and his home-made brown bread. They opened another bottle of wine.

'How was the meeting?' Toby inquired.

'Bloody awful,' Miriam replied.

Toby smiled and helped himself to more bread. Miriam might be irritable now but after more wine and some fruit she would become sleepy and pliable. He would not make love with her, he was tired after groping with Louise in the car, but he enjoyed the reassurance of knowing that his wife and his mistress were sexually available to him. Tomorrow morning, after Miriam had brought him a cup of coffee in bed and gone to work, he would make love with Louise if he felt like it. He was a fortunate man and he knew it.

Thursday

LOUISE, driving back to her cottage after teaching a morning tutorial, had every hope of seeing an empty orchard. Instead, as she rounded the bend that Mr Miles had found so treacherous, she was greeted by the irritating sight of the big blue van and a washing line strung between two of her apple trees. Brightly coloured blouses and shapeless grey underwear were bobbing among the blossom. Louise swore, turned her car down the drive, jerked on the handbrake and marched purposefully towards the orchard.

'Anyone home?' she demanded truculently.

The van rocked. First the dog put his head around the door, and when he saw Louise wagged a welcoming tail. Then the old lady herself emerged. She was wearing a man's smoking jacket in deep plum patterned silk and midnight-blue silk pyjama trousers. 'You again,' she said.

'I think you should move on today,' Louise said clearly. 'This *is* my orchard and you have been here now for more than twenty-four hours. I think it's time you went. If you want a nearby site I can telephone Mr Miles at Wistley Common Farm for you. He sometimes has a vacant field.'

The woman observed her from under the mop of hair. 'Out all night,' she said. 'Did you go to a party?'

31

Louise found herself blushing. 'Of course not. I was at a meeting and then I went on to dinner with friends.'

'I'll trouble you for some fresh water,' the woman said. She reached inside the van and brought out the empty jug again. She jumped lightly down from the steps and strolled towards the gate, the dog at her bare heels. Louise took the jug and marched into the house. A couple of letters were pushed to one side as she opened the door into the porch. She filled the jug and stalked back down the garden path. The old woman was leaning on the gate.

'Beautiful day,' she commented. 'You must enjoy the birds at dawn.'

Louise, who never woke until long after dawn, said nothing.

'I was born here, you know,' the old woman said conversationally. 'In this very cottage.'

Louise could not help but be interested but she remained sulkily silent.

'The trees were younger then,' the old woman sighed. 'The trees were so much younger then.'

She put out an old mottled hand and rested it against a tree trunk as an owner might stroke a favourite dog. There was a strange familiarity between her and the tree, as if the tree were responding to her touch. Louise found herself trying to picture her orchard as a field of saplings, like girls ready to dance. 'I think you should go today,' she said, but her voice was no longer angry.

The old woman nodded. 'As you wish,' she said. 'Whatever you wish.'

Louise felt suddenly deflated, as if she had triumphed in some small act of malice.

'What was your meeting?' the old woman asked.

Louise shrugged. 'It's a committee I belong to. We're

trying to encourage older women to go on university degree courses. Every year we organise an open day and then for those that are interested we run introductory courses. This year we're focusing on women in science and industry.' Louise heard her voice sounding flat and indifferent. 'It's a *very* important issue,' she said.

'And where did you go for dinner?'

'To my friends' house – Toby and Miriam. I used to rent their flat before I came to live here. Miriam and I were at university together. Toby and I . . .' Louise abruptly broke off. 'Toby is her husband,' she said.

'Drives a white Ford Escort car, does he?'

'Why?'

'I've been past a few times. Quite often there was the white Ford Escort parked outside.'

'Yes,' Louise said shortly.

The old woman smiled at her benevolently. 'Quite a friend you are!' she observed.

Louise could think of no response to make at all.

'And what d'you teach, at the university?' the woman inquired pleasantly.

'I have an experimental post. I'm a specialist in women's studies seconded to the Literature department on a year's trial.'

The old woman nodded. 'Well, I must get on,' she said as if Louise were delaying her with gossip. She started towards the van.

'But you *are* leaving today?' Louise confirmed.

The old woman turned and waved the gaudy jug. 'Just as soon as I get packed,' she said. 'As you wish.'

Louise nodded and turned and went into the house. She picked up the letters and went to read them in her study. The van, solid and blue, obscured the view of the common which she usually found so soothing. She opened the letters without needing to tear the flaps, glanced at them and put them under a paperweight. She switched on the word processor and picked up the phone to speak to Toby.

'She says she's leaving.'

Toby, collecting books for a seminar for which he had failed to prepare, was rather brisk. 'Good. End of problem.'

'I feel like a bully.'

'Napoleon!'

'Napoleon?'

'You can't make an omelette without breaking eggs,' he said bracingly. 'Napoleon said it.'

'She's so very old. And she was born here. She says she was born here.'

'She probably says that everywhere she goes. Look, I have to go. I'm supposed to be taking a seminar on industrialisation and I've put *Das Kapital* down somewhere and I can't find it.'

'Call me later,' Louise urged. 'I feel a bit desolate.'

'Do some work!' Toby recommended. 'Sarah's waiting for your Lawrence article, she told me this morning. I'll call you later. I might be able to get out to see you this evening – Men's Consciousness group is finishing early.'

'Oh!' The half-promise was an immediate restorative. Louise often dreaded being alone in the cottage. On cool summer evenings when the swallows swooped and chased against an apricot horizon the cottage seemed too full of ghosts, other people whose lives had been lived more vividly and more passionately than Louise's. They had left a trace of their desires and needs in every sun-warmed stone, while Louise flitted like a cold shadow leaving no record. Louise felt half-invisible, looking out of the window across the common. She would pour herself a glass of wine and go out into the garden, sit in a deck chair on the front lawn and read a book, consciously trying to enjoy her solitude. Then she would turn around and look at the little cottage which seemed more lively and vital than herself.

It had been built as a gamekeeper's cottage, part of a grand estate of which Mr Miles's great-grandfather had bought a small slice. Louise thought of a man like Lawrence's gamekeeper, Mellors, letting himself quietly out of the gate that led to the common and walking softly on dew-soaked grass to check his rabbit snares. Impossible for Louise to speculate what a man like that would think as he walked down the sandy paths between the ferns, a dark shadow of a dog at his heels. Impossible even to imagine him without the gloss of literature on him. Louise was not even sure what a gamekeeper did for his day-to-day work, she was far better informed about his sexually gymnastic nights. But that was fiction. Everything she knew best was fiction.

The gamekeeper had left when the big estate was sold up. Mr Miles had told her that the cottage was used by his own family and then housed farm labourers. He knew one of his father's workers who had lived there with his wife and their seven children. Louise had protested that they could not possibly have all fitted into the two little bedrooms.

'No bathroom,' Mr Miles had reminded her. 'So three bedrooms. Girls in one room, boys in another and parents in the third. I used to come down for my tea with them sometimes. It was grand.' He smiled at Louise, trying to find the words. 'A lot of play,' he said. 'Like foxcubs.'

Louise sometimes thought of that family as she went to sleep alone in her wide white bed. A family where the children played like foxcubs, with four boys in one room and three girls whispering in another and a great marital bed which saw birth and death and lovemaking year after year.

She pulled up her chair and sat down before the word processor.

Nothing came.

Outside in the orchard, the blossom bobbed. The blue van was as still as a rock, planted like a rock, embedded in the earth. The old woman was clearly not packing, she was not moving around at all. She was doing nothing and Louise feared very much that when Toby visited in the evening the van would be there still, and the old woman, who guessed so quickly and knew so much, would see Toby's white Ford Escort car pull up the drive and watch him get out and let himself in the front door with his own key. Louise thought that with the old woman's bright eyes scanning the front of the cottage she would not feel at all in the right mood to go upstairs with Toby if he wanted to make love.

She was quite right. The van was still there as the sunset dimmed slowly into a soft lavender twilight. Toby's tyres sprayed gravel as he pulled up outside the cottage. Louise opened the door at once to draw him in, hoping that the old woman would not see them.

'Evening!' the old voice called penetratingly from the bottom of the darkening garden.

Toby turned at once, ignoring Louise's hand on his sleeve. 'Good evening,' he replied.

'Oh, come in,' Louise urged. 'She said she was going, but she's still here. I'll talk to her tomorrow and get her moved on. Come inside now, Toby.'

'I'll just say hello,' Toby said. 'I'm curious.' He handed Louise the bottle of wine he was carrying and strolled down towards the orchard. The old woman was leaning against the garden gate, her dog sprawled over her bare feet, keeping them warm.

'Hello.' Toby smiled his charming smile at her.

The old woman nodded, taking in every inch of him: his silk shirt, sleek trousers, casual shoes, and his jacket slung over his shoulder.

'And are you at the university too?' she asked, as if continuing a long conversation.

'Yes,' Toby said engagingly. 'I'm in the Sociology department. Louise teaches feminist studies in the Literature department so we're colleagues. But tell me, what are you doing here?'

The old woman looked around her as if the briar roses were leaning their pale faces forward to eavesdrop. 'I've come here to write,' she confided softly. 'To write my memoirs. I wanted somewhere quiet where I could work.'

'Really? How very interesting.' Toby was not interested at all.

She nodded. 'I was born in 1908. My mother died when I was four. Her health had been broken, you see, by the force-feeding.'

Toby, whose attention had been wandering, suddenly clicked on, like a searchlight. 'Force-feeding?'

The old woman shook her head. 'You wouldn't know. It's all over and forgotten now. But they were terrible days for the women suffragettes.'

'I do know,' Toby said hurriedly and untruthfully. 'I've studied that period. Was your mother a militant suffragette?'

The old woman suddenly gleamed at him. 'She was! She was! And after her death, they took me in. They called me the youngest recruit of them all! They used to pop me

37

through the scullery windows to check the houses were empty. We cared about pets, you know. If there was a budgie or a canary I'd open the front door and we'd get them out before we fired the building.'

Toby could feel his heart rate speeding. 'Let me get this straight,' he said. 'You were working for the WSPU – the women's suffrage movement. And they used you, as a little girl, to help them in their attacks on property?'

The old woman nodded. 'It was like the greatest adventure in the world for me. I used to love going out at night with them, on the raids.'

'And you can remember it all?'

'Remember it?' the old woman laughed. 'I've got a trunk full of photographs and newspaper clippings. I've got my diary and my letters. And *her* diary and her letters too.'

'Whose diary?' Toby asked. He had a feeling very like drunkenness. He could feel his head swimming and his breath coming too fast. 'Whose diary have you got?'

'Why, the diary of the woman who adopted me,' the old woman said nonchalantly. 'Sylvia, Sylvia Pankhurst.'

Toby waded back to the house like a drowning man gasping for the shore. In his fevered imagination he saw the book he would write, the definitive book on the women's suffrage movement and the inside story of the life of Sylvia Pankhurst. It would be illustrated lavishly with previously unseen photographs. He would quote extensively from her private papers – letters, diaries. He would collate and index them all into chronological order and then deposit them, perhaps at Suffix, perhaps in London. They would be called the Summers collection and he would publish a guide to them. The book would go into many editions. There was a huge and growing interest in anything about the women's movement, not just in England but worldwide. He would get a teaching post far better paid, far more prestigious than Suffix could ever offer. He could go to Cambridge, or Oxford. He leaned against the front door for a moment, hyperventilating with fantasy.

Oxford, hell! He could go to America! What would the University of California not give for him, and for the Summers collection? He would be able to name his price. The increasingly complex, increasingly competitive world of sociology would be left behind him. He would be into gender studies, he would be an expert on the women's movement. He was a new man, every inch of him was a new man. He could enter this deliciously easy growth area and leave sociology with its growing emphasis on computers and complicated statistics behind him.

The door opened behind him. 'Are you ready to come in now?' Louise asked sulkily. 'I've opened the wine.'

He turned to her, elated, full of his plans. Then some cautious instinct made him hesitate. 'She's quite a character,' he said casually. 'D'you know why she's here?'

Louise passed him a glass of red wine. 'It's her route, isn't it? She knew my aunt. She probably comes here every year.'

'Oh.' Toby forced the excitement to drain from his face, he controlled his voice so that he sounded nonchalant. 'Like a gypsy. They always travel the same route, don't they?'

'I've no idea,' Louise said. 'Ask Miriam, it's more her area than mine.'

As usual, a reference to Miriam signalled Louise's greatest displeasure. Toby leaned back on the sofa and invitingly patted the cushion beside him. 'Come and sit here,' he said.

'I've been thinking about you all day. I couldn't get you out of my mind.'

Louise could never resist that tone of voice from him. She crossed the room and sat close. Toby slid his arm around her shoulders. His mind was working frantically. He would borrow or buy a tape recorder and persuade the old woman to talk before a microphone. He would make her go through every photograph and every newspaper clipping and identify each one, and all the people in the pictures. He would give each photograph a reference number and cross-refer each one to the tape recording. Then he would lead her through her childhood, from her earliest memories of her mother, through her contact with the Pankhursts and her relationship with them all.

He had lied when he said he had studied the period. He had a nodding acquaintance with the history of the struggle for women's votes, but no more than any man who has read a couple of history books and lived with a feminist. Both Louise and Miriam would have been better prepared and better suited to interview the old woman. Miriam had taught a women's history course at evening class, and Louise specialised in women's studies. Toby did not care. The world was full of better-qualified, better-read, more learned academics and he could not give way to all of them.

There is a point in every academic's life when he or she realises that a career in a university is as unjust as the upward struggle in any large corporation. Those that survive are those that learn to exploit career opportunities. Those that do well are as unscrupulous and ambitious as any City executive. Toby was not going to hand over the research opportunity of a lifetime simply because he was the wrong gender and had no interest in the topic.

'So she's told you nothing of her plans?' he asked softly.

40

Louise kicked off her shoes and rested her bare feet on the end of the sofa. Toby observed that she had painted her toe-nails a deep sexy red.

'She's supposed to be leaving,' Louise said. 'She said she'd go today. I'll make sure she goes tomorrow. I'm at home all day. I'll pack her up and drive the van myself, if need be.'

Toby smoothed his lips along Louise's sleek head. When he had first met her and Miriam, Louise had worn her straight hair very short in an unbecoming crop. It had made her face look pointy and sharp. Of the two women, Miriam with her great mop of a shaggy perm and her wide easy smile was undeniably the more attractive. But over the years Louise had grown her hair into a pageboy bob which went well with the increasingly smart clothes she wore. Miriam, who had no time for regular visits to the hairdresser, let the curl drop out of her hair till it was flat and straight . Now she tied it back at the nape of her neck with a leather barrette when she remembered, or an inelegant elastic band; and cut it with the kitchen scissors every month or so.

The faces of the women had changed too. Miriam's sexy wide-mouthed grin had faded over eight years of arduous and depressing work. When Toby came home late at night and found her dozing in an armchair, a Home Office report open in her lap, he often thought she looked older than her thirty years. Older, and tired and sad. He would wake her and send her up to bed then, full of nostalgic regret for the girl she had been, who used to get drunk on a pint of weak lager and lime at lunchtime, and lie in the sun and refuse to go to her seminars.

Louise's pointy face had grown rounder and more relaxed. The successful reception of her PhD thesis, the publication of her book, and her particularly lucky slide into her lectureship had put the gloss of a successful woman on her. Her move to the country had given her more time to herself, and Toby was agreeably surprised to find that she seemed to be spending this time on personal grooming, of which the claret toes were the latest example. Louise contributed to a quarterly paper of feminist theory. Toby had just read her essay which explained that feminists now could legitimately wear any kind of garment, adopt any sort of adornment. The old dreary dress codes of puritan drabness could be rejected. Apparently feminists could now enjoy their femininity. Indeed, any kind of aping of male dress style – whether boiler suit or power dressing in a tailored jacket – was a betrayal of their true sexuality. Lace underwear, even stockings and suspenders, was part of a woman's personal choice and a legitimate statement of her individual power.

Toby found this development of feminism intensely enjoyable. No enthusiast had greeted the Second Wave more ardently. He slid an exploratory hand under the collar of Louise's shirt and felt the thin strap of something which might be a bra, or might be some kind of teddy or body stocking. He knew himself to be a remarkably lucky man. His youth had coincided with the period of time where women demonstrated their emancipation by leaving off their underwear, refusing to shave their body hair, and part-icipating in promiscuous sex. A state as near to Paradise as the mid-twenty-year-old Toby could imagine. Now he was older and his tastes were more refined he had the remarkable good fortune to discover that feminism had taken a develop-mental turn. Body hair was now removed, personal adorn-ment was a sign of confidence and pride, and although promiscuity was out of fashion, celibacy – that spectre of the late '80s – had never caught on. Provided a man was prepared to wear a condom (and Toby was always thoroughly prepared), he could expect to find most serious intelligent women dressed in underwear appropriate to a *fin-de-siècle* Parisian brothel, and open to invitations of the most imaginative nature. Toby let his hand stray downwards to Louise's right breast. She seemed to be encased in a kind of silky lace. 'Shall we go upstairs?' he asked politely.

Louise smiled in assent and led the way. She glanced over her shoulder to the blue van in the orchard. It was still and quiet. No lights were showing. Perhaps the old woman was having an early night prior to a long journey at dawn tomorrow. Louise resolutely put her from her mind and opened the bedroom door.

Miriam and Toby's bedroom at home was functional – part library, part sleeping area. Toby often worked in bed and the floor and table on his side were often littered with papers and books. The telephone was Miriam's side with a notepad and pencil for late-night emergency calls. Toby loved the contrast of Louise's orderly female room. There were no frills or lace, nothing fussy, but the room had a groomed elegance – like Louise herself. There was a pure white quilt on the modern brass bed. There were complicated and faintly erotic prints on the freshly painted walls. On Louise's uncluttered dressing-table were a few small bottles of perfume. On her bedside table was a promising bottle of aromatherapy massage oil. The electric blanket had been switched on since the late afternoon; Louise disliked cold sheets. Toby undressed without haste and laid his clothes carefully on a chair. Louise stripped down to her lacy teddy, threw back the covers of the bed and spread herself out for his view.

'Gorgeous,' Toby said appreciatively, and slid on top of her.

He did not stay there for more than a moment. Toby's lovemaking followed a certain pattern which both Miriam and Louise had learned. He moved easily from one position to another with the woman on top, or at his side, but rarely beneath him, a position which had been unpopular with feminists in the old days, when Toby learned his erotic skills. He varied the rhythm of his movements from very fast to languidly slow. He neglected no erogenous zone with his fingers or his tongue with the meticulous thoroughness of a man checking off a mental list. He talked to Louise (or Miriam) not only about his feelings and desires, but he also inquired courteously as to their progress. 'Is this good? And this? Do you like it when I do this? And this?' Whether he was trying to please or inviting congratulations, it was impossible to say.

When he was ready to come to orgasm which, with Louise (and Miriam), was these days rather soon, he would smile a peculiarly attractive smile and take Louise's (or Miriam's) hand, lick the middle finger and place it lovingly but firmly on her clitoris. Thus prompted, Louise (or Miriam) would caress herself to a climax while Toby gave himself up to the bliss of his ejaculation with a clear conscience.

Today, as other days since Louise's move to the cottage, their lovemaking was pleasant rather than overwhelming. The night before, in the car, they had been desperate for each other's touch. The fact that the half-hour was stolen from Miriam's meeting spiced the taste of each other's mouths. In the morning, in Toby's spare bedroom, Toby had chosen a little light sensual teasing, but had refused to make love. He often chose to withhold himself from either his wife or his mistress for Toby was a true gourmet, he liked the taste of desire, he did not have to consume the whole banquet. Also, as his relationship with Louise and

Miriam had become part of his domestic routine, he found he enjoyed the knowledge of their desire for him even more than consummation. He liked leaving them aroused, he preferred them dark-eyed and slightly breathless to slack and satisfied. He enjoyed playing with Louise in the morning and then catching sight of her at work, knowing that she was still turned on. Both women serviced his ego as much as his libido.

Toby and Louise on her big bed made love with a sense of familiar enjoyment rather than excitement. Perhaps they were sated, perhaps their minds were distracted by the old lady at the bottom of the garden. But Toby knew that the problem went deeper than that. By some unfortunate trick of fate he now only became deeply excited if there was a possibility of discovery. The car in the lane on the South Downs in the evening light was as dizzy an encounter as any of their earlier moments. Louise in Miriam's house – when Miriam might return at any moment – was Louise at the very pinnacle of her desirability. Louise in her own house, with the front and the back door safely locked, was too secure to give him that swift, sweet illicit thrill. It was an encounter as safe as those of his marital bed. He went through the erotic motions, and he reached a climax. But it was nothing like the pleasure of having Louise under Miriam's very nose.

Toby did not know it, and Louise would never have admitted it – not even to herself – but it was exactly the same for her too. They had, both of them, become addicted to guilt and mistaken it for love.

Toby and Louise ate cheese, biscuits and soup sitting either side of the kitchen table. Toby glanced at the clock.

'I have to go,' he said. 'I said I'd be home at ten.'

'Have you been here?' Louise asked. She always practised the permanent mistress's courtesy of priming herself on his deceptions.

'No. With a graduate student,' Toby said. 'James Sutherland, playing pool.'

'You smell wrong,' Louise cautioned. 'Not smoky enough.'

'He has a pool table at his house.'

Louise raised her eyebrows. 'Our students *are* going up in the world,' she observed. 'Which one is he?'

'The one who drives the white Porsche,' Toby said grimly. 'God knows where they all get their money. D'you know, I teach a group of undergraduates who are sharing a house – but they're not squatting, they're not even renting it, they're buying.'

Louise nodded. 'The student bar has started stocking Lanson champagne. God! When we were undergraduates we used to save up for Friday nights and then get drunk on cider and gin.'

Toby chuckled. 'Did you really?'

'We called them "Happies".'

Louise remembered wrongly. She had mostly stayed sober to study. It was Miriam who was the sybarite in those days. 'Miriam and I used to drink three each and then fall off our bar stools.'

'I never saw you fall off your bar stools,' Toby said with regret.

'You met us in our finals year,' Louise reminded him. 'Our salad days were over then. It was all continuous assessment when we were students. We were on the rack from September to June.'

'But more thoroughly assessed,' Toby prompted.

46

He and Louise had fought an easily defeated campaign to preserve the university's practice of continuous assessment, in which students demonstrate their learning and research skills with work written over weeks of preparation. In practice, the conscientious ones worked themselves into a stupor of fatigue with week after week of late nights and early mornings, while the lazy ones drank to excess and fooled around until two days before the deadline when they went into a frenzy of last-minute labour. The results were broadly comparable.

The university, weary of supervising students rushing to extremes, had instituted the convention of a finals exam fortnight so that all the breakdowns and alcoholism and suicides were concentrated into one short, manageable period.

Louise and Toby had fought this change on the grounds that it was a deviation from the radical nature of the university. Of course, no-one had ever proved that continuous assessment was more or less radical than examinations, and once continuous assessment was adopted as the Conservative government's policy for GCSEs it had rather gone out of fashion as a Cause. Nonetheless Toby and Louise still loyally paid lip service.

'I learned more in my final year than I did in the other two put together,' Louise said.

'I wish I'd had that opportunity,' Toby sighed, hypocritically hiding his pride in his own degree. 'Finals fortnight at Oxford was madness.'

He glanced at the kitchen clock, drained his glass of wine and stood up. 'See you tomorrow.'

Louise followed him from the kitchen to the sitting room and passed him his jacket. She was attractively dressed in a silky dressing gown. Toby had a moment's regret that he was leaving her to go into the cool summer night and drive home to Miriam who would be irritable and worried from her meeting at the Alcoholic Women's Unit.

'I'm not coming in to university tomorrow,' Louise reminded him. 'I shall make sure the old woman moves on and then I'll work here all day. I'm overdue on that Lawrence essay.'

Toby hesitated. It would be fatal to his plans if the old woman disappeared again into the lanes of Sussex with her precious bundle of primary sources and her irreplaceable oral history. But he could not think of any reason to stop Louise from moving the trespasser on her way. All he could do was delay her. 'I'm free in the morning,' he said. 'I'll come out and have breakfast with you. I'll bring fresh croissants and the newspapers.'

Louise lived far beyond the restricted village paper round which was organised by Mrs Ford from the village shop and delivered only to her particular favourites. Louise adored reading the *Guardian* over breakfast. Toby had played one of his strongest cards.

'Oh, how lovely!' she exclaimed. 'To what do I owe the honour?'

Toby smiled his engaging smile. 'Oh, I don't know. I just thought we could spend the morning together. Don't get up before I arrive and I'll bring it up to you in bed. I'll be here by nine.'

Louise wound her arms around his neck and kissed his cheek and his ear. 'Lovely lovely man,' she said softly.

'Promise you won't get up?' Toby demanded cunningly. 'I don't want you to spoil the mood by worrying about the old lady. You stay in bed until I come.'

'Promise.'

He released her and she watched him walk from her front

door to his car. Then she shut the front door and went to the kitchen to clear the plates from supper. She was thoughtful. This was the first time Toby had offered to bring her breakfast since the move to the cottage. In the old days, in her little studio flat, he had often climbed the stairs with his copy of the *Guardian* and croissants hot from the bakery in a greasy paper bag, after Miriam had left for work. The transition of this tradition to the cottage could only indicate his increasing commitment.

She wiped down the pine table with a sense of fluttery excitement. Toby had been with her this morning, teasing, withholding, but playing with her and not his wife. He had been with her all evening, and now he was coming to breakfast. His movement towards her was evident. Since the start of their affair Louise had wanted him to choose her. The underground half-conscious competition between close women friends meant that Louise and Miriam were always rivals. The women's movement's insistence on loving sisterhood had meant that both women totally ignored this. If challenged they would have denied any feeling of rivalry; but in fact Miriam was always worried that she had made the wrong career choice when she decided to work for the refuge and leave the academic life which had been so good for Louise; while Louise's sexual confidence would always be undermined by her memory of the three long summers when Miriam attracted scores of young men by doing nothing more seductive than lying on the grass and picking daisies. Only one thing could restore Louise to a proper sense of her own worth – Toby.

Louise went through to her study to collect the vexing copy of *The Virgin and the Gypsy* to re-read once more in bed. A glimmer of golden light from the bottom of the orchard caught her eye. Now there was a woman who seemed to need no man at all. No friend, no husband, no lover, certainly not the husband of her best friend. Louise stood for a little while in the darkness of her study looking out at the friendly little light, considering the old lady. There was a woman who seemed powerfully self-contained. Not a property-owner like Louise, not a career woman like Louise. Not a sexual object like Louise – left alone again, despite her silky sexy dressing gown. A woman who had avoided all the opportunities and all the traps open to the modern woman. A woman who had been born into a society markedly less free, a woman who enjoyed none of Louise's opportunities and enhanced consciousness but who was, nonetheless, an independent woman in a way that Louise was not.

Louise speed-read the whole of *The Virgin and the Gypsy* before she went to sleep. Although she had taken English Literature as her BA and was now a women's specialist in the Literature department, Louise was quite incapable of understanding either fiction or poetry. All of it was judged purely on its attitude to women. She had learned the jargon and skills of literary criticism. She could point to an adjective and detect imagery. But the heart of her interest in writing was neither the story nor the telling of it, but its attitude to the heroines.

Any work of fiction could thus be simply de-constructed and simply scored on a grade of say one to ten, entirely on the basis of its position on women. The language might be living vibrant poetry, the story might bypass Louise's critical pencil and plunge straight into her imagination, but still she would work through the pages going tick, tick, tick in the margin for positive references to women, and cross, cross, cross for negative imagery. A piece of blatant sexism would be flagged with a shocked exclamation mark. *The*

Virgin and the Gypsy was spotted with outraged exclamation marks by the time that Louise's bedside clock showed midnight and she had finished re-reading it.

She closed the book carefully and put it on her bedside table. She set her alarm clock for quarter to eight. She had promised Toby that she would not get up before he arrived with her breakfast but she was not going to be found in bed in her brushed cotton pyjamas, her hair tangled, and her mouth tasting stale. When Toby arrived, thinking he was waking her, she would have already showered with perfumed shower gel, cleaned her teeth, brushed her hair, and changed into silk pyjamas which matched the dressing gown she only wore for Toby's visits.

She glanced towards the darkened window. There was a pale wide moon riding in the skies over the darkened common. An owl hooted longingly. Up the little lane came the strangled roar of a Land-Rover in the wrong gear: Mr Miles driving home after a late night at the Holly Bush. The sound of the engine faded as he turned the corner towards his solitary darkened farm and then everything was quiet again. Louise turned on her side and gathered her pillow into her arms for the illusion of company, and slept.

She dreamed almost at once. She was in Toby and Miriam's house but the road before their front gate was a deep brown flood of a river. At the edge of the churning waters, where the waves splashed and broke against the front doorsteps, was a tossing flotsam of paperbacks, their pages soggy and sinking in the dark waters, their covers ripped helplessly from the spines and rolling over and over in the turbulence of the flood.

Louise began to be afraid but then realised, with the easy logic of dreams, that she could go out of the back door, into the little yard and through the backyard gate, where she put out the dustbins on Thursdays. From the backstreet she could go to the university, to her office, where there were plenty of books to replace those that were rushing in the flood past the house, torn and soggy. She went quickly through the kitchen and flung open the back door.

It was the very worst thing she could have done. With an almighty roar, like that of some wild and uncontrollable animal, the flood water rushed towards her, far higher and more violent than it had been at the front. Louise fled before it as it tore the notes from the cork pin-board and clashed saucepans in their cupboards. The larder door burst open and packets of cereals and rice tumbled out into the boiling waters. Toby's wine rack crashed down and the bottles broke, turning the water as red as blood and terrifyingly sweet. Louise ran for the stairs, the red waves lapping and sucking at her feet as the current eddied and flowed through the ground floor of the house. She screamed as she grabbed the newel post at the bottom of the stairs but there was no answering call from above. She was alone in the whole world with the hungry waters after her.

She staggered up the stairs as a fresh high wave billowed in through the kitchen door. With a crash the front door fell in and the two rivers merged, swirling, in the hall. The scarlet waters' terrible load of tumbling books chased Louise up the stairs, past Toby and Miriam's bathroom and bedroom, up the little stairs to her own flat.

There was someone in her bed. A man. For a moment Louise recoiled in fear, and then the crash behind her, as the stairs gave way, made her run into the room and fling herself on him, terrified at last into desire. She was screaming, but not for help. She was screaming: 'I'm sorry! I'm sorry! I'm sorry!'

Louise wrenched herself from sleep with a gasp of terror.

Her pillow, gripped in her arms, was damp with warm sweat. Her hair was plastered to her neck as if she had indeed been washed by the waters of that strange dream flood. She swallowed painfully, her throat was sore. She unclenched her fists, she released the pillow.

Her bedroom was very quiet. The clock ticked very softly. She looked towards the window. Dawn was coming, the first she had ever seen in the country. In the soft pearly light of the early morning a few solitary birds were starting to sing. Louise raised herself up in her bed and looked down towards the orchard. The blue van was there, with a tiny wisp of smoke coming from the skewed chimney. The van was rocking slightly as the old woman inside moved about, making breakfast for herself and the dog. Louise sniffed. She could smell a safe warm smell of woodsmoke. She felt enormously comforted at the sight of that battered blue roof and the presence of another person nearby. She dropped back to the pillows again and fell asleep like a child that is reassured by the sound of her mother in the next room. There was, after all, nothing to fear.

Friday

TOBY WAS PROMPT, anxious that Louise should not have broken her promise and moved the old woman on. Before he let himself in at the front door he put down the packages on the doorstep and went quietly down to the caravan in the orchard.

The old woman was sitting in her doorway, face turned upwards to the weak morning sunshine. She smiled at him when she saw him but she did not move. The dog raised his head and lifted his ears and gave a soft warning growl.

'Hush,' the old woman said gruffly.

At once the dog dropped down to watch Toby in silence.

'I'll come and talk to you later,' Toby said. 'If I may.' He smiled his most charming smile. 'I'm longing to hear about your childhood. Could you spare me some time this morning?'

The old woman looked thoughtful. 'I promised her I'd leave,' she said regretfully. 'She doesn't want me in her orchard. I should be moving on today. I'm about ready to get packed.'

Toby let himself through the gate, the words spilling out in haste. 'Oh, don't go, don't go. There's no need for you to go. I'll talk to Louise. She doesn't really want you to go. You needn't leave for a week or so. I promise.'

The old woman smiled at him. 'As you wish,' she said gently. 'I'd rather stay. I've some problem with the van that needs sorting. Mr Miles'll do it for me. I could get it fixed here and then move on later.'

Toby nodded. 'You do that. I'll be out later. In about an hour.'

The old woman graciously assented. 'All right, then. I'll be here.'

Louise, watching the two of them from her bedroom window, wondered what Toby wanted with the old woman. If it had been Miriam seeking her out then Louise would have known that she had found her a settlement place, a bed in a refuge, a council site. But Toby – Toby never did anything for anyone but himself.

Louise slipped into bed and arranged herself attractively on the pillows as the front door opened and Toby's footsteps sounded on the stairs.

'Darling,' he said as he came into the room and laid the *Guardian* on her white counterpane. 'Darling.'

'The old woman's van has got some mechanical problem,' Toby said after he had made efficient but perfunctory love to Louise, unpacked the croissants and drank coffee, all in a rather bohemian mess in Louise's wide white bed.

Louise watched him, her eyes hazy with post-coital content.

'She told me Mr Miles would fix it for her if she could stay a few more days. I said I was sure you'd let her.' Toby put on his little-boy-pleasing face. 'I was sure you wouldn't really mind.'

'I do mind,' Louise said abruptly. 'I don't want her here. I didn't ask her to come here. And I particularly dislike the

55

way she interferes. She talks to you, she watches my front door and knows when you're here. God knows what arrangements she has in there for hygiene. Mr Miles has a thousand empty fields. If she's on such good terms with him, why doesn't she go up there?'

Toby reconsidered rapidly. As long as he knew where the old woman was, it would actually be more convenient if she were not on Louise's doorstep. A casual remark from her about Sylvia Pankhurst, and Toby's research would have to be shared with Louise, and the rewards shared too. But if she were safely housed away from Louise then he could develop the interviews at a leisurely, appropriate pace, and Louise would not find out about it until he had a contract from a publisher and an exclusive agreement with the old lady.

'That makes sense,' he said. 'Why don't you ask Mr Miles? He owes you a favour for breaking the fence.'

'I'll phone him,' Louise decided. 'I'll phone him this morning.'

Toby got dressed slowly while Louise showered for the second time that morning and then emerged from the bathroom rubbing her hair dry with a towel. He cleared the breakfast things away while she dressed and when she came downstairs he was washing up.

'Thank you,' she said, slightly surprised.

Toby shrugged off her thanks. 'You've got enough to do. I want to see this problem with the old lady solved before I go to work. Call Mr Miles now, I can help him move her.'

Louise gave Toby a long level scrutinising look. 'Thank you,' she said again. She dialled the number on the kitchen telephone. It rang for a long time and when Andrew Miles picked it up he was breathless from running from the yard.

'It's Louise Case. I'm sorry to trouble you but I have a problem here.'

'Oh aye,' Mr Miles said cautiously. Louise had telephoned him when her septic tank overflowed, when her rainwater drains had blocked and flooded her study, when her water-pipes froze, and when the coal merchant had failed to deliver her coal. To all these minor crises Mr Miles had responded as a good neighbour, and graciously received Louise's envelopes containing excessive amounts of cash. But he had learned that Louise's charm – to which he was deeply susceptible – generally indicated work which needed doing at once, often in the middle of lambing.

'I have this old woman camping in my orchard,' Louise said.

'Well, you would,' Mr Miles replied. 'It's May.'

'Is that her name?'

'The month. She always camps in your orchard in May. June she goes on to Cothering Farm. Every year.'

Louise exhaled her rising irritation. 'I didn't know that.'

'Oh, yes.'

Mr Miles seemed to think the call had ended. He was about to put down the telephone.

'Wait!' Louise said urgently. 'I want her moved.'

There was a shocked silence.

'She can't stay here, there are no . . . facilities. She has a dog, and she needs wood for her stove. She's right at the bottom of my garden!'

Mr Miles sighed.

'Surely you have a corner of a field or somewhere she could go?' Louise asked plaintively. 'All those fields of yours are empty.'

'Hay,' Andrew Miles said succinctly. 'Those empty fields

are hay meadows. They are not empty. They are growing hay. You can't put a van on a hay crop.'

'Somewhere there must be a corner for her?'

'She can come if she likes. But she's always stayed in your orchard before. She was born there.'

'Will you come down and tell her?'

'I'll come down just before dinner,' Andrew Miles said grudgingly. 'But I doubt she'll listen to me.'

'Not until tonight?'

'Dinner midday.'

'Thank you,' Louise said. But he had already hung up.

Andrew Miles's Land-Rover pulled up behind Toby's clean white Ford Escort and coughed to a standstill. Louise came out of the front door, Toby behind her. Louise introduced the two men. Andrew looked over Toby with one brief, encompassing glance. Toby in his turn saw a man in his middle forties, weathered into a broken-veined tan. A tall man, all bone and muscle with beaky hard features and a pair of hard blue eyes. His thinning fair hair was crushed down by a flat cloth cap with the shine of age on the peak. He was wearing working trousers very unlike Toby's well-cut chinos, and a brushed cotton coloured shirt with the nap worn away at the collar.

'Well, then,' he said.

Louise led the way down the garden to the orchard gate. 'Hello!' she called.

The old woman poked her head out of the van door and looked at the three of them. She nodded to Andrew Miles with a small knowing smile, but she said nothing.

'Mr Miles here has a field where you could park your van,' Louise began. Unconsciously she had raised her voice to the determinedly bright tone that is appropriate for the disabled and old and those too weak to protest. 'A lovely big field where you'd be more comfortable.'

The old woman looked at Andrew. 'The bottom field where your dad kept the pigs?' she asked. 'I told your grandad and I told your dad I'd not stop there.'

'Any field you like. You're in the way for Miss Case, here,' he said gruffly.

The old woman looked quickly at Louise. 'How am I in your way?'

'You're not!' Louise said quickly. 'But it is my orchard, and you are trespassing, actually.' She felt her voice weaken. 'It is my land, you know, and there isn't really room for you here.'

'He said I could stay.' The old woman jerked a dirty thumb at Toby. 'Your fancy-man. He said I could stay.'

Toby flushed under Andrew Miles's look of interested inquiry. 'Well, I was just thinking . . .'

'I can't move anyway,' the old woman said. 'The gears are gone. I couldn't get up that hill. I've got no first or second gear. I was going to ask you to fix it for me.'

Andrew nodded. 'Not today I can't,' he cautioned. 'Later I will.'

The old lady nodded as if the problem were solved. 'When the engine's fixed I'll move on,' she said. 'Not to the pig field. I go on to Cothering next. I'll go when the engine is fixed.'

Louise would have been happier with an undertaking as to when the engine would be fixed but both men had nodded and turned away. The old woman spoke to Louise in a conspiratorial undertone. 'He's a handsome man. Any woman would be proud to have him in her bed. I can see why you like him.'

'Toby?'

'Andrew Miles,' the woman said, her voice loving every syllable of his name. 'And such a pretty farm, and owned freehold, you know. You've been wasting your time with that girl's blouse Toby. If I were your age I'd be tucked up in the big feather bed in the farmhouse b'now and a couple of babies in the cot, too.'

Louise turned away and followed the men back to the house. They were standing in the drive beside Andrew's Land-Rover. Louise felt extraordinarily uncomfortable.

'I'll need to look round,' Mr Miles said. 'I'll have to find a reconditioned gear box. It's a big job. I can come down and do it later in the week.'

'That'll be great,' Toby agreed eagerly. He was heavier than Andrew Miles, better dressed, rounder-faced, richer all over with the smooth glossiness of a well-serviced urban man. But beside the beaky farmer he looked strangely insubstantial. 'Louise can't really work with the van there.'

'I thought she worked in the dining room?'

'It overlooks the orchard.'

Andrew Miles looked at Louise as if he would ask her what work took place in the dining room but needed a clear view of the orchard. 'Landscape painting?'

'No, I'm trying to write an essay on Lawrence,' Louise said. 'But I can't concentrate on anything when I keep seeing the van.'

'Oh, writing. I thought you were a teacher.'

'I teach at the university and I write as well.'

He opened the door of the Land-Rover. It creaked loudly and a few flakes of paint fell like dark green snow. 'Got to get home,' he said. 'Pigs want feeding.'

'Thank you for coming,' Louise said. 'I really do appreciate it. You're such a good neighbour!'

Andrew Miles nodded without smiling. Louise, feeling that she had been gushing, retreated to the front door. Toby stood by his car, to ensure that Mr Miles crashed his Land-Rover into reverse gear and backed safely away from its shiny whiteness.

They went back into the house. 'Coffee?' Louise offered. 'Or do you have to go?'

'Actually, I think I'll pop down and have another word with your old lady. She was talking to me last night about her childhood. I was thinking, I might do a bit of oral history research on her. It's something I've always wanted to do. If she's going to be here for a few days I could take the opportunity.'

'You hate oral history,' Louise pointed out. 'You said it was worse than local history in encouraging people to be egotistical about their boring past, trying to pass tedious personal gossip off as interesting facts.'

'Oh, yes,' Toby said with an easy laugh. 'But if she really was born here and adopted in London then she does have a story. Quite different from all the people who worked in newspapers before computers, or served in shops before supermarkets. She might be really quite interesting.'

Louise shrugged. Her dream of the flood-tide carrying books, the old woman's admiration of Andrew Miles, and Toby's sudden attentiveness all conspired to make her feel off-balance. She felt as if the calm certainties of her life as a career academic and adulterous lover were all being questioned at once. 'Talk to her if you want to,' she said. 'But if Miriam rings me, are you supposed to be here?'

'I'm in the library at university,' Toby said. He knew that the naming of Miriam was a warning of Louise's displeasure, but his inner joy that he had successfully laid claim to the old lady's story without challenge from Louise was too great.

'You do some work,' he urged. 'Don't worry about the old lady. She'll be no trouble to you now.' He smiled at her and went down the garden path to the gate to the orchard. Louise turned and went back into the house.

'*The Virgin and the Gypsy*, a patriarchal myth of rape and female growth,' Louise typed into the keyboard. The words came up on the screen, each letter trotting out behind the cursor like a reliable friend. Louise paused. She had the start of an idea – that Lawrence portrayed the young women as waiting for an event in their lives, that Yvette in particular was shown as a girl awaiting transition into womanhood. There was some concealed pun, Louise thought, in the girls having attended 'finishing' school – and the sense that their travels ended at the start of the book. Lawrence affected to know better – that the two women were not finished, they were not even started until they were sexually active.

So far so good (tick tick in the margin) but then Lawrence went further and implied that sexual development was the only future open to them. Their conversation was mainly about adornment and husband-catching. Their social life was all courtship. And their inner life was the progress from unknowing virginity to maturity which could only be achieved through sexual intercourse with a knowing man. All this was very bad indeed (cross cross cross in the margin, and often '!').

Louise thought she could write a convincing essay dividing Lawrence the rebel – against the bourgeois society, which was good (tick tick) from Lawrence the sexist – against

62

women except as sexual objects, which was bad (cross cross cross). But when she came to write the first paragraph she found that between her and the screen came an entrapping maze of images. The snowdrop-flower of the mother's face, the gypsy lashing his horse to reach the house before the thundering flood of the river, Andrew Miles's gentle smile at the old woman, and her own dream of rising water and the man in her bed. A man to whom she had cried 'I'm sorry! I'm sorry!' A wronged man, the wronged man. The wrong man.

Louise had never screamed at any man, least of all Toby whose control over his own temperament inspired a calm, almost balletic response from her. Toby was so charming, so consciously sexily charming that he inspired Louise to be charming too. She could never have flung herself at him screaming 'I'm sorry'.

In the end she wrote, 'It is almost impossible to construct a feminist reading of D.H. Lawrence's works, immured, as he is, in the sexism of his generation and class', which felt like the start of an appropriate revenge on a dead author who had filled her night with unacceptable but irresistible images of desire and then given her a dream of a wronged man in her bed and a scarlet flood of spoiled books.

The phone ringing abruptly at her elbow made her jump. She picked it up, half-expecting Andrew Miles with some news of a gear box. But it was Miriam.

'I can't talk,' she said. 'I'm in a rush. I wondered if I could come and stay with you tonight? I'm up to my ears and I want a break.'

'Of course,' Louise said. Miriam often stayed a night in her cottage. Sometimes she came with Toby, sometimes alone. 'Lovely.'

'I've been doing the finance books of the refuge all morning and the walls are closing in on me. Hell! Louise, d'you remember when we said we'd never get office jobs?'

'It's hardly an office.'

'It's office work. It just happens that it's done on an old school desk in a cramped room without any qualified help. This does not make it any better, surprisingly enough. Shall I bring food?'

'I'll go into the village and shop,' Louise said. 'I might as well. I'm not getting anything done here.' She paused and then asked with clever deceit, 'Will Toby come too?'

'I've lost him,' Miriam replied. 'He's not at home and he's not in his office. Can I be a bore and bring him if he wants to come?'

'That's fine,' Louise said. 'I'll make enough for three and we can pig out if he doesn't come.'

'Thanks,' Miriam said. 'I'll go to my meeting now. If they ask for a treasurer's report they can see my notepad. I can't make head or tail of it myself.' She giggled, her old feckless undergraduate giggle, and put down the telephone.

Louise pressed the 'Save' key on her word processor and shut the machine down, preserving its one solitary sentence, and went out into the garden.

Toby and the old woman were sitting on her steps. She had a large cardboard box on her lap and she was showing Toby one yellowing piece of newspaper after another. Louise waved and was surprised to see Toby stuff a newspaper clipping back into the box and come quickly forward.

'I've just had Miriam on the phone. She's coming out for dinner and to stay overnight. Will you want to stay too? I have to shop.'

The thought of his wife and mistress under the same roof again was always a temptation for Toby, but then he remembered a meeting on graduate students which he was supposed to chair. 'Damn, I can't,' he said. Besides, it would give him a chance to go to the library and take out everything they had on the suffragette movement. 'Got to chair the humanities programme meeting.'

'I'll shop now then,' Louise said distantly. 'Shall I buy something for lunch?'

Toby glanced back at the old woman with her tempting box of cuttings sitting on her steps in the sunshine. 'No, I've delayed you too much today, anyway,' he said. 'I'll finish up here and go.'

Louise nodded rather coldly. 'See you Monday then.' She waved a casual hand and then went back up the garden to her car. She and Toby were accustomed never to display affection before strangers, but she was irritated by having to be discreet in her own garden.

Wistley village was built along one main street with the village green a bulbous lump on the west side of the road. In older days it had been the village children's playground when they had tumbled out of the little school beside it. They would buy everlasting gobstoppers or barley-sugar spirals at the village shop and put down their jackets for goalposts in winter, wickets in summer. People who lived adjacent to the green endured the bruising of plants in their front gardens by the flying trespass of a boundary shot or a wildly kicked goal. Often the game was interrupted when an irate gardener burst from a cottage and chased a child across the green and across the road. The children ran like a yelping pack to the common and then dropped into the bracken and lay low.

Since 1972 the village children had been bussed to the

big school twelve miles away, and the weekday village was as desolate as Hamelin after the piper. The old school house had been converted into a rather imposing-looking residence, with white gables and mock Georgian bow windows and a double door. The new owner, a retired captain of marines, had put up a name plate which read 'Wistley Manor', a rather unfortunate misreading of history in a village which had always escaped a resident squire and which had been, for a brief exciting period in the late eighteenth century, organised as a radical labourers' co-operative.

No-one objected. The Methodist chapel, which had held services since the great Wesley himself had preached on the green and led a deafening chorus of hymns, was deconsecrated in the early '80s and converted into a house which then called itself 'Wistley House'. This small piece of one-upmanship amused the village and put the Captain's nose badly out of joint. The two households sent each other Christmas cards of engravings of their houses and signed inside, 'from all at Wistley Manor' or 'from all at Wistley House', and the question of social predominance was never conclusively settled.

The small Norman parish church survived, though the old vicarage had been sold to a wealthy couple from London who had it done up and maintained, but hardly ever visited. The village children stole daffodils from the immaculate lawns on Mothering Sunday. The vicar, with no home in the village, now commuted from nearby Hallfield, with two other villages in his charge. Wistley had morning communion every third Sunday and some people blamed the poor attendances on the difficulty of predicting whether this particular Sabbath was sacred in Wistley or not.

The majority of people in the village lived in a small council estate on the south side of the green. The houses were pale concrete. They had won an award for imaginative design in the late '70s and were notorious for the perennial leaks in the flat roofs. Some of the long narrow gardens were bright with skeletal climbing frames in primary colours. Others were packed with wigwams of peas and beans and obedient rows of potatoes. Many grew nothing but long grass and mysterious bits of engines. One or two had gone very modern indeed and concreted the lot, speckling the concrete with a pattern which was supposed to look like cobblestones or hand-laid bricks. Most of the men worked in Hallfield at the fruit packing and bottling factory. Many women went to Hallfield for part-time work, but some cleaned or nannied in the nearby large renovated cottages and houses.

There was a thriving corner shop run by the widow Mrs Ford which sold newspapers, magazines, sweets, cigarettes, and a small supply of tinned and dry goods. There was a butcher who also stocked teas and groceries. Most of his trade came from the larger cottages and houses. It was cheaper to catch the bus to the supermarket at Hallfield than pay his inflated prices. Only his mince was reasonable and his sausages, though suspected of excess amounts of cereal or worse, were cheap. There was a small greengrocer's, whose owner was planning to retire shortly. The competition from nearby farm shops and fields of pick-your-own fruit was proving too much. And there was a tiny off-licence which made a living from opening in the evening and selling everything that anyone might want after six. A mobile fish-and-chip van stopped outside the shop on Fridays and Saturdays.

There were two pubs: the Holly Bush, which was used by people from the council houses and boasted a successful darts team, and the Olde House at Home, Wistley, which had been opened in 1973 and boasted many darkened beams

– some of them even made from real wood – faded prints, a good menu of bar food, and three different types of beer. Andrew Miles, a connoisseur of public houses, had been thrown out of the Olde House at Home, Wistley, on Christmas Eve, 1989, for caressing the landlord's wife's bottom, and remained permanently banned.

Louise, who was planning to make a chicken casserole for herself and Miriam which could go in the Rayburn now and need no attention until they were ready to eat, bought chicken pieces at the butcher's, and onions, potatoes, red peppers and tomatoes at the greengrocer's. On her way back to her car she was stopped by Captain Frome of Wistley Manor.

As an unobservant newcomer to the village, Louise had no idea that Wistley Manor was, in reality, a new house, with a snob name. She always felt herself to be in the presence of a genuine squire of the manor when Captain Frome spoke to her. She had attended a sherry party at his house, shortly after moving in to the cottage, and had felt herself simultaneously insulted and flattered by his weighty paternalist flirting. She believed that he was born and bred in Wistley Manor and heir to a long tradition of rural squires. She felt he was the sort of man who would know what gamekeepers did during the day. She had no idea that he knew even less about the countryside than she did.

'See you've got that old rogue parked on your patch!' Captain Frome said, lifting his hat to her, and then taking the carrier bags easily out of her hands.

'There's no need,' Louise protested. 'I can manage perfectly well.'

He smiled. Louise's objections were to him the usual flutterings of a damned pretty woman. 'Don't know why you encourage her!'

'I don't encourage her!' Louise said, stung. She fumbled in her handbag for her car keys. 'She just arrived without permission. I'm trying to move her on.'

'Outrageous really.' He waited by the car door while Louise opened it. 'And once you get one coming, they'll all be here. Gypsies, tinkers, hippies. We can't afford it in a little place like this. All sorts of difficulties it causes.'

'She moves on in June,' Louise offered, taking the bags from him and stowing them on the passenger seat.

'Nearly a fortnight! I'm surprised you don't have her moved on. She'll be burning your fence for firewood and chopping down your trees next.'

'Her van needs repairing, Mr Miles is doing it for her. Then she's moving on. I can't really get rid of her before then.'

'Police'd move her on PDQ. Pretty damn quick,' he translated.

'I don't think I want to call the police in,' Louise said firmly. 'She's just an old lady.'

He gave a short sceptical laugh. 'I hope you feel the same when all her family arrive! Half a dozen vans all in your orchard. One old lady is no problem. A small camp is something different.'

'A camp?'

'She's probably a scout for the whole family.' He raised his hat to her. 'I could mention it at the Parish Council meeting, they could find a proper site for her.'

Louise was still reeling at the thought of a small camp in her orchard. 'Yes,' she said vaguely. 'If you think it would help. But she did say she was moving on.'

'Give an inch, they take a yard, these people,' he said. 'Good day.'

*　　*　　*

Miriam arrived as Louise was clearing up the kitchen.

'I'm glad to be here,' she announced. 'It's been a B of a week.'

Louise poured her a glass of wine from the open bottle. 'Why so bad?'

Miriam shrugged. 'Oh, I don't know,' she said. 'Perhaps I'm getting too old for it. Or perhaps it really is getting worse. When I started working at the centre I genuinely believed we could make a difference. But all I do is sustain the problem. For every woman I can get rehoused there are six I have to send back to their husbands to get beaten again. There's less and less money available and more and more people needing help, and I can't get the staff. I used to have more volunteers from the university than I could handle. But I went up and gave a talk the other day and a girl asked me what *she* would get out of it? I ask you! What she would get out of working in a women's refuge!'

'What did you say?'

'I flannelled on about sharing your privileges, and a sense of duty to the community, and she looked at me as if I was speaking Chinese. Then I said it would look good on her CV for a future employer and her eyes lit up at last. That's all she was interested in.'

'So will you take her?'

Miriam made a face. 'Fat chance. She won't volunteer until she's done her finals so that she gets the entry on her CV but doesn't have to waste her precious time. She asked me how much I earn and when I told her she made a little face and said she didn't think she could manage on that and that she couldn't consider community work as a career.'

'Surely it's always been tough,' Louise said. 'From the very start.'

'Yes. But at the start in the '80s there was a genuine

feeling that poverty and abuse of women could be solved. Since then, post-Thatcher, there's a sense that poverty and cruelty is natural. There's nothing anyone can do about it. The job for police or for social workers is to make sure that it doesn't spill into the posh areas. It's happening everywhere. The charities working with the homeless have to stop people sleeping in boxes where rich people might fall over them. My job is about containing violence in people's homes, not curing it. I get enough money to rehouse women who might be murdered. The ones that get knocked about have to go back.' Miriam sighed. 'Anyway.' She changed the subject. 'I saw the van. You still have your old lady?'

'She's due to leave, as soon as Mr Miles fixes the gear box,' Louise said. 'I'm actually becoming accustomed to her being there. I had a bad dream in the night and I woke up and saw her light at the bottom of the orchard and it was comforting.'

'What facilities does she have?'

Louise shrugged. 'How should I know? I've never been in. I give her a jug of fresh water now and then.'

Miriam looked rather severe. 'You mean, there's an old woman living in a broken-down van in your orchard and you haven't even checked if she has the facilities to cook and clean? What about her toilet? What about washing?'

'I don't want to know about her toilet,' Louise said, irritated. 'I expect she is managing how she has always managed. She appears to be a seasonal event around here. My aunt apparently knew her and let her stay. Now I've inherited her along with the cottage. At least Mr Miles says she can stay on his fields. Next year I'll make sure I have the fence up by May, and that gate bolted.'

'But what if she were to be ill? Or have a fall?'

'She doesn't look like the sort of old lady who has falls,' Louise said unkindly. 'She looks like the sort of old lady who would have to be pushed.'

'Oh really, Louise!'

Louise scowled. 'I can't be responsible for her, Miriam. I really can't.'

'Well, someone ought to be,' Miriam said. 'Would you mind if I went and had a word with her? There are permanent sites in the county, I checked before I came out. I brought a leaflet with a map, just in case she didn't know.'

Louise hesitated, wondering whether the old lady would speak of Toby. She shrugged. It would be Toby's own fault for getting so intimate with her. 'If you must. I was just about to serve supper.'

'I'll only be a sec,' Miriam promised and slipped out of the kitchen door.

The sun was low on the horizon, casting a pale yellow light across the garden and greenish shadows. Small bats circled and dipped in the air, moving almost too fast to be seen. The night-scented flowers made the garden sweet and dreamy. Miriam walked slowly across the grass where the daisies had already closed their pink-tipped faces against the dusk. Her anxieties and irritations with the imperfect world drained away from her. She breathed in. The air was clean and sweet, still warm, and with the promise of warmth for tomorrow, and for four months of tomorrows.

The summer had always been Miriam's favourite time of year. No-one who had ever seen her sprawled in the grass outside the library with a book over her sleeping face could doubt the natural order of things which made the sun always shine on her. Punctual and reliable in autumn and winter with essays well-written and cogently argued, her work went to pieces in spring and disappeared completely during the summer term. Her midsummer essays were always late and always crumpled and dusty as if they had been written in a garden under a tree, resting on the grass messy with fertile pollen. Her hair, tidily brushed in the dark months, took on glints from the sun, and grew wild and curly around her face which became first flushed and then freckled and then brown.

In the long summer vacations Miriam would always go abroad. She and Louise hitch-hiked or travelled by train to the south of France, Spain, or Italy in long idyllic holidays only marred by the delay of drafts of money from home, or by the occasional wet day when Miriam would droop and exclaim at the impossibility of the Mediterranean being cold.

Abstemious for the rest of the year, Miriam was a glutton and a drunkard in summer. She would eat a pound of peaches in one sitting. She would drink lager in pint glasses. And in summer, Miriam was joyfully wanton.

It was no accident that she had found her radical feminist conscience in the darkening autumn of her last year at university and that in her final summer she had been too harassed by exams to respond to the weather. Then she had taken the job in the women's refuge and all her subsequent summers had then been marked by the stuffiness of the cramped office and the rancid smell of her sweating clients. For three weeks every year Miriam and Toby went cycling in France and once again Miriam would lie in the sun and melt into Toby's kisses. But these were holidays from reality. Miriam's adult self was wintry and serious.

The old lady was sitting on her steps, watching the sun go slowly down. The windscreen twinkled with the yellow light as if it were clean. Her lined face was golden in the light, she looked like some wise old priestess at a shrine where anyone in need could go for assistance. She smiled as she saw Miriam approaching as if she knew all about her.

'Hello,' Miriam said pleasantly. 'I'm Miriam Carpenter, a friend of Louise's. I work with homeless women in Brighton. I just popped out to see if there was anything I could do to help you.'

The old lady smiled at her, her face crazing into a thousand wrinkles. 'What help could you possibly give me?' she asked.

Miriam, more accustomed to needy clients, failed to hear the arrogant emphasis. 'I could help you get on a housing list,' she said eagerly. 'Or get this van on to a permanent site where you could have running water, and showers and toilets. That'd be something, wouldn't it? They have electricity at the sites. You could have a television.'

The old lady chuckled. 'I don't want any of that.'

Miriam felt checked. 'Medical care?'

The old woman grew suddenly grave. 'I won't be needing that,' she said. 'Nature will take its course.'

'You might have a fall,' Miriam suggested. In Miriam's world women over sixty were always falling and needing replacement hips, just as women of forty were always getting hot and needing hormone replacement therapy. The female body was in continual need of attention and assistance.

The old lady put her hand out to Miriam. Miriam stepped forward and clasped it. The touch of the old lady's hand was warm and dry as a snakeskin. 'I've not got long to live,' she said gently. 'Just a month at the most. So I don't need anything, but it was kind of you to offer. I just want to be left in peace.'

There was a short stunned silence. 'You're dying?' Miriam asked incredulously.

The old lady nodded, her eyes on Miriam's face. 'That's why I wanted to be here,' she said gently. 'In this orchard. I was born here and I've been here every May for the last thirty years. I had a fancy to die here. Die here and have my van burned with my body.'

'You're a Romany,' Miriam said, her voice very gentle with respect.

The old woman smiled at her. 'I like the old ways. I want to die here, where I was born. Do you think she'll let me?'

'What about a hospice?' Miriam asked.

'A hospital? No, I don't like hospitals.'

'No, no, a hospice. A special place, like a rest home. People go there when they are very sick, going to die, and the staff are specially trained to understand and to be with you, to control the pain and help you.'

The old lady looked slightly alarmed. 'That doesn't sound much fun. I wouldn't like one of them at all.' She pressed Miriam's hand gently between her own. 'It's hard for someone like you to understand, I know,' she said. 'But really, I just want to go quietly, in my own bed, in the place I was born. I want to be on my own,' she insisted. 'No-one fussing around me, and someone to burn my things when I'm dead.'

Miriam, who had counselled a thousand women distressed by less, felt her throat tightening. 'You're very brave.'

The old woman smiled. 'Will you help me – to stay here and die as I've lived? As I want to die?'

Miriam blinked rapidly. 'Yes,' she said. 'Of course. I'll

settle it with Louise and if you change your mind I'll see if I can book a place in the hospice if you need extra help. Do you have enough to eat? Fresh water?'

'I'll thank you for a jug of fresh water,' the old woman said meekly. 'I've been thirsty, but I didn't like to go to the back door in case I was intruding.'

Miriam took the jug without comment and hurried to the kitchen door. The kitchen was filled with rich-smelling steam. Louise had taken the casserole from the oven and was adding a generous glass of wine to the gravy.

'She needs water,' Miriam said with emphasis, filling the jug at the kitchen sink.

'She always does,' Louise replied, stirring and tasting with relish. 'She must drink a gallon a day.'

Miriam said nothing but took the jug out to the van again.

'Don't say nothing to her about me dying,' the old woman said to Miriam. 'I don't want to worry her. I don't want to make a fuss. If you can get her to let me stay, that's all I want. Can you do that?'

Miriam had been strictly trained in client confidence. 'I won't tell anyone until you say I may,' she agreed. 'Can I book a place in the hospice in case you need it?'

The old woman smiled as if she were giving Miriam a concession. 'If it would make you feel better,' she said. 'But I shan't go anywhere else. I want to die here.'

'You shall do it as you want!' Miriam promised. 'I have to go in now. Do you have everything you need? Do you have enough food?'

'I've had trouble lighting my stove today. I'll just eat some cheese and biscuits tonight. I don't need much. I'll have a hot meal tomorrow or the next day.'

'I'll bring you out some of what we're having,' Miriam

76

promised. 'We're having chicken casserole. Would you like some?'

'Thank you,' the old woman said with dignity. 'That would be very nice.'

Miriam smiled and was about to go back to the house.

'And do you teach at the university too?' the old woman asked.

'No. I work at a refuge for women who have been beaten by their partners. And I work with women alcoholics and with women who have been abused.'

The old woman looked shocked. 'A young thing like you!' she exclaimed.

Miriam smiled. 'I'm not so very young. I'm thirty.'

'Thirty,' the old woman said thoughtfully. 'But how long have you been doing this?'

'Since I left university. Nearly nine years now.'

The old woman looked at Miriam with a strange expression. Miriam stared back, trying to read the face. She looked as if she were pitying Miriam. This was a sensation so strange that Miriam felt almost offended. For the past nine years Miriam had been in a position to pity others. The reversal of the roles made her feel disorientated and uneasy.

''Bout time you did something for yourself then,' the old woman remarked. 'Nine years on other people's troubles is much too long.'

'I enjoy my work,' Miriam said, steadfastly smiling.

The old woman snorted. 'Lady Bountiful,' she said spitefully. 'You should look to what's going on in your own backyard. It's not very long, my dear, before you're dead and buried and all you'll have done is worry about other people's troubles.'

Miriam shook her head, trying to keep the smile on her

face. 'I do make a difference,' she said. 'I get women rehoused, I help to change their lives.'

'Pot calling the kettle black,' the old woman said churlishly. 'You should be rehousing yourself, my girl. Change your own life.'

Miriam began to understand why Louise did not want this woman in her orchard. 'I'd better go,' she said. 'I'll bring you your dinner in a moment.'

The old woman smiled, her good humour undisturbed. 'You run along. Find someone else to worry about. *I'm* all right.'

Louise was reluctant to let Miriam out of the door with a plate of chicken casserole, fearing that she would set a precedent and the old woman would arrive for breakfast, lunch and dinner thereafter. But no-one could ever stop Miriam from doing what she knew to be right. Louise let her go.

'You must let her stay here, Louise,' Miriam said firmly. 'She told me something in confidence which I can't tell you, but you really do have to let her stay here.'

'What d'you mean?' Louise demanded. 'She's going as soon as the gear box is fixed. That's the agreement.'

Miriam shook her head. 'I want you to promise me that you'll let her stay. I promise you she'll not be here longer than a month. I give you my word, Louise. It's just a month.'

Louise put their own plates down and plonked salt and pepper in the middle of the table. She poured more wine. She looked sulky. 'You wouldn't be so keen if it was your garden.'

'I probably wouldn't,' Miriam admitted honestly. 'But she's where she wants to be. Listen, I'm making arrangements for her accommodation. If the problem is not resolved in a month I'll find her a place in the h . . .'

'A place in the h . . . ?'

Miriam shook her head. 'I really can't say. But I promise you that she won't be with you for more than a month.'

Louise sighed. 'I don't want her. I don't see why I should *have* her.'

'Well, you've got her. Just put up with her for a month. Twenty-eight days. It's not much to ask. And it's not as if you do a lot for the homeless.'

'All right,' Louise conceded grudgingly. 'But she's to go in a month without fail. And if anyone tries to join her –' Louise was thinking about Captain Frome's warning of family camps. 'If anyone tries to join her I'll have them all moved on.'

'She doesn't have anyone travelling with her. She specifically told me that she wanted to be here on her own.'

'All right then.'

The two women ate in silence.

'She told me a funny thing,' Miriam said. 'She told me I should change my own life, look at my own backyard.'

Louise glanced up, a forkful of casserole poised.

'It's true,' Miriam said. 'I spend all my life organising other people and I never look at what I'm doing. At where we live. At Toby and me.'

'But you're all right, aren't you?' Louise had no false delicacy warning her not to tread in difficult areas. Miriam had shared the difficulties of her relationship with Toby from the very beginning. Louise's intimacy with them both was reinforced by the fact that she always heard of every marital squabble from both sides. On many occasions she had acted as unpaid (and untrained) counsellor, explaining

Miriam's feelings to Toby and vice versa. That her insight into Toby's feelings came from her love affair with him did not seem, to Louise, to disqualify her from taking a neutral viewpoint. And indeed, Miriam had always found Louise supportive and sympathetic. There were few things Louise enjoyed more than dissecting her lover's psychology with his wife.

'We're all right,' Miriam agreed. 'But nothing more than all right. We share a house. We often eat together. We sleep in the same bed. Sometimes we make love. It's OK but you couldn't say it was wildly exciting. We're not close any more, if you know what I mean.'

Louise nodded encouragingly. 'Is he withdrawn?'

'Not him,' Miriam said. 'It's me. I can't even tell you why. I'm really busy all the time, and the work I do – well, of course it's depressing. I'm home after him in the evening and then I spend an hour on the telephone. I'm out of the house before him in the morning. We saw more of each other when you were there, actually. We always had dinner together then.'

Louise hid her pleasure. 'Don't the two of you eat with Hugh?'

Miriam shook her head. 'Toby doesn't cook like he used to,' she said. 'Last time he did a proper meal was when you came.'

Louise nodded her head, looking concerned but feeling exultant. It was as she had thought. The marriage was a three-way relationship. With her withdrawal everything had changed. She felt a thrilling desire to jiggle the pillars of the temple like an experimental Samson and see if the whole thing came down.

'If you could have anything you wanted,' she asked, invoking the old game they used to play when they were undergraduates and thought that everything was possible, 'anything in the world, what would it be?'

Miriam put her fork on her plate and rested her chin on her hands. For a moment she did not look like Miriam, thirty years old and stuck in a rut of social work and unsocial hours. She smiled. 'I'd buy a bike,' she said. 'A mountain bike with loads of fancy gears and I'd pack a bag, and I'd take the ferry to Europe and I'd bike all around the world. Everywhere it was sunny. And I'd never come home again.'

Louise smiled indulgently. 'Lovely,' she said.

Saturday

THE PHONE RANG ABRUPTLY on Saturday morning, jerking Louise from sleep. She could hear Miriam downstairs, moving around the kitchen, making coffee and toast. Miriam never slept late any more, she was out of practice. Her conscience would wake her from the deepest, most restful sleep and remind her of work she had left unfinished: work which never could be finished while men and women treated each other with contempt.

'Frome here,' the Captain's upper-class authoritative voice boomed in Louise's ear. 'Sorry to call so early, I had some news I thought I should tell you.'

'Oh yes, Captain Frome,' Louise said, sitting upright and rubbing her face into wakefulness.

'We had the community policeman at the Parish Council meeting last night. It seems that your old lady may be joined by some friends, just as I thought. We all felt you should be warned.'

Louise raised herself in bed and looked anxiously out of the window. The blue van was still solitary in the orchard. The dog dozed at the steps. A small pile of wood, dead branches from trees, had appeared at the other side of the steps. Hazy violet woodsmoke shimmered from the aluminium chimney. Louise could smell the smoke, and behind the smoke the delicious smell of bacon frying. 'Friends?'

'There's some kind of gang of travellers – the usual sort of thing. Apparently they're headed our way. The police are keeping a general eye on things. But I told the community policeman about your old lady. He thought she might be some kind of advance guard, to soften up the do-gooders. I said you were taking a proper attitude to it. I said you were moving her on.'

'I am,' Louise assured him hastily. 'In a month. I've said she could have a month.'

'I thought you said she would be gone by June?'

'I did . . . er . . . her plans have changed.'

'Well, they'll be here before then!' the Captain exclaimed. 'They'll be here within days! The neighbourhood watch are leafleting houses, advising people to lock up their fields and paddocks. You'd be well advised to move her on and get that fence of yours repaired before they're all camped in your orchard.'

'Oh God,' Louise said wearily.

'D'you want me to come around and sort it out?' the Captain demanded, trying to conceal his eagerness.

'No, no! Thank you, but no. I have a friend, a social worker, she can find the old lady somewhere to go. She said she had a place for her. She's staying with me. She'll sort it out.'

'Social worker, eh? I'd have thought you'd have done better with a firm word from me.'

'Oh, thank you,' Louise said distractedly. 'But I really think . . . I'll telephone if I need you, if I may.'

'Very well, very well,' the Captain said rather distantly. 'See what you can do. The whole Parish Council is concerned at the line you're taking. You don't want to be seen letting the side down now, do you?'

'No! Of course not.'

'Newcomers to the country always have to be particularly careful,' he advised kindly. 'You think you're doing the right thing but in fact you're putting a lot of backs up. Take my word for it. Let's do this as it's always been done and get the gypsies moved on.'

'I'll phone you,' Louise responded weakly. 'Goodbye.'

Miriam tapped on the door and came into the room, a cup of coffee in her hand. 'I heard the phone.'

'Thank you,' Louise said. She took the cup. 'That was the local bigwig. Apparently there's a convoy of travellers headed this way. Everyone thinks they're coming to my orchard. I've got to get the old lady moved on and the fence put up. Miriam, this changes everything.'

'You could put a gate in,' Miriam suggested. 'She *has* to stay for a month. I promised her she could.'

'But what about all the other travellers?' Louise found her voice was rising. 'And there's the village to think about as well. I don't want to upset everybody.'

Miriam shrugged. She was a city dweller, she had no idea of the mafia-like power of village society. 'The other travellers won't come here,' she said. 'What is there for them? A tiny little orchard and the company of an old lady? They'll be on their way to a rave somewhere.'

'Oh God,' Louise said again. 'They'll be holding a rave in my orchard!'

Miriam laughed aloud. 'No, all you've got is one quiet old lady for a month. This is just the panic of the bourgeoisie with property values under threat. Calm down!'

'Well, I'm getting a gate put in,' Louise said firmly. 'I'm not having the fence open to anyone who fancies driving in. And you must make her promise that she is nothing to do with these others.'

'OK. OK. I'll make you some breakfast. Toast?'

'Please.' Louise got out of bed and pulled on her fraying towelling dressing gown. The silky one with the matching pyjamas was in the bottom drawer waiting for Toby.

She picked up the telephone. She knew Andrew Miles's three-digit number by heart. Again she waited while the phone rang and rang. Just as she was going to give up, he picked it up. He was breathless. 'Yes?'

'It's Louise Case.'

'Hold on a minute.'

Louise heard him shouting at a dog to get out of the kitchen with those dirty paws and then he picked up the phone again. 'Yes?'

'I've just had Captain Frome on the telephone,' she said.

'Oh, him.'

'He says there is a convoy of travellers headed this way.'

Andrew Miles said nothing.

'I want a gate put across the gap in the fence,' Louise told him. 'The neighbourhood watch people are advising everyone to close up their paddocks and fields.'

There was a suppressed snort on the other end of the telephone which sounded like Andrew Miles trying not to laugh. 'A bit difficult on a two-hundred-acre farm and a common with common rights,' he pointed out.

'Yes, but about my orchard . . .'

'All right,' he said. 'I've got a hurdle I can put across. I'll come down now.'

'Thank you,' Louise said. 'And the gear box for the van?'

'I've not found one yet,' he said. He had forgotten all about the van. 'I'll ring a couple of garages and then I'll come down.'

'Thank you,' said Louise again but he was already gone.

By the time Louise was dressed, in well-cut jeans and a

crew-neck cream cotton sweater, Andrew Miles's Land-Rover had already shuddered to a halt outside and Miriam had opened the front door to him. 'Hello, come in.'

Andrew hesitated. He had never been inside the house since Louise had moved in. All their business had been conducted at the overflow end of the septic tank, or pacing the boundaries. 'Louise will be down in a moment,' Miriam said with her meaningless social-worker smile.

Andrew heel-toed his Wellington boots off and stepped over the threshold, leaving them in the porch. His knitted socks were thick and grey. He wriggled one adventurous toe back out of sight from a small hole. Miriam was too polite to stare but she was unused to people taking their shoes off before entering a house like faithful Muslims in a temple.

Louise came downstairs and recoiled slightly at seeing Andrew Miles, so big, and with such big woolly feet, in her dainty sitting room. 'Oh, hello.'

'She asked me in,' Andrew said gracelessly.

'Coffee?' Miriam offered.

Andrew gave Louise a quick embarrassed look. 'If you have the time,' Louise said. 'I expect you want to get on. You're always so busy.'

'Haymaking,' Andrew explained quickly. 'Soon,' he added more honestly. 'I'll start on that hurdle.'

He backed out towards the door and stepped into his Wellington boots again.

Miriam looked curiously at Louise. 'Is that your drunk neighbour? I thought you said he was old.'

'I never said old.'

'Take a cup out to him,' Miriam commanded. 'You can't drag him down here and then not even pass the time of day.'

86

'I pay him,' Louise said. But she poured coffee into a mug and went out into the drive.

A black-and-white collie observed her silently from the cab of the Land-Rover, too well-trained to do more than beam at her and stir a silky tail.

'Coffee?' Louise offered, and handed Mr Miles the mug.

He was untying the hurdle from the back of the Land-Rover. But he straightened up and took it from her. Louise noticed for the first time that his eyes were an unusually dark blue, as blue as periwinkles. The old woman was right, he was an attractive man; but hardly an appropriate partner for her. Louise smiled at the thought of life in Wistley Common Farm. His life was an antithesis of hers. Their hours, their pastimes, even their thoughts were in complete contrast.

Andrew Miles drank the scalding coffee at speed.

'Is it going to rain?' Louise asked in her light social voice.

'The forecast's bad,' he replied. 'Rain from midday and some thunderstorms tonight. I'll go down and see Rose before I leave. Make sure she's all right.'

'Rose?'

Andrew Miles looked surprised. 'Rose,' he repeated. 'In the van.'

'I didn't know her name.'

'Rose Miles.'

He handed the mug back to Louise with a word of thanks and then continued unloading the hurdle.

'Hang on a minute,' Louise said, struggling to understand. 'Did you say Miles? Is she a relation of yours?'

'She told you she was born here,' Andrew said reasonably.

'I thought she was a gypsy.'

He smiled. 'Born in this house, married a gypsy. She

went away when she was twenty or so. But she always comes back here for the summer.'

'She's one of your family?'

Andrew shrugged vaguely. 'She was born a Miles. She's an aunt or something. I'm not very good on that kind of thing.'

'Well, then, she should certainly be at your farm,' Louise said suddenly. 'Not here.'

Andrew smiled. 'I really would like to oblige you, Miss Case,' he said formally. 'But it's her wish to be here. I can't move her on. I have no authority over her.'

Louise felt reproved. 'Captain Frome says there are travellers coming this way.'

Andrew nodded.

'They might come in here when they see the van.'

'They wouldn't break down a fence. That's damage and trespass. They'll come on up to my farm.'

Louise's eyes widened. 'What will you do?' she asked. 'Have you warned the police?'

'I'm renting them a field,' Andrew Miles said pleasantly. 'We're going to have one of these – what d'you call them? – raves. There'll be dancing and I've said they can have fires and cook. It'll be a bit of a party. I like a bit of a party.'

He humped the hurdle from the back of the Land-Rover on to his back and carried it around to the break in the fence, not seeing Louise's astounded face. He leaned it against the surviving fence and carefully broke away the damaged wood and put it into a pile.

'Rose can have that, I suppose,' he said to Louise. 'Unless you want it for kindling.'

Louise flapped her hands dismissively at the wood pile. 'You can't possibly do this!' she exclaimed. 'There will be all sorts of people. You don't know what you're getting yourself

88

into. They'll be dealing in drugs and they'll be in trouble with the police, and they'll be impossible to move on. They'll damage your land. Their dogs will eat your sheep.'

'Oh, I don't think so,' he said gently.

He reached in his pocket for some baler twine and started lashing the gate to the fence posts with three loose loops.

'Why are you doing this?' Louise exclaimed. 'Why let these people come to your land?'

Andrew went to the other end of the gate and experimentally lifted and opened and then closed it. He twisted a loop of twine to fasten it shut.

'No hinges,' he explained. 'You'll find it a bit heavy to shift. But she's not going anywhere till I get the van fixed. At least it closes the gap for you, if that's what you want.'

'Thank you,' Louise said distractedly. 'But why are you letting them on your land? Everyone in the village is against it!'

Andrew straightened up and smiled at her. 'I like a bit of a party. It's not often we get a chance for a bit of a party round here.'

Louise was speechless for a moment. 'Captain Frome will go mad.'

Andrew smiled warmly at her. 'He doesn't matter,' he said with the confidence of a man who lives in his own house, his father's house, with his own land stretching for miles all around him. 'He doesn't matter at all.'

He opened the hurdle gate, picked up the broken fence rails, and strolled down the orchard towards Rose Miles's caravan. He dumped the firewood on the little pile, kicked off his Wellington boots and left them by the steps, tapped on the open door and stepped inside, ducking his head, as a man confident of his welcome.

Miriam called from the front door. 'Telephone!'

Louise went numbly in. 'Hello?'

'Frome here again,' the voice boomed. 'Sorry to trouble you twice in one morning. I've got some news I thought you should have. The travellers are definitely headed your way. They're about forty miles from the village now. The police are setting up a roadblock and they're warning everyone to lock their gates. Are you secure?'

'Secure?' Louise asked helplessly.

'All bolted up?'

'Oh yes, Mr Miles came down and tied a hurdle on the gap.'

'Tied? That won't do. You need a chain and a padlock.'

'Mr Miles says they'll be going past. They're on their way to his farm. He's rented them a field.'

There was a stunned silence. 'I assume this is not some kind of a joke,' the Captain said icily.

'No, no,' Louise said. 'He just told me.'

'Is he still with you?'

'Yes, but . . .'

'I'll be up there at once,' the Captain said and the phone suddenly clicked off.

In the van Andrew Miles was sitting on Rose's bed. She was perched like a bright flighty hummingbird beside him. Today she was wrapped in a purple silk kimono, with a broad sash at the waist of pink shot silk scarves.

'Forgot your gear box,' Andrew said. 'Do it soon.'

'No hurry,' she said pleasantly.

He smiled at her, his blue eyes twinkling. 'Thought not. Will you move on in June?'

She shook her head. 'I've come home to die,' she said simply. 'I've got a month at the most.'

90

Andrew chuckled. 'You said that at Bluestone Farm three years ago,' he reminded her. 'They let you stay all summer and gave you all the cracked eggs. D'you remember? You ate like a lord. They kept hoping you'd get salmonella but you were still there in October.'

'Oh aye,' she said. 'Laugh at an old woman. But you'll burn my van and my things, won't you, lad? When I go?'

'When you go I will,' he promised. 'But I don't reckon it'll be this month.'

'Pretty girl,' Rose remarked, nodding at the cottage.

Andrew looked surprised. 'She's hardly a girl,' he said. 'Miss Case.'

The old woman shook her head. 'You've not looked,' she said positively. 'Under the lah-di-dah and the books and the big head. She's a pretty girl. Do nicely for you, get you the cottage back and all. Your dad always regretted selling it.'

Andrew shook his head, smiling. 'Tell my fortune?' he suggested mockingly. 'Will I marry a rich girl? How many babies?'

'Time you were wed,' the old woman said determinedly. 'Your liver can't stand you being a bachelor much longer. And that's the very girl for you.'

'She's got a man of her own,' Andrew objected. 'And a job at the university.'

Rose screwed up her wrinkled face in disgust. 'He's a nothing! Hardly a man at all. And he does nothing for her, you take my word for it. And that job of hers is a bit of nothing too. What she needs is a good man and a couple of chavies. Then you'll see.'

'How d'you know he does nothing for her?' Andrew asked curiously. 'Have you been eavesdropping?'

'I know what I know,' Rose said, retreating rapidly into sibylline wisdom.

'If you've been hanging around under the windows listening, or opening letters, or spying, you'll get into real trouble,' Andrew cautioned her. 'I won't help you stay here if you're pestering Miss Case.'

'Miss Case! Miss Case!' the old woman jeered. 'Her name's Louise, and if you had any sense you'd take her up to the farm into the big bedroom and start as you mean to go on.'

Andrew flushed a deep brick red. 'That's enough,' he said. He stood up but kept his head stooped to allow for the low roof of the van. The van rocked like a ship at sea when he moved to the door and stepped into his Wellington boots. The dog sat up and sniffed cautiously at his boots and trousers.

'Don't you like the look of her then?' the old woman demanded tauntingly from the interior. 'She's got a pair of cream pyjamas in pure silk, and a long silky dressing gown to match. And every night she's alone in that big bed of hers with nothing but a book to keep her warm.'

Andrew patted the dog and then straightened up. 'She'd never look twice at me,' he said very quietly. 'She pays me as an odd job man. She'd never look twice at me.'

'She's burning up for you,' the old woman alleged. 'I hear her at night, all on her own. She cries into her pillow for sheer loneliness. In her silk pyjamas, in that big bed.'

Andrew stared at Rose like a puzzled large animal. 'Well, that isn't right,' he said fairly. 'A pretty girl like that, crying herself to sleep.'

Rose nodded. 'Throwing her young years away on her books and that feeble bloke,' she reminded him.

Andrew shook his head again as if someone had told him of a new and wasteful farming practice. 'That's not right,' he repeated. 'Not right at all.'

Rose gleamed at him. 'No,' she said. 'She needs a man to give her babies, before it's too late for her.'

Andrew nodded. 'Yes, I can see that she'd need that.'

'And someone to love her,' Rose said, her voice a seductive spellbinding whisper. 'A man to take her to bed and see her right, keep her warm at nights and make her laugh. It's not right that she's stuck with that girl's blouse Toby Summers.'

Andrew hitched his trousers and glanced towards the house. 'She could surely do better than him,' he said fairly.

'She could do no better than you,' Rose stated. 'And I've told her so as well.'

'What did she say?'

'She smiled,' the old woman said mendaciously. 'She smiled and blushed.'

'Oh,' Andrew said. 'Really?'

'Blushed like a little rose.'

Andrew Miles walked thoughtfully up the orchard through the garden gate to his Land-Rover parked in the drive. An old but shiny Rover was parked behind him, blocking him in. Captain Frome got out.

Andrew gave a small grunt of annoyance and straightened his cap on his head.

'Good day!' Captain Frome said cheerily. 'Glad to see you've got that hurdle up. Good man! I brought a chain and padlock up for the young lady. We really have to batten down the hatches!'

Andrew nodded and opened the door of his Land-Rover with a loud creak.

'I've heard the most nonsensical rumour,' Captain Frome went on heartily. Louise and Miriam appeared at the front door; he lifted his hat to them. 'Heard that you might be thinking of renting a field to some bunch of weirdos. A great convoy of them are headed this way. You wouldn't give 'em house room, would you?'

'Now who told you that?' Andrew asked curiously.

Captain Frome slapped him on the shoulder. 'Village gossip,' he said. 'It's quicker than jungle drums. I've been telling everyone you're too good a man to get mixed up in that kind of racket.'

Andrew smiled slowly. 'Could you move your car, Captain?' he said gently. 'I have to get home. Pigs need feeding.'

'Certainly, certainly,' Captain Frome said. 'We can't keep the . . . er . . . pigs waiting, can we? But I can tell the neighbourhood watch that you're not involved?'

Andrew got into the Land-Rover and slid open the window. 'You keep them informed,' he recommended pleasantly. 'Is Mr James still the chairman?'

'Yes. James, good man, a responsible landlord. He's promised to close the Olde House down for the day if the convoy comes through.'

'You can ask him when I can come back and drink in his pub,' Andrew said. 'It's been three years last Christmas, and they open all day now on Saturdays. It would suit me.'

'My dear fellow,' Captain Frome said. 'I'll certainly mention it. Especially if you're . . . er . . . holding the line up here. What were you . . . er . . . banned for?'

'Patting his wife's bum,' Andrew admitted. 'But I was drunk.'

'Good Lord,' the Captain said. 'Well, I see. I see James's position too, actually . . .'

'Three years for a quick feel?' Andrew demanded. 'That's got to be wrong.'

94

'Well, I hardly know,' the Captain dithered. 'I mean, a chap's wife!'

Andrew started the engine and crashed the gears. 'Not very often I ask the neighbourhood watch for anything,' he said reasonably. 'And it's your lot who want me to chain up my fields. And she isn't what you would call a looker.'

'Yes,' the Captain said uncertainly. 'Well. Good man. Consider it done.'

Andrew smiled a winning smile and waited for the Captain to back his Rover out of the way before turning the Land-Rover and driving off.

Miriam and Louise, still standing in the doorway, watched him go. 'Damn,' Louise muttered. 'I haven't paid him. I'll have to go up to the farm later.'

The Captain approached them. 'Good day!' he said, lifting his hat.

'This is Miriam Carpenter – Captain Frome,' Louise said politely. 'Will you come in?'

'No, thank you. I've just stopped by to check on your old lady,' Captain Frome said. 'And if I may, I'll check that your gates are secure.' He reached into one capacious pocket and brought out a large padlock and chain. 'This is for your paddock gate, and this . . .' he produced another smaller version '. . . this is for your garden gate.'

Louise looked blank.

'The neighbourhood watch has set up a special fund to buy these,' he explained. 'We're taking the threat very seriously. Wistley is a precious piece of architectural heritage. We can't have hordes of hippies running all over it. And the dirt, and the litter!'

'No,' Louise said uncertainly.

'So here's a leaflet the police have given us on fighting the convoy menace with a special hotline number to telephone if you see or hear anything suspicious, here's your padlock and chains, and with your permission, I'll just pop down and see your old lady.'

'Why, this is a military operation!' Miriam commented, her voice carefully neutral.

The Captain glowed, his purpose in life restored. 'It has to be!' he exclaimed.

He raised his hat again and bustled down the garden path towards the orchard. Miriam raised an eyebrow at Louise. 'I wouldn't live in the country for a million pounds,' she said firmly.

They watched the Captain as he approached the van door. Warned by some innate intelligence, the dog stood up and barked loudly. The Captain, one eye on the dog, opened the gate and went into the orchard but kept well back from the van.

'Hello?' he shouted. 'Hello?'

Rose appeared, magnificent in purple silk, at the head of the steps. 'You're trespassing,' she said at once.

The Captain was lost for words.

'Move on,' she commanded. 'You're upsetting my dog. He's a valuable dog, highly strung.'

'Good God!'

She favoured him with a wicked knowing grin. 'Trespassing,' she said again. 'I know your sort. Give them an inch and they take a mile. You're on my land.'

'I have permission from the landowner, Miss Case.' The Captain gulped air. 'I just wanted a word with you.'

'You're on my land,' Rose proclaimed. 'Trespassing on my land. It's her garden but my orchard. And you're trespassing on my site.'

'This is outrageous!' the Captain exclaimed.

'I think so,' Rose said quickly. 'Harassing an old woman who has done nothing more than come home to die.'

'Die?'

'And trespassing!'

'How can I be trespassing?' he demanded. 'Miss Case admitted me to her property.'

'This is not her property,' Rose said slowly and clearly. 'It's mine as it happens. Now clear off.'

Captain Frome, his mind whirling, took one step forwards. At once the dog flung itself to the far end of its thin leash and rattled out a volley of loud threatening barks. Captain Frome retreated behind the garden gate. The dog subsided on to his haunches and beamed the wide white-toothed satisfied grin of a dog whose bluff has not been called.

'I shall be taking this up with the authorities,' Captain Frome warned from the shelter of the closed gate. 'And I daresay the police will be taking a close interest in you. If you think your friends are going to follow you to Wistley for some sort of orgy you have another think coming, Madam.'

Rose stared at him. 'You're barmy, you,' she said. 'There's never been an orgy in Wistley. It's not that sort of place. Or at least it never was until you came here. I think it's disgusting at your age.'

The Captain's forehead flamed scarlet. He made an odd popping noise in his throat. Then he turned from her and stamped up the garden path, past the front door, slammed into his Rover and wound down the window.

'Outrageous,' he called to the two women in the doorway. 'Miss Case, I warn you that woman is laying some kind of claim to your property. I shall be looking into it at once. She says she has come here to die. Most unhygienic. We

97

had that sort of thing in India. We won't have it in Wistley. I shall inform the police and the neighbourhood watch. And I advise you in the meantime to keep a very close watch on your personal property, anything moveable. Washing on the line, parcels in the porch, garden tools, anything. I know these people.'

He started the engine with an angry roar and backed the car quickly out of the drive.

'What?' Louise said as he drove away. 'Did he say she was claiming my property?'

Miriam watched the departing car with irritation.

'Did he say she'd come home to die?' Louise asked.

'Oh, what does it matter what he says?' Miriam demanded irritably. 'He's just a little tinpot colonel. He's just saying anything to upset you about an old lady who's doing no harm at all.'

'She's a thorough nuisance,' Louise said with spirit. 'And he's a responsible citizen and practically the squire of the village.'

The rest of the weekend passed rather awkwardly. Toby, joining the two women at teatime on Saturday, found them in a state of unspoken tension. Miriam thought that Louise was selfish and materialist. Louise had never before come into conflict with Miriam's determined beneficence. As soon as Toby learned that the old woman had told Captain Frome that she was terminally ill he confessed his interest in her, and unpacked from his car his little tape recorder, and his brand new box of blank index cards.

'I've got interested in her childhood,' he said. 'She has a connection with the Pankhursts. I want to get her on the record.'

'The Pankhursts?' Miriam exclaimed. She glanced at Louise, who knew more than any of them about the early suffrage movement.

'It's very rambling and incoherent,' Toby said swiftly. 'But I thought I'd give her the benefit of the doubt and take some notes.'

'Shouldn't Louise . . .'

'Or you, Miriam?'

'I wouldn't want either of you to waste your time,' Toby said firmly. 'Not at this stage. I'll show you my notes if I get something that makes sense, and then discuss it with you both. It's probably nothing.'

He slid towards the front door, doing his best to conceal his excitement but he could not help but be aware that Rose's imminent demise was the best thing that could have happened. Rose would be dead before the royalty cheques arrived, and her papers – records, diaries, and cuttings – would belong exclusively to him. There would be no danger of a later, better-informed scholar asking Rose more searching questions and obtaining better information. Toby would have cornered the market in the old lady's memory, and once she was dead, no-one could come after him and check up and argue.

'I'll go down and see her, then,' he announced, ignoring the frosty atmosphere. 'I'll be a while. But I'll cook dinner for us all when I come back.'

Neither woman looked up as he left. Louise was reading *Lady Chatterley's Lover* in the hopes of it inspiring some insight into the Lawrence essay. Miriam was reading the *Guardian* which Toby had brought with him.

'So long,' Toby said cheerily. 'And tough shit,' he added as he closed the front door and they could not hear. The greatest disadvantage in Toby's lifestyle of having a wife

99

and a mistress who were close friends was that when he did not enjoy the blissful pleasure of two women, liking each other and indulging him, he suffered the huge discomfort of two women, irritated with each other and furious with him. Toby had ridden out worst storms. He would survive this one.

He was surprised to find the van door closed. He called 'Hello' from the gate but did not like to come closer because the dog, which was sulking under the van with its back turned to the increasingly cool breezes which were blowing up the hill, raised its lip and growled softly at him. The second time he called the door creaked open.

'Yes?' Rose asked. 'It's a good deal too busy here, shouting and people visiting all day. It was better when the old lady was alive.'

'I *am* sorry,' Toby said charmingly. 'It's just that I'm so keen to talk to you. I am fascinated by your story. May I come in?'

She shook her head. 'I couldn't settle to it today, I'm that worried.'

Toby was alert. 'Surely you could settle to it,' he said. 'Those interesting newspaper clippings?'

'I'm not well,' Rose said. 'You'll have heard that.'

Toby composed his face into an expression of sincere concern. 'I *did* hear,' he said. 'I was so sorry. It made me think how lovely it would be if we could preserve your memories in a beautiful book so that you will have left your mark on the world.'

'I need my burying clothes,' Rose said thoughtfully. 'Something special.'

Toby gritted his teeth on his impatience. 'I could give you some money,' he offered. 'For the time and trouble you will be spending on our project. Not very much of course,' he added hastily. 'But enough for some clothes. Perhaps fifty pounds?' He saw her face and said quickly, 'A hundred?'

'Let's go and buy them,' Rose said. 'Let's pop down to the village and buy them now.'

'And then come back and do some work?' Toby confirmed.

Rose was thrusting her feet into a pair of grimy sandals. 'When my mind's at rest,' she said. 'I have to see my burial clothes in my drawer before I can think about anything else.'

Toby drove tight-lipped down to the village. He felt conspicuous with Rose sitting beside him swathed in purple silk with her shock of white hair and her alert bright face. He noticed vaguely that there were posters on the village lampposts and a big poster nailed to the tree on the village green in dayglo orange which said: KEEP MOVING ON, HIPPIES! YOU'RE NOT WANTED HERE.

'No clothes shops,' Toby said after a swift survey.

'Not here,' Rose said. 'I meant to go to Hallfield. Drive on.'

Toby developed a white line around his mouth and drove on. He had to slow down and stop three miles outside the village where two police cars were blocking the road and exiting traffic had to trail around them.

'What's all that about?' he asked.

Rose shrugged.

In the closeness of the car Toby became aware of a stuffy grassy smell about her. He opened the window. Altogether it was turning into a most disagreeable afternoon. They drove into Hallfield and Toby followed the signs to the car park but Rose stopped him. 'Drop me in front of the shop,' she commanded. 'And wait. We'll be quicker that way.'

Toby went down the broad street and, sighting a rare parking space at the side, pulled into the gap. Rose put out her age-spotted hand, palm up. 'A hundred pounds I think you said?'

For a moment Toby thought of reneging, but the box of clippings and the unseen diary of Sylvia Pankhurst were like jam in the larder to him. 'I'll have to get the cash,' he said unwillingly.

There was a branch of his bank with a cash dispenser on the other side of the road. Toby went over to it, uncomfortably aware of the stares at Rose, dogging his steps in her violently purple kimono tied with the pink shot silk scarves. Rose crowded close and watched him tap in his number and the card and then the money come out. 'That's a useful thing,' she remarked. 'Where d'you get the cards from?'

'You have to have a bank account first,' Toby said crossly. He thrust the smooth, warm notes at her with regret. Rose licked a forefinger and flicked through them. 'They get smaller and smaller,' she said.

'What do?'

'The notes. I remember when a five-pound note was as big as your hand. You knew you were spending money then.'

Toby strode back to the car. Rose's general recollections were of no value at all. Any old woman would say the same. He did not want to indulge her nostalgia. He had no interest in her except as source material. 'I'll wait here,' he said.

Rose smiled, 'Shan't be long,' and disappeared into the shop.

*   *   *

102

Toby leaned against his car and waited. It was an unusual experience for him. Since the advent of feminism none of the women he knew expected him to join them on shopping expeditions. Since women did not dress to please men, then men's opinions were clearly superfluous. Indeed, once this theory had been elevated into doctrine, any comment on a woman's appearance was an insult to both the man and the woman, and under some circumstances could constitute sexual harassment. How such a state could evolve in a mere ten years had never bothered Toby. He merely reaped the benefits of being able to neglect the little politenesses which had been compulsory for men a generation ago. He had never been required to compliment a woman on a new outfit, or notice and praise a new hairstyle. No woman had ever sulked because he had failed to notice a new dress. Of course he had never bought an item of clothing as a present for any woman and this had saved him a good deal of boredom and enormous amounts of money. Both Miriam and Louise were far more careful with their own hard-earned salaries than they would have been if they had been brought up as spendthrift conventional women with free access to his. When they shopped for clothes they bought swiftly and efficiently without troubling him for his time or opinions.

Toby waited for what seemed like hours. Occasionally he sighted Rose, who waved to him as she crossed the road to try yet another shop, but when she came back to the car she was empty-handed.

'No good,' she said shortly.

Toby opened the car door and Rose dropped into the seat with a little sigh of exhaustion.

'Why not?' Toby asked as patiently as he could.

Rose shook her head. 'So dreary,' she said. 'All greys and navy and cream. I like a bit of colour.'

'Surely, to be buried in . . .' Toby suggested.

'A nice bright red,' Rose decreed. 'Go out with a bang. Sylvia always wore colours. She loved her clothes.'

'Did she?' Toby asked, ambition suddenly revitalising him. 'Sylvia Pankhurst? Was she vain about clothes?'

'Oooh!' Rose exclaimed. 'A peacock! But then she was the feminine one, of the two of them.'

'The feminine one?' Toby backed the car into the main road and headed back for the village. 'Of the two Pankhurst sisters?'

'There were three sisters,' Rose volunteered. Toby longed for his blank index cards, his little dictaphone and his coloured pens.

'And Sylvia was the feminine one,' he prompted.

'Not among the Pankhurst sisters,' Rose said. 'They were all keen on their clothes. I meant with her girl friend. The American. The one that dressed like a man.'

Toby let out a small yelp and veered sharply into the middle of the road. 'Sylvia Pankhurst was gay?' he asked breathlessly. The implication of this was greater than his ferreting brain could take into account. It could provide a new heroine for the gay women's movement. He could write a book which would become a classic text for gay women, linking forever women's rights with lesbianism. On the other hand, and perhaps more commercially viable, would be a scandalous deconstruction of the Pankhursts and the suffragette movement (and by implication, *all* feminists) by showing that the first great feminist heroine (or at any rate, the only one he knew of) was in fact a raving dyke.

Of course Toby did not say 'raving dyke', even to himself. He had been too well-trained. But there was a gap in his mental sentence, like a crossword puzzle clue: 'A politically incorrect and abusive term for lesbians, two words, (6,4)'.

'Gay? She was happy enough,' Rose said equably.

They turned the corner and there was the police roadblock marked by yellow signs saying: WISTLEY VILLAGE, ACCESS TO RESIDENTS ONLY. On either side of the road the trees were unwillingly sprouting the orange dayglo posters which read NO HIPPIES IN WISTLEY and DRIVE ON, HIPPIES.

'Where are you going, sir?' The policeman bent down to Toby's window and took a good look at Rose, who bared her teeth at him in a grin more threatening than pleasing.

'Wistley village,' Toby said deferentially. Policemen always made him feel guilty. Despite compulsory attendance with Miriam at a number of political demonstrations where police had often outnumbered marchers and were sometimes prevailed upon to help roll up banners and offer lifts home, Toby always felt nervous around policemen. 'Wistley village, officer.'

'Are you a resident, sir?'

'No, just visiting.'

'And is this lady a resident?'

Rose beamed horridly at him. 'Squatting,' she said helpfully. Toby closed his eyes briefly and then laughed a light inconsequential laugh. 'Please pay no attention,' he said. 'We are both guests of Dr Case. I am Dr Summers and this is Miss Pankhurst.'

'Dr Case's address?' the policeman asked, impressed as the police always are by professional status, and with no ability to differentiate between GP and PhD.

'Wistley Common Cottage.'

'Just a moment, sir.' The policeman went back to his car and spoke to someone on his radio. Toby assumed he was checking the address. He came back, putting on his hat again. 'That's fine, sir. Sorry to inconvenience you.'

105

Toby smiled weakly. Rose beamed. They drove on into the village, past a group of watching children who had appeared from nowhere and gathered to laugh at the policemen, and up the deserted main street, empty of passing traffic. The Olde House at Home was shuttered and closed. The Holly Bush's door was shut and the curtains were drawn. Every gate was padlocked. Every garden shed was bolted and double-locked. Houses which had little ornamental shutters had fastened them tight. Curtains were drawn. It was a village which had frightened itself into siege.

'Stop!' Rose suddenly shouted.

Instinctively Toby jammed on the brakes but not a curtain twitched at the squeal of the tyres. 'What is it?'

'There it is!' Rose cried longingly. 'My burial gown.'

Toby looked along the line of her pointing finger. Rose had seen through the high bolted wrought-iron garden gate of Wistley Manor to where clothes swung and blew on a rotary line. There was Mrs Frome's scarlet chiffon dressing gown, a gorgeous affair of layers of floaty chiffon trimmed with thick silky red ribbons and inches of ruching at the hem. 'That's it,' Rose said again. 'That's what I want.'

Toby experimented with his light inconsequential laugh. 'It *is* nice,' he said, as one might speak to a child. 'Now let me think! I wonder where we could find something like it!'

'Why?'

'So that we could get it for you . . .'

'I don't want something like it,' Rose said reasonably. 'I want that one.'

Toby laughed again and looked at her for confirmation that she was joking. Her face was completely serious. Toby looked back at the chiffon gown. 'You can't have that one,' he said patiently. 'That one belongs to someone else. I don't know who. We'll see if we can find you something *like* that one. That'll be nice, won't it?'

Rose gave a brief sardonic laugh, and got out of the car.

'Now hang on a minute . . .' Toby began hastily.

Someone had been putting up posters all over the village. The telegraph pole adjacent to Wistley Manor's garden wall had two dayglo orange posters, one on top of another. The lower one said: NO HIPPIES, NO GYPSIES. The upper one said: NO BLACKS, NO YIDS. Someone had clearly had second thoughts about this, and there was a ladder beside the telegraph pole, which someone had left standing while he went in search of pliers to cut down the second poster. In the morality of the middle-class England of the early '90s it was acceptable to abuse hippies and gypsies but not yet permissible to abuse blacks and Jews. Or at any rate – not publicly in posters. After all, the former threaten rural property values while the latter do not. This is what is known as successful assimilation and multi-cultural society.

In one brief horrifying moment Rose had hitched up her purple kimono, tucked it into the pink belt, scurried up the ladder, swung her leg over the rounded top of the wall and dropped out of sight.

Toby moaned softly and went to the garden gate and peered through the wrought-iron lilies. Rose had the chiffon negligee over her arm but she was also helping herself to some large beige silk French knickers and a couple of capacious bras. 'God, no,' Toby said quietly. 'Miss Pankhurst!' he called softly. 'Miss Pankhurst! I think you should come away now.'

Rose, her arms full of someone else's laundry, started towards the wall, and then stopped.

'I can't get out,' she hissed. 'There's no ladder this side.'

Toby moaned a little louder. 'Oh God!' He tugged at the

gate. Captain Frome had locked it, and there was a new and shiny chain and padlock around the latch and also, for safekeeping, around the hinge. It rattled loudly but it did not yield.

'Hush!' Rose snapped irritably. 'Idiot. Someone'll hear.'

Toby cast a swift look up and down the deserted village street. The children were all gathered at the roadblock, half a mile down the road. The village green was empty, the owners of substantial properties were all bolting up their garden sheds for fear of gypsies maddened by the sight of the elegantly stripy lawns raiding their Black and Decker mowers. Toby swarmed up the ladder and sat astride on the top of the wall. He stretched down as far as he could reach. 'I'll pull you up,' he said.

Rose came to the foot of the wall, trampling zinnias, begonias and bright expensive bedding plants and held up her right arm, her left still clutching her swag. Their fingers barely brushed.

'You'll have to come down,' she said.

With a cry like a wounded rabbit, Toby leaned down to the street side of the wall and hauled up the ladder, straining under the weight of it. Then he dropped it down into the garden side of the wall, breaking the buds of prize-winning roses. Rose raced up the ladder, handed Toby the trailing wispy booty and then helped Toby see-saw the ladder back to the street side of the wall. She set off down with an agility surprising in a woman of eighty afflicted with a terminal illness. At that precise moment Captain Frome came out of his French windows into his garden and saw Toby sitting astride his handsome polished flint garden wall, with his arms full of stolen washing.

'You!' he yelled in the stentorian shout that had pacified

a whole sub-continent. 'What the hell d'you think you're doing?'

Only Rose knew what she was doing. Without wasting a moment she dropped from the ladder into the street and flung herself into Toby's car. Toby clung to the top of the wall, frozen in horror as Captain Frome, his eyes bulging and his face flushing, galloped down the garden.

'Name?' he demanded. 'And get down from there.'

Toby gave a short despairing wail and dropped from the wall to the street. He picked himself up and hobbled to his car as Captain Frome tore down the garden path and flung himself at the gate. Alas for precautions! He could not open his own gate without three separate keys. Plunging his hands in his pockets and bellowing in impatience, Captain Frome found one key, unlocked the gate, and then another for the first padlock. But by the time he had fitted the third key in the lock Toby's car had roared, the tyres had squealed and Toby and Rose and the Fromes' washing had disappeared up Wistley High Street.

'I saw you!' Captain Frome bellowed. 'And I'll know you again!'

In his rage he had not thought of the registration number, nor had he spotted Rose. He turned from his gate and ran back into the house to telephone the convoy hotline number and to alert the neighbourhood watch that not even roadblocks and offensive and illegal posters were enough to deter the scourge which had descended on the hapless village and was even now wreaking havoc on unprotected lingerie.

The frosty atmosphere at the cottage had melted under the two women's mutual disapproval of Toby's attitude to Rose. They dissected his ambition and his exploitation of the old woman very thoroughly and found themselves in complete accord.

'I think I'm really growing away from him,' Miriam said. 'We married much too young of course . . . and somehow everything was different then. Toby, me, you.'

Louise nodded. Toby was a shared problem, like the disappointing child of intellectual parents. They liked it when he was difficult almost more than when he published an essay, gave a public lecture, or gained promotion. There was more to talk about then. 'He's certainly got more ambitious recently,' Louise said. 'More individualistic.'

Individualism was a very serious character flaw. Louise's ambition and her lucky rise through the university hierarchy was unobjectionable because her promotion increased the numbers of women in the university and offered a good role model to other aspiring women. Toby's more effortful ascent brought no benefits at all for women and thus could only be a source of pleasure in the most individualist and private sense. It was nice for his wife that he was earning more money, and nice for his lover, but for them as women it was actually to be decried.

'Of course he's brilliant,' Miriam said loyally.

Louise nodded. 'And right-thinking.'

In the current climate a man working in the humanities had to be both brilliant and right-thinking or give up his post and carve out a career for himself in the bolder frontiers of right-wing journalism. Toby would have loved to have been irritating in print once a fortnight, but he had neither the originality nor the courage to take on the women's movement as a whole and certainly would not dare to challenge such opponents as his wife and his lover.

'But he can't just *use* Miss Miles.'

'I'll speak to him,' Louise said. 'She *is* my guest.'

'I'll speak to him,' Miriam agreed. 'He can't sacrifice his sense of respect for other people for egotistical ambition.'

The two women nodded at their accord and Miriam went back to her newspaper while Louise read her book in an agreeable silence. After a little while Louise looked up. 'Lawrence is really quite disgusting,' she commented. 'All of this stuff about Mellors' phallus, it really is quite fetishistic.'

Miriam nodded. She had not read Lawrence for years. She hardly ever read novels now, and poetry – which she had loved – she could no longer understand. Unless it was cathartic poetry written by women exploring scarifying experiences, she could not see the point of it. Rhyming poetry actually offended her as a waste of time and energy which could have been better spent on pamphlets.

'And the sex is absurd,' Louise went on. 'In this part here they've just made love, but Lady Chatterley didn't want to. Then she does want to and they make love again, and then they make love again. That's three erections between tea-time and dinner. It's physiologically impossible. It's ridiculous.'

Miriam smiled faintly, as if she were remembering something equally physiologically impossible. 'Oh, I don't know.'

'He's a thirty-nine-year-old man with a weak chest and heart,' Louise said firmly. 'He simply couldn't do it, and Lawrence knows it. It's just male exaggeration, just as Lawrence goes on about how big Mellors' penis is. Just male vanity.'

The smile died from Miriam's face. 'I suppose so,' she said. 'But isn't the point of the story the magic of love? Not really realism? About the lady and the gamekeeper in a sort of triumph through sex against an unfeeling class-bound society?'

Louise snorted and put three crosses in the margin.

'Exactly so,' she said. 'It's a Mills and Boon novel written by a man. The magic of love. What's that supposed to be? Have *you* ever experienced it? It's a myth.'

Miriam looked down at the *Guardian* again. 'I suppose it is.' She spoke almost with regret. 'But I do think that there are times when something – chemistry perhaps, or hormones, or sexual desire – can give you a feeling that is really quite magical. When you're just mad for someone and nothing else in the world matters.'

Louise smiled with affectionate contempt. 'You're a romantic,' she said. 'Would you melt and flame and flutter?'

'Given half a chance,' Miriam said. 'But the women's refuge doesn't give you quite the scope of a gamekeeper's hut in the woods. Anyway, I think my melting and fluttering days are over.'

'Melting and fluttering are illusions,' Louise said firmly. 'They're designed to keep women subservient through their emotions. I don't think any woman of sense would melt and flame and flutter. Lady Chatterley is a real subservient character – firstly to her family, then to her husband, and then to her lover.'

'Have you got a man at the moment?' Miriam asked with sudden apparent irrelevance. 'Are you still seeing what's-his-name, Michael?'

Louise nodded. A few years ago, unable to keep a full secret from Miriam, she had invented an imaginary married lover, with the proviso that she did not want to talk about him.

Miriam, a true friend, prompted confidences but did not demand them and kindly hoped that Louise was sexually satisfied and privately worried that she was lonely.

'Still him?' Miriam said. 'D'you think he'll ever leave his wife?'

Louise had the grace to blush slightly. 'I think he will,' she said. 'Their marriage was always a bit, I don't know, empty. I think he will leave her soon.'

'Would you have him here?' Miriam asked, looking around at Louise's orderly sitting room. 'Would you live with him?'

'I'd love it,' Louise said. 'It's lonely here, sometimes. Especially in the winter, when it gets dark so early and it's so quiet. It would be good to have company. Some nights I put on the radio just to hear another voice, and I actually wait to hear Mr Miles drive past at closing time. It's ridiculous. I wait to hear the noise of his Land-Rover and then I know it's bedtime. It would be bliss to have him here. I've waited so long for him, it's the only plan in my life I haven't completed. My work is right, I have a place of my own, I'm earning better than I ever have before. It's just him – the one thing I've not got.'

Miriam looked uncomprehending. 'I'd love to have time to be lonely,' she said. 'The phone's always ringing and I live in a house with two men. The place is never empty, it's never quiet, and it's never how I like it.' There was a short silence. 'You don't think it's a bit ... a bit obsessive?' Miriam asked cautiously. 'How you are about him? You don't think you're a kind of typical mistress, waiting and waiting while he fobs you off with excuses?'

Louise closed her mouth on an angry retort. 'We're going at my speed,' she said. 'I didn't want more commitment at the early stages. I wasn't ready for it. It's only just now that I feel ready to move on. He'll come to me when he and I agree the time is right.'

Miriam nodded but she did not seem convinced. 'Fine,' she said. 'It's just that you hear of an awful lot of women who think that the man is coming to them, and then they're forty or fifty and he's still not arrived, and they never meet anyone else.'

Louise shook her head emphatically, pushing away the dreary vision. 'Not me,' she insisted. 'I've not got problems with dependency. I'm a liberated woman. I love this man and we have a relationship but it's an open relationship. But I have other men. I have a mature and independent life.'

'But you don't really get involved with other men,' Miriam pointed out. 'That guy from Leicester who I thought was so nice. You hardly spent any time with him at all. He was really interested in you and you only saw him at the conference and didn't get in touch later. You're not truly free if you're not free to fall in love.'

'Fall in love!' Louise mocked. 'Melt and flame and flutter?'

'Not melting or flaming then – but you know what I mean. Intimacy, openness.'

Louise shook her sleek head. 'I don't believe in it,' she said. 'I believe in comradeship and sexual compatibility. All the rest is just a patriarchal myth to keep women in their place, waiting for men, putting up with their neglect or abuse. *You* of all people should know! You see that stuff over and over again! "He only hits me because he loves me so much."'

Miriam nodded. 'I suppose so. But *you're* waiting. You're not really free if you're waiting. You're putting up with neglect while he stays with his wife. You said yourself you were lonely.'

'We're not a conventional couple, you can't make those sort of definitions,' Louise said confidently. 'I'm working towards the relationship I want with him. I accept the limitations on the relationship for now because they give me freedom and space. When I am ready and he is ready he'll

114

come to me.' She glanced at the clock. 'Toby's a long time.'

'I hadn't noticed,' Miriam said. 'When did he go?'

'More than an hour and a half ago.' Louise stood up and stretched. 'Damn. I'd better take the money for the gate up to the farm.'

'I'll take it for you,' Miriam offered. 'I'd like a walk.'

In her first months at the cottage Louise had bought a pair of expensive walking boots and marched along all the local footpaths and bridleways. But after her first enthusiasm she found that she preferred to observe the countryside, and the small seasonal changes, from her windows. The landscape – so important to town dwellers – rapidly became nothing more than an obstacle between where she was and where she wanted to be. The four miles down the road to the Wistley shops might be a flower-fringed lane, no wider than a car, where cow-parsley and meadow vetch wiped their pollen on her car doors in midsummer. But it was a nuisance to have to drive every time you wanted a newspaper or a pint of milk. The twenty-mile drive to the university through the high clear hills of the Sussex downs was completed by Louise in an efficient trance. She listened to the radio, she thought about her work, she daydreamed of Toby. She hardly saw the pale earth turning green or the wheeling gulls.

'Are you sure? I can just as easily drive up there.'

Miriam nodded. 'I'd like to see the farm,' she said. 'Is it OK to just go round? Should I ring up or anything?'

'He's always there. I knock on the back door, and if there's no reply I go round to the yard,' Louise said. 'He's often in the barn doing things to animals. Sometimes he's out on the tractor, but generally he's in the yard or the barn.'

Miriam pulled on a light jacket. 'Does he live there on his own?'

'Yes. His father died about five years ago, I think.'

'I'm surprised he's not married.'

'I don't think he's the marrying type. He's got a bit of a reputation in the village, they talk about him in the shop sometimes. And he drinks of course.'

'Gorgeous eyes,' Miriam said.

Louise suddenly felt a stir of interest. She looked at Miriam more closely. 'Gorgeous eyes?'

Miriam smiled. 'A girl can look,' she said. 'And he does have the most deep blue eyes, that wonderful navy blue. Like Robert Redford.'

'Wistley Common's Robert Redford!' Louise put her hand in her pocket for the envelope. 'Here you are. Try and control your restless desires. I think you'd frighten him to death!'

Miriam smiled. 'I'll come back over the common,' she said. 'I'll be a while.'

Louise nodded and turned back to *Lady Chatterley's Lover*. It was one of the long descriptive passages about scenery, page after page containing nothing to which she could possibly object.

She had never thought of Andrew Miles as a desirable man before Rose had spoken of his bed and Miriam mentioned his eyes. She had thought of him as useful – a competent neighbour who would put up gutters and deliver her sacks of coal when the coal lorry could not manage the snowy lane. She sometimes bought eggs from him, and he knew the name of the septic tank contractors. He put up the fence for her, and mended a window hinge. It was comforting to know that a man as large and competent as Andrew Miles was up the road. His routine was known to her, the strangled roar at night of his Land-Rover taking the hill was as regular as a clock bell chiming for half past eleven, except at weekends when he was later.

116

She could not have survived in the cottage, especially the winter, if he had not stopped once or twice a week at her door to ask her if all was well. When her power had cut off suddenly in the night, it had been Andrew Miles at half past seven the next morning who had told her about the trip switch on the fuse box which would put the power back on. When there was a brief flurry of snow in February he drove down the lane in his tractor beating a clear path so that she could get to work. He told her she might telephone him from the university before she drove home and he would meet her in the Land-Rover in the village and ferry her to and from her cottage until the thaw. She always paid him excessive amounts of cash in unmarked envelopes; but she had never thought before that he was a man who might be seen as desirable rather than useful.

It was the same revelation as Toby. Louise had seen him in the bar and been introduced to him. But it was only when Miriam turned to her and whispered behind an indiscreet hand, 'At last, a bit of real talent!' that Louise had suddenly seen him as sexy. Then he had dazzled them both. Five years older than them, the gloss of Oxford and a fellowship at Bristol still on him, while they were nothing but under-graduates, he was a star in their tiny firmament. Louise, peaky and shy, smiled at him and watched him. Miriam, in her late summer bloom, glowed when he looked at her and seduced him without effort.

Louise turned the pages irritably. Lawrence was still going on about the state of England and the way one countryside replaced another, the mean dirty mining vil-lages overwhelming and obliterating the open country. Louise skipped to the end of the chapter. She was only interested in prosecuting Lawrence as a sexist. Anything else was irrelevant. She wondered for a moment what Mr

Miles would think of Miriam and felt unreasonably uneasy. Mr Miles could not seriously be of any interest to Miriam whose taste in men had always been for skinny intellectuals. Miriam, with her social conscience and her sharp feminist mind, could not possibly be attractive to Mr Miles whose tastes must surely run to the broad-hipped and bucolic. Nonetheless, Louise glanced at the clock and wondered whether Mr Miles would invite Miriam into the farmhouse for a mug of tea. She felt even more impatient with Lawrence, who believed that sensuality could smash the barriers of class and education.

Toby drew up outside the cottage. He was speechless with anger. Rose beside him was quite unconcerned. '*That* was a good afternoon's work,' she said with satisfaction as if they had enjoyed a peaceful shopping trip together. 'Thank you for driving me.'

Toby opened the car door and got out. He was inwardly raging.

Rose leaned into the car and gathered up the Fromes' laundry from the back seat. She slammed her door and set off down the path. Toby watched her go. She still had his hundred pounds in her pocket.

At the van door she greeted her dog, climbed the steps and then turned and waved. Toby stood still and then limped into Louise's house. He had hurt his ankle when he jumped down from the wall and he very much wanted a drink.

'You were a long time,' Louise remarked. 'Where have you been all this while?'

Toby dropped into a chair and nodded, saying nothing.

'Miriam's gone to the farm for a walk,' Louise said. 'You only just missed her.'

118

There was a short silence. 'She'll be an hour at the least,' Louise prompted. She was not feeling desire for Toby, but she had a need to reassure herself that what she had said to Miriam was right – that her lover was turning to her, that he preferred her to his wife, and that he would ultimately come to her.

'I'm absolutely exhausted,' Toby said. 'May I have a bath?'

'Of course. There are clean towels in your bedroom.' Louise paused. 'Shall I scrub your back?'

Toby got to his feet with a little grunt of discomfort. Louise watched him limp to the stairs. 'Are you all right?' she asked. 'Have you hurt yourself?'

'She's a public nuisance,' Toby exploded suddenly. 'I've had a bloody awful afternoon. I've sprained my ankle running around after her and I'm no further forward at all. She's rolled me over for a hundred pounds and all I have to show for it is an absolutely wasted afternoon.'

Miriam would have been familiar with the irritable tone of Toby's voice. He was intolerant of physical discomfort and on camping holidays if it rained, or if he scraped his knuckles or banged his elbow, he would be suddenly gripped with temper which only comfort and sympathy could abate. But Louise had never seen him like this before. His tone with her was always urbane, and detached. Toby scowling and red-faced like a crossed toddler was a new, less attractive Toby. He always laughed at her misfortunes, laughed affectionately, as if they did not much matter and she was silly and rather endearing to make such a fuss. But now, in his own discomfort there were no grounds for comedy.

'Bloody woman,' he said again, and turned and limped upstairs, dramatically favouring the sprained ankle and clinging to the banister.

119

Louise looked after him thoughtfully, and let him run his own bath and scrub his own back.

Miriam arrived at the back door of the farm and knocked. There were two short barks from a dog and a shout from indoors, bidding her enter. She opened the door with the old-fashioned latch and stepped into a large scullery. There was a row of pegs with foul-weather gear hanging up, and below them a muddle of Wellington boots. There was a handsome tea trolley bearing cardboard trays of dirty eggs, speckled with straw and grey-white hens' droppings. There was a dog basket in the corner of the room and a large old-fashioned white kitchen sink with an enormous boiler hung above it and a hard-worn towel beside it. Either side of the sink was a brand new washing machine and tumble dryer. The collie barked once more, but kept its place in its basket.

The inner door to the house opened and Mr Miles looked out. 'Oh! hello,' he said. 'Come in.'

Miriam hesitated and then undid her neat brown boots and left them side by side in the doorway before crossing the threshold to the kitchen. She felt rather like a tourist visiting a temple barefoot, anxious to conform to the courtesies and yet feeling ridiculous.

Mr Miles was eating his tea. A large brown loaf stood on the table with two thick slices carved from it. He had a broad wedge of pie on a plate with a pile of bright green tinned peas and boiled potatoes. A brown teapot stood on the table with a sugar bowl and a bottle of milk. He had a book propped against the butter dish and the radio was tuned to Radio Four.

'I'm sorry to disturb you,' Miriam said. 'I brought you

this from Louise.' She held out the envelope. Mr Miles pocketed it.

'Would you like a cup of tea? Something to eat?'

Miriam hesitated. 'I shouldn't interrupt your meal,' she said.

Mr Miles merely waited for a direct answer to his invitation.

'I'd love a cup of tea,' Miriam admitted.

'Cup behind you, help yourself,' he said and sat down again at his place. He switched the radio off and when Miriam had taken a mug from the dark wood Welsh dresser he pushed the milk bottle and teapot towards her.

Miriam poured herself a cup and then tasted it. It was very good quality Lapsang Souchong. She looked at Mr Miles with surprise. He shut his book, carefully marking the place, and continued to eat his meal with neat movements. Miriam thought she had never seen a man with such calm presence.

She looked around her. The kitchen floor was stone-flagged with bright rag rugs like scattered islands of warmth. The ceiling was low with the dark heavy beams making it lower; Miriam thought that Mr Miles must have learned to duck his head every three paces. Behind her was the Welsh dresser and a large wood-burning kitchen range. To her right was a small casement window with a view over the nearest fields and then, as the land fell away downhill, the rolling side of Wistley Common, green and fresh in the May sunshine.

At the back of the room was a kitchen sink with a large expensive dishwasher beside it. A small white-painted door led to the larder and beside it another dark wood door with a latch led to the rest of the house. Miriam guessed the place was an old Elizabethan farmhouse with later additions. She

121

would have loved to look all over it, but glancing at the owner's unperturbed bulk she thought she did not have the nerve to ask.

Mr Miles finished his meal and folded a large slice of bread and butter into a quarter and downed it in two great bites. He poured himself another cup of tea and waved the pot invitingly at Miriam. She took another cup, not from thirst, but to prolong the visit.

'This is nice,' Mr Miles said. 'Not often I have company for tea.'

'Have you always lived alone?'

'With my dad and mum before she died, and then with him. He went five years ago. Cancer.'

'I'm sorry,' Miriam said.

Andrew Miles shook his head. 'He was glad to go, he was grieving for her. He thought he'd be with her after death. Cancer's a disease from grief, don't you think?'

Miriam felt rather bemused. 'I don't know,' she said. 'I've never thought of it.'

Andrew nodded. 'I think it is,' he said. 'Very rare in the animals. Only in the ones that can love. I've had a dog die of cancer but never a sheep.'

'Don't sheep love their lambs?' Miriam asked, feeling wonderfully out of her depth.

'For a while,' he pronounced. 'But they've got terrible memories, sheep. Most forgetful animals. Some of them never get the knack of caring for the lamb at all. It's as if they forgot they just had it. A lot of nuisance, that is.'

'Nuisance?'

'Someone else has to rear them. Another sheep if they're lucky. Me, if they're not.'

'You hand-rear lambs?' Improbable images of Little

Boy Blue and Bo Peep flashed across Miriam's urban imagination.

'Yes.'

'Isn't it frightfully hard work? Do you bottle-feed them?'

'I bottle-feed them. It's always hard work at lambing. No-one gets much sleep at that time of year.'

'Why not?'

Mr Miles looked carefully at her as if to make sure that she was not teasing him with feigned ignorance. 'You have to wake with the sheep,' he explained. 'Make sure the lambs come all right. Help them if they need it. Pair up the lambs with the right mother, make sure she doesn't reject them. Get orphaned lambs fostered on to other mothers. All sorts.'

'I never knew,' Miriam said. 'I thought farming was all machines these days.'

Andrew Miles smiled one of his rare friendly smiles. 'Not on this farm,' he said. 'I've only just got a television. Anyway, we have sheep and cows and hens. You can't really mechanise beasts.'

'What about battery farming?'

He looked shocked as if she had said something terribly vulgar. There was a brief embarrassed silence. 'I wouldn't do that,' he said finally.

Miriam waited for an explanation of why not; but he said nothing more. 'I don't know anything about farming or the country,' she heard herself say apologetically.

'What's your line then?'

Miriam's work sounded curiously evanescent to herself as she tried to explain. 'I run a refuge for women whose partners are violent to them, in Brighton. And I work with alcoholic women who are trying to give up drinking. And I work with women who keep getting involved with the wrong sort of man.'

123

Andrew Miles looked enormously impressed. 'What do you do with them?'

'I counsel them. I help them to change.'

He looked at Miriam as if she were some kind of rare animal which had strayed into his kitchen. 'Change?'

'Women who drink or who seek violent men or uncaring men have to change themselves before they can properly leave,' she said. 'Otherwise they just find themselves in a similar situation with another man who is as bad. It becomes a pattern for them. I counsel them how to change their emotional patterns so that they can truly change their lives.'

'Well now,' Andrew Miles said, enormously impressed. 'I never heard of such a thing before. And where did you learn to do that?'

Miriam smiled. 'I go on courses. I'm still learning. I shall be learning all my life.'

'And you're Miss Case's friend?'

Miriam nodded. 'My husband and I used to share a house with her. We're staying with her this weekend.'

A guarded, almost frightened look came across Andrew Miles's face at the mention of Toby. 'Oh, I couldn't live in a town,' he said suddenly.

Miriam, who did not follow the connection, looked surprised. 'Why not?'

He pushed back his chair from the table and started stacking the plates in the dishwasher. 'So complicated,' he muttered half to himself. 'All these people sharing houses and changing their lives and learning.'

Miriam laughed her seductive giggle. 'We don't do it all the time,' she said. 'Sometimes we do nothing.'

Andrew looked up at her. 'I would hope so,' he said firmly.

Miriam brought her mug over to the dishwasher, tossed

the dregs in the sink and put it in the top rack. Andrew Miles returned the milk and butter to the larder, put the bread in a bread bin and wiped down the table. There was an intimate domestic atmosphere generated by this sharing of tasks. Miriam suddenly wondered, unprompted, what Andrew Miles would be like in bed. She smothered a giggle by bending to pick up a table mat which had fallen to the floor.

'Would you like to see the beasts?'

Miriam nodded. 'If I'm not delaying you?'

He led the way from the kitchen to the scullery, stepping into his boots and pulling his cap on over his thinning golden hair. He waited for Miriam to fasten her little boots and then led her out of the back door. He showed her the hens scratching in the yard and the little wheeled hen coops. He showed her a couple of guinea fowl which his mother had kept and which had survived her. There were lambs in the field nearest the house and two of them hurtled towards the gate when they saw him. Miriam petted them but Andrew thrust his hands in his pocket and would not touch them though they bleated for his attention.

'They're so sweet,' Miriam said.

'They're for eating, they're not pets,' he said firmly. 'They'll have to forget they're hand-reared.'

'Can't you keep them?'

'I'll keep the yow,' he said. 'But the little tup'll have to go.'

In a further field there was a small herd of creamy-coloured cows. 'Charolais,' he said proudly. 'That's a pedigree herd, that is. French cows.'

'Why not English?' Miriam asked.

'Less fat on Charolais,' he said. 'The cooks don't like meat with fat any more. It has to be lean. All the English varieties, good English cows, are too fatty. So we farm lean beasts now and the taste is all wrong.'

'Why?'

'It's the fat that flavours the meat,' Andrew Miles said solemnly. 'But you can't tell them that. Someone decides that fat is bad for you and nobody eats decent beef any more.' He shook his head at the folly of fashion in food. 'I can give you the finest steak you've ever tasted off these fields – but I'd go out of business if I tried to farm English beef. It's all French. It's all tasteless. And now they're all going vegetarian.'

'Toby cooks a lot of lentils,' Miriam agreed.

Andrew's eyes widened in silent horror. 'Yes,' he said. 'I imagine he would.' He turned and gestured at a field beyond the cows. 'Here is where we're going to have the party when I get the hay in.'

'A party? You mean you really are having the travellers here?'

He looked at her. 'Why not?'

'Well, the whole village seems to think that it's a dreadful thing. Louise had Captain Frome on the telephone twice and then he came out while you were there.'

'Captain Frome's not the whole village. Some of them at the Holly Bush are rather looking forward to it.'

'Looking forward to it?'

'When the hay is in.'

'What's the hay got to do with it?'

Andrew Miles looked at her once more, as if she were pretending to an ignorance which no adult could reasonably have. Then he pointed to the field where the tall grass was speckled with flowers. 'When that's cut, and all the other hayfields, you can put wagons on it, or tents, anything you like. It's just grass. It'll grow. And when the hay is in there's a little break, like, before harvest and shearing. That's when people always had parties, in the old days. You'll have heard of haymaking?'

'In books, yes.'

'Well, after haymaking, and later again, after the harvest is in, people have their shows and their parties. That's how it's always been. So when they telephoned me and asked me if I had a field I said they could come, either after haymaking or after harvest. And they wanted to come soon. I think it'll be fun.'

Miriam giggled again. 'They're going mad about it in the village.'

Andrew Miles shook his head. 'Not all of them. A few of them, the newcomers, they're all upset about it. But the other farmers and the lads in the Bush, they're not worried.'

'It may be more than a few people in vans,' Miriam warned him. 'It's not so traditional these days. They'll probably have huge electronic speakers and the music will go on all day and night. And there's certain to be drugs being sold.'

'Well,' Andrew said tolerantly. 'They're just kids after all. They deserve a bit of fun.'

Miriam could think of nothing more to say. 'Thank you for showing me round. I'd better get back now.'

'D'you know the way?'

'Yes, I'll go over the common.'

Andrew touched his finger to the cap he habitually wore. 'Would you like to come to the party?' he asked pleasantly. 'It'll be next weekend. I'd be very pleased if you would come. I've asked Miss Case already.'

Miriam smiled at the thought of this formal invitation to a rave. 'I should love to come,' she said. 'Thank you for asking me.'

Andrew nodded and headed towards the yard, his dog at his heels. At the gate the hand-reared lambs stood and bleated appealingly. He paused and thrust his hands deeper into his pockets to prevent himself caressing them, and then went on to the barns. Miriam turned down the track that led to the common and started to walk back to Louise's cottage, three miles downhill.

Sunday

TOBY PAID ANOTHER VISIT TO THE VAN on Sunday
morning while Louise and Miriam fetched the Sunday
papers from Mrs Ford's shop. As soon as they had turned
out of the drive in Louise's car Toby skipped over the front
doorstep carrying a cup of tea, down the garden path, and
through the orchard gate. He found Rose prepared to be
gracious. She drank it, sitting on the step of her van, watching the sun burn off the early-morning mist. Toby, cramped
and chilly sitting on the dewy grass and eyed in a baleful
way by her dog, thought that few scholars had endured
more in the course of research.

Rose was prepared to be obliging. She brought out the
box of newspaper clippings again and showed them, one at
a time. They all described raids on empty houses where
windows had been smashed or fires laid. From the outraged
tone of the newspapers you would have thought that mil-
lions of pounds had been lost. But in fact the fires were
rather small and easily contained. And the windows were
quickly replaced.

'It wasn't the amount of damage, or the expense,' Rose
said. 'It was to give them the sense that we were everywhere.
Like the IRA.'

Toby glanced up from a particularly trivial cutting. 'Hardly like the IRA,' he objected.

Rose shook her head at his stupidity. 'The IRA didn't really care about a telephone box in Milton Keynes,' she said. 'The point is to make the population feel that the terrorists can go anywhere they want. That nowhere is sacred. That they have so many members that they extend everywhere. That's basic terrorist theory. I'd have thought you'd have known that, a bright boy like you.'

Toby shifted a little in the damp grass. The dog sniffed at his ankles as he stretched out and he drew them back up towards him swiftly.

'Did you say you had some diaries?' Toby asked.

'I'll show you them later.' Rose was quite absorbed in her bottomless box of little pieces of newspaper. 'Here, I did this one. It says, "Entrance was effected through a small, unfastened scullery window", and it says later: "These reckless harpies must be employing children or even trained monkeys for the successful accomplishment of these acts of violence". That was me!' she said proudly. 'Me!'

'I wonder if I could take the diaries away with me, to read carefully?' Toby asked.

Rose did not lift her delighted face from her box. 'Oh no,' she said.

'I should be tremendously careful with them. I know how precious they are . . .'

'No.'

'I have to see them, study them, in order to understand them properly,' Toby said. 'I have to read them and re-read them or else I can't do the book at all.'

Rose looked up at him. 'As you wish,' she said helpfully. 'I wanted to write it myself, anyway. I'll have a bit of a clear out and burn the stuff that's no good and then I'll write the rest.'

'No!' Toby yelped. 'Don't burn anything. *Please* don't burn anything until I've had a chance to look at it. *Please,* Miss Pankhurst – you don't know what people might find interesting. All sorts of things which you might think are boring would be very interesting to historians. I'll read every word, I'll take tremendous care of them. I'll bring them back to you the very moment I have read them.'

'Oh, very well.' Rose suddenly lost interest. 'You can take this box now if you like.'

'I'd like to start with the diaries,' Toby said hopefully.

'This box or nothing,' Rose said, holding it out.

Toby almost snatched it from her. 'Is it all suffragette clippings?' he asked, looking at the depth of the box and the cream-coloured drifts of newsprint.

'Oh no,' she said. 'I popped all sorts in there over the years. Dress patterns, recipes, stories that I liked the sound of. But you can read it all if you want to, as you say. It will be fascinating to you even though it's quite boring to everyone else. It's just a lot of junk to everyone else but, as you say, you'll be reading every word.'

Toby forced a smile on his face. 'Thank you,' he said. 'I'll bring it back the moment I've finished.'

'You needn't bring it back,' she said. 'I was turning it out anyway. You can sort it and keep what you want.'

'I will,' Toby promised. 'And then we'll look at something else, shall we? The diaries and the photographs?'

Rose nodded. 'All right.'

'Could we perhaps have a little glance at the photographs now?' Toby asked winningly, keeping a firm grip on the box.

'No,' Rose said decisively. 'They're under a box of hats

131

that wants turning out. You can see them when you've finished with the newspaper clippings. I'll be ready for you then.'

'All right,' Toby agreed. 'I'll read them at once and be back soon. Perhaps tomorrow.'

Rose smiled at him, her malicious old-crone smile. 'You'll need your eyes tested,' she said. 'You'll need your head tested too.'

Toby managed a pleasant laugh.

'Which woman is it to be, then?' Rose demanded suddenly. Toby, struggling to his feet and cautiously putting his weight on the sprained ankle, gave a little whimper of discomfort. 'What d'you mean, Miss Pankhurst?'

'Can't go stringing them both along forever, can you?'

Toby looked at her blankly.

'Unless you're more of a man than most you can't satisfy two women,' Rose said clearly. 'It's a rare man that can satisfy one. So which will you have? Louise or Miriam?'

Toby tried an urbane smile. 'It's not quite like that,' he said pleasantly. 'Louise is our very good friend, and Miriam is my wife. It's not a question of choosing between the two. I am married to Miriam and Louise is a dear, dear friend. These days I think everyone accepts that a man and a woman can be friends.'

Rose shook her head. 'That girl needs a man,' she declared. 'A man in her bed and a baby on the way. She needs someone to warm her bed at night, not a quick poke and then an empty house. And Miriam needs some fun. She looks downright miserable. And you're the one that has brought all this about. So you'd better think carefully what you're doing, my boy. You're bringing neither of them any good at all.'

Toby gritted his teeth and kept the smile on his face. 'I

think these days we don't really believe that a woman *needs* a man and a baby,' he said. 'Of course Louise will make her own choices as an informed adult. She has her own life to live. I think neither you nor I can say what's best for her, can we, really? And Miriam is absolutely free to live how she wishes. We have an open and adult relationship. I assure you she does the work she wants and she lives as she wants.'

A fugitive memory of Miriam as he had first met her with her curly wild hair and her larky eyes swam up from his past and challenged his view of her as a woman who had fulfilled her potential. Toby put at once from his mind the knowledge that his wife was deeply unhappy.

'All three of us are very happy in our own ways. Not your ways perhaps, but they do very well for us. You needn't worry about us, I promise you, Miss Pankhurst.'

'You're a selfish little puppy,' Rose said levelly. 'You'd better make your mind up, one or the other; or you'll lose both and serve you right.'

Toby bit back a roar of rage at this old woman daring to lecture him. 'I'll think about what you've said,' he replied, smiling till his cheeks ached. 'I hear what you're saying. I've taken it on board. I thank you for your concern for us, and I promise you I'll think about it.'

Rose grunted in disdain and stamped into her van and slammed the door behind her. Freed from her presence, the dog came out from under the steps and snarled at Toby's feet. Toby limped hastily to beyond the garden gate and shut it with a bang. Between the pain in his ankle and the bruising to his ego he felt thoroughly battered. He trailed back to the house with his huge box of newspaper clippings in his arms in an advanced state of sulk. If he had not admired Rose and liked her so very thoroughly – as any researcher should feel towards his subject – and if he had not been a committed feminist and she a woman, he would have absolutely hated her.

Miriam and Louise bought armfuls of newsprint: the *Sunday Times*, the *Observer*, the *Independent* and the *Sunday Telegraph*. It did not occur to either of them to buy any of the tabloids though they both spent some time reading the lead stories and furtively turning the pages until Mrs Ford's indignant glare drove them from the little shop. Neither woman had bought a tabloid newspaper for ten years. Tabloids maintained a reprehensibly sexist attitude towards women, and whatever the news they carried neither Miriam nor Louise would ever stoop to support them. Miriam could see the *Daily Mirror* at work since someone in the refuge would always buy it. She would read it, clandestinely, during the morning, and while she was generally outraged by its attitudes she found herself reliably entertained. However she would never have bought it for herself.

In the doorway of the shop they met Captain Frome. 'It seems we've won the first battle,' he said loudly enough for the other customers in the shop to hear. 'The police turned a convoy of ten vans – ten, if you please! – back at the roadblock and they've gone over the border into Hampshire. We've won the first battle, if we remain vigilant we'll win the war.'

There was a rustle of polite interest in the little shop.

'We'll show 'em,' Mrs Ford said militantly, earning herself a swift approving smile from the Captain.

'They may try and regroup, of course,' Captain Frome warned. 'But I think we've got them on the run.'

One of the women in the shop said, 'Seems a shame,'

under her breath but Captain Frome was too grand to acknowledge such suppressed heckling.

'Neighbourhood watch meeting, Tuesday night, six thirty sharp,' he said, handing a poster to Mrs Ford with a commanding nod. 'Hope you'll be there, Miss Case?'

Louise glanced uncomfortably at Miriam. 'Unfortunately I have a meeting at the university on Tuesday,' she said.

'Cut it! Send your apologies!'

'You're reporting on the Science and Industry Sub-dean's attitude,' Miriam reminded her sharply.

'I really have to be there,' Louise said weakly. 'But I'll telephone you the next day if I may and see what was decided.'

Captain Frome nodded but he was dissatisfied. 'Do you wish to register a proxy vote, or nominate someone to vote for you?'

'What would we be voting on?' Louise asked.

'Further actions, of course.'

'Oh, of course,' Louise said vaguely. 'Well . . . would you like to be my proxy, Captain Frome?'

He nodded. 'Very well. We do need to stick together, I think.'

'Hounding innocent people from pillar to post,' a woman murmured quietly behind the rack of groceries. 'Moved on all the time. Doesn't seem right. Half of them with kiddies. Where are they supposed to go?'

Captain Frome raised his voice slightly. 'I think I speak for the whole village when I say that we're not some kind of Butlins holiday camp for every ne'er do well who can get his hands on a caravan.'

'Do you know,' Miriam suddenly interrupted, her voice loud and icy, 'I've never heard anyone say "ne'er do well" before? I thought it was something people only said in books.'

There was a snort of laughter from behind the groceries. Miriam took the newspapers from Louise and walked past Captain Frome and out of the shop.

'Oh,' Louise said feebly. 'Good day, Captain Frome.'

Miriam was waiting beside Louise's car in a state of barely repressed rage. 'What a pompous oaf!' she spluttered.

'He represents the village's feelings,' Louise said, hastily unlocking the car so that Miriam's noisy disdain could be shut inside and muffled.

'No he doesn't,' Miriam said abruptly. 'He represents the propertied classes. All the working people and the farming people are perfectly happy for the travellers to come. Mr Miles is looking forward to the party.'

'That is absolutely absurd,' Louise said, starting the car. 'Mr Miles knows nothing about raves. He's been conned into providing his land by some sharp operator. He knows nothing about raves or what is going to happen. Everyone in the village is behind Captain Frome, he has organised an enormous protest meeting. I *live* here, Miriam. I know what's going on.'

'No, you don't,' Miriam argued, as if she had totally forgotten about female consensus and about women's natural ability to listen and share information. 'All you know about is what that pompous old windbag says. You should listen to Andrew. He says everyone at the pub is quite happy about it.'

Louise drove too fast up the lane towards her house. 'I'm not that intimate with him actually. We've only ever talked about odd jobs.'

'Well, he's a damn sight more interesting than Colonel Blimp,' Miriam said. 'He's a sensible generous warm-hearted man. Not a stuffed shirt trying to find something to do to fill in his retirement.'

'Oh, really!' Louise cried in irritation. 'You hardly know either of them.'

'I know a nice man when I see him,' Miriam said. 'And I'd put my faith in Andrew Miles any day.'

Louise felt herself gripped with a quite unreasonable fury. If she had believed in the existence of jealousy between feminists she would have recognised this savage rage at Miriam's sudden intimacy with Andrew Miles. Louise's whole world was abruptly turned upside down if Miriam should find a man such as Andrew Miles attractive. Miriam who had Toby, who had been the pinnacle of Louise's desires for nine years. It made no sense at all that Miriam, with Toby as her husband, her intellectual companion and her lover, should find Andrew Miles, an uneducated uncouth farm labourer, so extremely attractive.

Louise drew up in front of her cottage and jerked on the handbrake. 'I think you go out of your way to be different,' she said. 'Andrew Miles has probably never even heard of feminism or activism or the Second Wave. He probably doesn't have an idea in his head beyond the weather and the price of corn.'

Miriam laughed. 'All the better for that,' she said perversely. 'I'm sick of feminist men.'

Miriam and Toby left at midday after a leisurely breakfast reading the newspapers. Miriam, who knew she had been unreasonable with Louise, cooked eggs and bacon for the three of them and made coffee and toast. Toby, who was anxious to avoid question or challenge about his relationship with Rose or the contents of Rose's big box, laid himself out to be entertaining, reading out snippets from the Sunday newspapers and commenting with insight and sarcasm. He could be very amusing when he wished and Miriam and Louise laughed and prompted him to further irony at the expense of the government. Much of what he mocked was funny, but the decline of the pound against other currencies and the steady downward spiral of the recession could only ever be amusing to people, like Louise and Toby, with small mortgages, guaranteed wages, and a contract of employment. Their amusement was founded on the smugness of being politically correct and financially secure. Miriam laughed with them but knew that her work and her salary was more uncertain, and the projects which she espoused – the safety of women – were not dear to this government's heart.

Toby and Louise cleared the breakfast plates away and washed up in quiet harmony while Miriam went upstairs to pack her weekend bag.

'I'm sorry about yesterday,' Toby apologised, finally referring to Saturday afternoon when he had limped home after his shopping trip with Rose and locked himself in the bathroom for two hours. 'Sometimes I really need space. Thank you for having the consideration to give me that space. You're so aware, Louise, so sensitive.'

In fact Louise had sulked downstairs while Toby had bathed and sulked upstairs, but this small rewriting of recent history made their mutual irritability appear in a more becoming light.

'What was the matter?' Louise asked, still being sensitive and aware.

Toby shrugged. 'Oh! I don't know! Having to shop with Rose. She borrowed a hundred pounds off me, you know, and I don't expect to see it again. I suppose I'm just not used to being around demanding women.' He gave Louise a sexy small smile. 'You've spoiled me,' he said.

Louise flapped at him lightly with the tea towel. 'I know it. But you are getting on well with her, are you? You will get some material out of her?'

Toby caught her hand, took the towel from her, and turned her palm upwards and kissed it very gently. Louise felt her whole body warm to his touch. They could hear Miriam moving around upstairs. Louise felt her nine-year habit of clandestine desire rising like a Pavlovian dog's saliva at the dinner bell. Sexual pleasure for Louise and Toby always meant the fear of being caught.

Toby bit the fleshy part of her palm. Louise leaned against the sink and dropped her head back, baring the smooth column of her throat. Toby moved closer and kissed down her neck, from her jawline to her collar bone; and where the crew neck of her jumper would hide any mark, he bit her soft warm skin and felt her responsive quiver.

His hands clasped her breasts and then stroked firmly down her body, but when Louise reached for his groin he stepped back. Toby had enjoyed years of this sort of encounter with Louise and he had trained himself to keep within the comfortable side of arousal. He was not going to drive home with Miriam suffering from cramps of lust. There was no possibility of making love to Louise, the most they could do now was a little adolescent dangerous snogging, and that was all Toby was prepared to do. He would touch Louise as intimately as he wished, but she might not caress him.

He captured her hands and came closer again. Louise's eyes were shut; unlike him, she had no cautious self-preserving boundaries. Toby enjoyed the sight of her absorbed sensuality. He felt powerful, masterful. He loved

139

arousing her in these stolen moments. And he loved to watch her struggling to hide her desire when Miriam reappeared. He felt like some cruel pagan god dispensing desire and withholding satisfaction. He kissed her soft inviting lips, he stroked his hand around her buttock and slid round to caress her thigh. A movement outside the kitchen window caught his eye. He lifted his face from Louise, and took his mouth from stirring hers.

Rose was there. She was watching him, staring without any embarrassment, as if he were some curious and not particularly attractive animal playing with itself in a glass case. Toby felt his erection collapse in a rush, and desire abruptly vanish. He stepped back from Louise and she slowly opened her eyes. Louise had her back to the window, she did not know they were being observed.

'You're too sexy,' Toby said feebly. His heart was not in it.

'Kiss me again,' Louise breathed. 'Oh God, I want you.'

Toby shot a quick glance at the window behind her head. Rose's staring critical face had gone. But he had no guarantee that she would not reappear like Jiminy Crickett the moment he laid his hands on his mistress.

He shook his head. 'I won't be able to stop,' he lied, playing the trump card of uncontrollable male desire, unreconstructed despite years of feminism. 'And Miriam'll be down in a moment.'

Louise drooped. 'I wish you could stay,' she said plaintively. For a moment, for half a moment, she felt a pang of resentment. Toby and Miriam were leaving together, going home to an empty house. If they so wished they could close their front door behind them and retreat to their battered double bed for the whole of the afternoon. Louise carefully turned her mind away from the possibility that Toby's

140

desire, aroused with her, might be satisfied with Miriam. She had learned early in this relationship never to speculate. Her own satisfaction would have to wait until Tuesday night in the back of the car if Toby was then willing, or else it would be her own insubstantial fingers in her cold big bed.

'Oh God, I wish I could,' Toby breathed, coming a little closer but keeping a wary eye on the window. 'I can think of nothing in the world better. I am crazy for you, Louise, I want you so much. I can't go on without you.'

He had said exactly the right thing. Louise's face took on that desirous tranced expression again. 'Oh, yes,' she murmured.

Miriam clattered down the uncarpeted stairs. 'Sorry I was so long,' she said brightly. 'I lost a sock. Why is it one always loses one? Why never the pair?'

'Isn't it Douglas Adams who proposes a corner of the universe filled with odd socks and biro pen tops?' Toby asked. He had stepped back half a pace from Louise at the first sound of his wife's footsteps on the stairs. He knew better than to jump guiltily away.

Louise looked from one smiling face to another.

'All packed?' Toby asked pleasantly.

They went to the front door, Miriam lagging a little to whisper to Louise, 'I'm sorry I was grouchy about neighbourhood watch. I hate that kind of thing. But I do really think that your Andrew Miles is a sweetie.'

'That's OK,' Louise said shortly.

'See you at the meeting, Tuesday?'

'Yes.'

Miriam and Louise hugged and then Toby came back from loading Miriam's bag in the back seat beside the precious box of cuttings. Miriam got in the passenger seat.

Toby kissed Louise goodbye, a careful unmeaning brush of the lips on her cheek.

'Thanks for a great weekend,' he said lightly. 'Call me, Monday.'

Louise stood on the doorstep of her pretty cottage and waved goodbye as they turned out of her drive into the lane. She felt unaccountably depressed but could not think why. She went back inside the house. The Sunday papers, heavy with words and bursting with opinions, were spread all around her tidy sitting room. Toby and she had forgotten the washing up and the greasy plates were drowned in cooling dishwater. The kitchen smelled of old cooking, and Louise felt tired all over. The long deception of Miriam, the long clandestine affair with Toby seemed suddenly pointless and unworthy. And if Miriam were genuinely tired of Toby, if Miriam who had lived with him and been showered with his love was sick of feminist men, was finding Toby himself wanting – Louise tossed pages of the newspapers from the sofa to the floor and put her feet up – if Miriam's final judgement that Toby was *not*, after all, the ideal man; then Louise could not think what she had been doing waiting for him for the past nine years.

Monday

MONDAY MORNING IT RAINED in steady grey sheets against Louise's study windows. The van in the orchard looked drenched and miserable. All the firewood for the stove had gone from beside the steps. Louise thought guiltily about Rose in her van with a damp dog listening to the rain on the roof while the last of the wood smoked on the little stove.

She switched on the word processor and read the uninspired title and one sentence: '*The Virgin and the Gypsy*: A Patriarchal Myth of Rape and Female Growth'. She pressed the 'Delete' button with a sense of relief and watched the words wiped from the screen. Louise typed urgently and the words flickered into life:

However attractive the notion of a relationship based on irresistible desire and spiritual compatibility, we know that this is a romantic dream. The union of the virgin and the gypsy of the title is as unlikely in real life as the union of Mellors the gamekeeper and Constance Chatterley, the lady of the manor. In real life we know that relationships are only meaningful if based on thorough equality – and such equality can only exist if there is equality of education and aspirations.

The dream of 'falling in love' and this love being all-powerful and transcending every objection of class, suitability and compatibility, is central to the romantic myth which has kept women in a state of slavish subservience for centuries.

Louise nodded at the screen and smiled slightly. Her fingers tapped rapidly. Last night, after reading *Lady Chatterley's Lover*, she had dreamed that a steeplechase race had been organised from Wistley village. A runaway horse had crashed through her fence, and then through her front door. In her dream Louise had run downstairs and somehow leaped into the saddle and the horse had turned and thundered from the cold and empty house outside into the rain, jumping hedges and even trees, up to Mr Miles's farmhouse. Louise had clung to the horse as it galloped along the narrow paths of the commons and then, as it had leaped higher and higher over more and more obstacles, she had opened her mouth and heard a great wild song spilling out from her lips. She had woken abruptly, to the sound of rain pouring from an overflowing gutter, in a state of elated sexual arousal mixed with intense irritation with D.H. Lawrence, and, less explicably, with Andrew Miles.

As women and feminists we have to challenge this myth [she wrote sharply]. We have to surrender romance, love, glamour, and belief in all-conquering desire in favour of reality. We can still enjoy friendship with men. We can still enjoy sexual intercourse with men. But we can no longer allow ourselves to be conned into the nonsensical belief that their attentions make us 'whole', or that sexual intercourse or making love is in any way some sort of spiritual activity. We understand the physiology of orgasm now, we have reclaimed our bodies. Now we need to reclaim our hearts.

There was a loud knock at the door. Louise pressed the 'Save' button on the word processor with a small triumphant flourish; and went to the front door.

Andrew Miles was standing in the pouring rain, the collar of his jacket upturned, his cap pulled down low over his blue eyes. When Louise opened the door he smiled at her, a new smile, an intimate smile.

'Hello, Louise,' he said.

Louise felt suddenly absolutely certain that he knew all about her dream. That he had come for her in this daytime rain, as the runaway horse had come for her in the storm of her dream. That at any moment he would swing her up into his arms and take her outside into the rain and that they would leap and fly and she would sing as she had done in her dream. 'What d'you want?'

He flinched a little from her abruptness. 'Nothing!' he said defensively. 'Nothing! But when I put that guttering up I promised to come and check it at the next big storm. I wondered if it was holding up under this rain.'

'It's overflowing,' Louise replied mechanically, still pushing her dream away from her. 'It woke me in the night.'

At the mention of the night Mr Miles flushed at once. He was thinking of Rose's tantalisingly vivid description of Louise's silk pyjamas and big empty bed. Louise, watching his colour rise, felt her own cheeks grow hot.

'You'd better come in,' she said brusquely. 'You're getting soaked.'

He did not move forward at the invitation but actually took a step backwards from the sharpness of her tone. 'Perhaps I'd better take a look at that gutter,' he offered. 'It may just be blocked with leaves.'

'I'll get the ladder,' Louise said.

She turned and went inside the house. The light aluminium ladder was stored in the cupboard beneath the stairs. She lifted it easily and brought it out to him. He was still standing in the rain, patiently waiting for her. He took the ladder with a word of thanks and then put it up at the south-east corner of the house where the rainwater was pouring from the gutter in a rich splashing stream. He put his hand up into the cold water and felt around in the down-pipe. The diverted water overflowed in a curtain down his sleeve and splashed on to Louise's newly laid flagstones.

Louise watched him for a little while from the shelter of the sitting-room French windows. Silhouetted against the grey sky, balancing on the top of the light ladder she could see the strength and bulk of his body. He looked curiously comfortable out in the rain with the water pouring around him. His cap was firmly jammed on his fair head, his collar was upturned. His legs, encased in rubberised trousers and thick Wellington boots, stood firmly on the ladder so that he towered over the sitting-room window. He looked like a giant, like some old Sussex chalk giant conjured from the rain, the storm, and Louise's unsatisfied desires.

Louise turned back to her study and the word processor. Her face looked tired and pale in the grey light. She felt weary of the essay and of the tough unromantic counsel it offered. She sat before the screen again.

The loud plashing of the overflow abruptly stopped; Louise could hear the water gurgling safely away. She heard Andrew Miles jump down from the ladder and then his knock at the front door. Louise sighed affectedly and went to answer it.

'That's fixed,' he said. 'There were handfuls of twigs in the gutter. I'm afraid you've got a couple of rooks nesting in your chimney. They're messy builders, they've left twigs all over your roof.'

'Rooks?' Louise asked.

He nodded. 'They've likely got a nest in one of the chimneys,' he said. 'You might have noticed a lot of soot coming down and some sticks?'

Louise shook her head. 'Apart from the sitting-room fire they're all boarded up. But I've heard some noise from the fireplace in my bedroom.'

He nodded. 'That would be them. You'll have to clear the nest out and put a cap on the chimney pot.'

Louise sighed with irritation. 'Can't I just leave them?'

He shrugged. 'They're noisy birds and they spread a lot of twigs around. And if a young bird falls down it'll be trapped in the fireplace and you'll hear it fluttering until it dies. You wouldn't want that.'

Louise found his assumption of her sensibility oddly touching. 'I suppose I'd better get it done. How do I get the nest cleared? Are there nest-clearing contractors?'

He gave a little cough to cover his laugh. 'I can do it,' he offered. 'I've got a brush I do the farmhouse chimneys with. And I can get you a chimney cap.'

'Thank you,' Louise said shortly.

Mutely he held out the ladder to her. Louise took it from him. His cap was dark with rain, his fair hair curling under it at the back was wet. Little rivulets of rain were running down his cheeks and under his collar.

'You're soaked,' Louise said. The sudden intimacy of the statement made her flush.

'Doesn't matter.'

Louise held the door wider. 'Would you like to come in? You could borrow a towel. Would you like a cup of coffee?'

He stepped out of his Wellington boots and put them carefully side by side in her porch. He took off his wet jacket and cap and hung them on the hooks. He carried the ladder in for her and put it where she indicated, under the stairs. He followed her into the kitchen, stooping a little under the white-painted beams. Louise thought that the cottage suddenly looked like a doll's house, a Wendy house built for play and filled with pretty insubstantial things. She filled the kettle and switched it on. Andrew Miles sat at the kitchen table and Louise put the biscuit tin before him.

'I was writing an essay,' Louise said brightly. 'On D.H. Lawrence, the writer.'

Mr Miles nodded. 'Not working today, then.'

Louise smiled. 'Not teaching,' she corrected him. 'It's my work to write as well as to teach.'

She made the coffee and put a cup before him and gestured that he should take a biscuit. Andrew Miles took two digestive biscuits, sandwiched them together and ate them in two big bites.

'Do you have a housekeeper?' Louise inquired suddenly, thinking of that appetite and the empty farmhouse.

Andrew smiled. 'Mrs Shaw comes up every morning. She keeps me neat and makes my dinner. She leaves it in the Aga for me.'

'Your work must be hard,' Louise said. She was thinking that it was lonely work, and lonelier still to come home in the evening, cold and sometimes wet, to an empty house. Lonelier even than her drive home to her cottage all cool and quiet, with no lights shining and no fires lit.

'It's what I'm used to,' Andrew Miles said, draining his

148

cup. 'I've never wanted any other life than farming. But some evenings it would be nice to have some company.' He drained his mug and put it down. Without looking at her, he said in a little rush: 'Perhaps you would like to come down to the village one evening with me and have a drink?'

Louise's first instinct was to say no at once, but there was something about his diffidence and his reluctance which made her hesitate. He was so very unlike Toby. He had none of Toby's easy charm, he lacked the confidence, he lacked urbanity. The way he had asked her – as if he had planned the words for some time and then nerved himself to speak out – prompted her to caution. And there was something very solid and honest about him, planted firmly at her table and looking at her with those remarkably dark blue eyes.

'That would be nice,' Louise said carefully. 'Perhaps when I've got this essay out of the way. I daren't take any time off before then.'

He sensed the rejection at once, and got to his feet. 'Of course,' he said, he sounded almost apologetic. 'I'll get that chimney cap and come around and clear the chimney as soon as the weather lifts.'

He went lightly in his socks to the front door. Louise suddenly wanted to delay him, to recall her rebuff.

'I'll be finished next week,' she said. 'By the weekend.'

He was stepping into his thick green Wellington boots. Louise owned a similar pair but hers had a neat redundant buckle on the side and cost almost three times as much.

'Well, you'll come up to the farm for the party, won't you?' he asked. 'They should be here next weekend. And we'll have a drink and perhaps a dance?'

'Captain Frome says they were turned back,' Louise said. 'They won't be able to get to your farm.'

He shook his head. 'They aren't due till next week. They're just travelling around. I said they couldn't come until I had my hay lifted. They knew that.'

'I think you're making an awful mistake,' Louise said earnestly. 'They're not at all the sort of people you're thinking about. They're town people, most of them, and the rave business is big business. They're professionals. And the people who come to the parties are not all travellers, or gypsies, not people you're thinking of. They're ordinary people with jobs and good incomes, they just get out their vans and go to raves at weekends.'

He smiled at her, and took down his jacket from the hook and put it on, turning up the collar before he pulled on the disreputable cap. 'I know,' he said gently. 'I read the newspapers, I listen to the radio. I'm not a complete peasant.'

Louise flushed redder than ever. 'I didn't mean . . .'

'They're straightforward businessmen,' he continued. 'They offered me an excellent price to hire two fields. They carry insurance and they've paid a deposit against damage. They're managing their own security. They're bringing their own catering truck, they bring their own portable toilets. I thought it might be a bit of fun, and it'll earn me more than the whole hay crop put together. I don't see the problem.'

'I didn't realise . . .' Louise said feebly.

Andrew Miles smiled. 'Most of them round here don't realise,' he said. 'Like your friend Captain Frome. He wants to live in the country, but he doesn't really want to be in the country as it is now. He has an idea of a place: perhaps he read about it in a book, perhaps it's where he had his holidays when he was a boy. It's Pooh Corner or the Wind in the Willows. He thinks of the country like one of those nature films – all animals and no humans at all. Or if there are humans then they're special people, not like town people. Quiet, and a bit stupid. They pull their forelocks to the local lords and they're grateful if he remembers their names. That's why Frome's always wanting to get us organised, to make the village prettier, to stop farmers hedging and ditching, to cancel the Hallfield market. Real farming is a dirty business, it's a noisy business, it's an industry not a postcard. He doesn't like mud on the road or having to drive slowly behind my tractor. He wants the country to be quiet and pretty. He wants a garden, not a work place.'

'He's not my friend,' Louise said uncomfortably.

'Doesn't matter,' Andrew said gently. 'I don't like people telling me who I can have on my land, or what I can do. I don't tell him who he can have to dinner.'

Louise suddenly had a vision of the country which was her home as a working community, not an attractive arrangement of scenery with an inconvenient absence of services. 'Have your family always lived here?'

'We've got headstones in the churchyard going back to 1425,' Andrew said. 'A long time.'

'You'd know what a gamekeeper does,' Louise remarked irrelevantly, thinking of her unfinished essay.

Andrew Miles chuckled. 'You're reading *Lady Chatterley's Lover*,' he guessed. 'I thought it was good. He's right about the gamekeeper. It's very realistic – not the . . .' he hesitated, a little embarrassed '. . . not the sex – that was all made up of course – but he was right about the pheasants. He knew about pheasants. I thought it was good.'

Louise had to adjust her picture of Andrew Miles yet again. She had never thought of him reading at all, she had almost assumed that he was half-illiterate, perhaps reading a tabloid newspaper, perhaps arduously scanning a farming magazine.

'You read novels?' she asked rudely.

'Sometimes. Mostly I listen to them,' he smiled. 'I've got a Walkman and I like to listen to novels when I'm in the tractor cab. I like Jane Austen best I think, but I like them all.'

He did up the buttons on his jacket. 'George Eliot is good for a long field,' he said. 'And Henry James is the best for harrowing. But that post-modernist fiction I just can't get on with. It's no good for ploughing at all.' He shot a mischievous grin at her astounded face. 'Thank you for the coffee, Miss Case. I have to go now, the pigs want feeding. I'll stop in to see that Rose is all right, on my way out.'

Louise opened her mouth to speak and found herself wordless. She let him go.

Andrew Miles pulled an armful of wood from the back of the Land-Rover and walked down the garden to Rose's van. Louise, from her seat before the word processor, watched him. He shouted from the steps and Rose opened the van door. Today she was huddled in a deep green velvet evening cape with the glamorous hood pulled up over her grey head for warmth. Andrew piled most of the wood into the van and dropped the rest by the steps. He went back to his Land-Rover for more, then he fetched a red petrol can, and went into the van. In a few moments Louise saw a thin plume of smoke coming from the chimney. He had got Rose's stove burning. Louise, abandoning all thought of the essay until he had gone, wondered uncomfortably if he thought badly of her, sitting warm in a centrally heated house while Rose huddled against the damp and the cold in a van at the bottom of the garden.

After a few minutes he emerged from the door. He was

laughing at something Rose had said. Rose patted him on the cheek with an easy, affectionate gesture and then waved farewell.

Andrew strode back to his Land-Rover, started the engine with the familiar badly tuned roar, and drove back up the hill to his farm.

Louise looked blankly at the screen. Then she remembered the meeting at the university on women in Science and Industry and telephoned the head of the department.

'I'm a member of the Fresh Start committee,' Louise said, wincing at the name. It always sounded to her like some kind of new soap powder. 'We're planning to target science and technology courses for our next open day. I wonder if I could meet with you and have a talk.'

'What about?' he said unhelpfully.

'About what we can do to make your department and other science and industry departments more attractive to mature women students,' Louise said pleasantly.

'In what way?'

Louise particularly did not want to complain about pin-up pictures which she had never seen. She had only Josephine Fields's assurance that the department was festooned with naked women astride burgeoning spark plugs.

'Any ways you think would be appropriate.' She paused. 'I think we all feel that there should be more mature women students in science and technology departments. The committee were wondering how best to encourage mature women entrants. Could I come and see you and we could have a talk about it?'

'Are you anything to do with that nutcase woman who has been stealing notices from the noticeboards?' the head of department demanded.

153

Louise thought. In theory, she was nothing to do with any nutcase woman who was a stereotype of the sexist male imagination and had never existed in reality. On the other hand, she recognised without difficulty a description of Josephine Fields joyously engaged in direct action.

'No,' she lied firmly. 'I don't know what woman you mean.'

'An ugly batty woman who has been going around my department, upsetting my lab technicians, and taking down posters,' he said bluntly.

'No,' Louise said again. 'I don't know anything about that.'

'Two o'clock today,' he said gruffly. 'Or next week sometime.'

'Today will be fine.' Louise knew that her voice was smooth and soothing. She couldn't help it. Any time she wanted a man to do something for her, she instinctively cooed. Twenty-nine years of training could not be overcome by sheer will. And anyway, it always worked.

'See you then,' he said. But he was already less gruff.

'I'll look forward to it,' Louise said sweetly. 'Pompous old fart,' she said to restore her sense of independence as she put down the telephone.

The paragraphs on the screen stared back at her looking more uncertain than ever before.

As women and feminists we have to challenge this myth. We have to surrender romance, love, glamour, and belief in all-conquering desire in favour of reality. We can still enjoy friendship with men. We can still enjoy sexual intercourse with men. But we can no longer allow ourselves to be conned into the nonsensical belief that their attentions make us 'whole', or that sexual intercourse or making love is in any way some

154

sort of spiritual activity. We understand the physiology of orgasm now, we have reclaimed our bodies. Now we need to reclaim our hearts.

Louise sighed deeply. She was not at all sure that she had reclaimed her body. She thought the sentence 'reclaim our hearts' was a bit purple and, in any case, she was not sure that it could be done. She had been in love with another woman's husband for nine years – not a very impressive record for a professional feminist. She pressed 'Save' again and shut the screen down. Her thoughts on Lawrence would have to wait.

She took a pile of students' essays with her into the sitting room and sat on the sofa, red pen in hand. She had set them the title, 'Clarissa: Willing Victim or Martyr?' Half of them were completely floored by the very question because they had neglected the preliminary precaution of reading the book. The other half had, quite intelligently, paid a substantial sum to the only student on the course whose mum had videoed the BBC film of the novel. Louise had heard that there had been 'Clarissa parties' where, by payment of small amounts of mood-inducing drugs to the host, you could go and watch the video. What *Clarissa* was like viewed through the bias of Ecstasy Louise could only imagine.

The essays were staggeringly lacklustre. The effect of Ecstasy while watching the video seemed to have negated any educational impact a grasp of the story might have caused. Those students who had flicked through the library copy of the novel and decided that it was something about people who wrote and wrote and wrote to each other, were as well informed as those who had blearily followed the story on screen through a drug-induced illusion of knowing everything.

The only students who had actually read the book – all 1499 pages – were the mature students, mainly women of thirty-five years and more who, plagued by their customary insecurity, had cooked supper for four, put the children to bed, loaded the washing machine, and then worked till three in the morning for a fortnight in an effort to get the work done. Louise tried to be fair, but she could not respect a woman whose academic work took place on a corner of the kitchen table, after everyone else had gone to bed. Despite her long membership of a committee to encourage mature women students to return to education Louise had a strongly held and strongly hidden belief that childbirth damaged a woman's brain. Unfortunately for them all, the over-anxious overworked students on her course could do nothing to disprove this.

Louise turned the pages idly, rewarding a good point with a red tick and a bad one with a cross. An occasional '!' marked her indignant disapproval. It was just like her reading of Lawrence. By lunchtime she had marked half of them, and after a miserable spinster lunch of a can of soup and a plate of crispbread and cheese she returned to the study and had another short go at the Lawrence essay. In the cool empty house, with the rain pattering on her window and a grey mist sliding up over the common, immersed in pointless unsatisfactory work, Louise kept herself busy: successfully distracting herself from the knowledge she was lonely and unloved; hungry and cold.

The meeting with Professor Edgeley of Science and Industry did not promise well. Louise made her way to his little room on the second floor of the Sci/Ind block, past posters which promised: GIANT PISS UP TONITE (NURSES FROM

GENERAL HOSPITAL INVITED!!!) CHEAP BEER. PARTY GAMES. STRIPPER. One chemistry lab was empty; Louise put her head around the door. It had the strange potent sharp smell of chemistry labs at her school and the same wooden benches with the little taps for bunsen burners at intervals along the stained brown benches and the swan-necked taps gazing down into grimy sinks at the end of each bench. The walls had posters pinned to them showing linkages of molecules and a pretty necklace diagram which Louise vaguely assumed was the plan of DNA. On one noticeboard at the back marked 'social' was an offensive poster. Louise tightened her lips. It was a picture of a half-naked woman in a hammock under a brilliantly blue sky. In the sky were printed the words 'AFL scrubbers – for cleaner skies'. Louise thought 'scrubbers' was deeply offensive to women, as was the woman's pose.

She went back into the corridor and walked briskly to the professor's room. She knocked on the door and went in.

He was sitting at his desk with a Tupperware container open before him, eating sandwiches, engrossed in a newspaper. When Louise entered he shot a guilty look at the little clock on his desk and rose to his feet.

'I'm so sorry,' he said. 'I had to teach an extra class and missed my lunch. Please sit down.'

Louise looked pointedly at the chair covered with library books and essay papers and made no move at all. He scampered round from behind his desk and thrust the papers and books to the floor. Louise smoothed her skirt down over her knees and sat down and crossed her legs. She thought she had him thoroughly rattled.

He bundled his lunch away into a desk drawer and smiled nervously at her. He was a large-built man with thin fly-away grey hair. He had small reading spectacles which he

157

put on the desk before him and touched from time to time with his long fingers.

Louise smiled her confident smile. 'I don't know if you're familiar with the work of the Fresh Start committee?'

He shook his head. 'No, I never, I haven't, that is to say . . . No.'

Louise nodded. 'We were founded about four years ago with the aim of attracting mature women students into higher education,' she said. 'The committee is chaired by a graduate of this university who now works with abused women in the refuge in the town, Miriam Carpenter. I am vice-chair. The deputy head of Sociology, Naomi Petersen, is a member, as are other women students, undergraduates, postgraduates, and a couple of women who work locally.'

Professor Edgeley looked overwhelmed rather than gratified by this flood of information.

'After being very successful in encouraging women to join degree courses in the humanities, we thought this year we would target science and engineering.'

'Why pick on us?' the professor demanded. 'I mean, why concentrate on us?'

Louise smiled calmly. 'What are your proportions of women students?'

He hunted under his newspapers for a memo pad. 'I looked it up. At the moment we've got in the third year, twenty-eight per cent; in the second year, oh, we did rather well, thirty-seven per cent; and in the first year, thirty-two per cent.'

Louise nodded. 'Rather a long way from the ideal of fifty per cent,' she observed calmly.

'I don't think fifty per cent would be ideal at all,' Professor Edgeley said with sudden spirit. 'The country doesn't need that many women scientists and engineers. There aren't that many openings in the pharmaceutical and cosmetics industry! And we don't have the applicants.'

'I think women scientists could do something other than work with make-up and medicine,' Louise countered with acidic sweetness. 'But I am interested that you don't have the applicants. I think we could help you with that.'

'No need! No need at all!' the professor said hastily. 'We find that the numbers rise and fall depending on the A-level syllabi in the schools, what's on telly, whether the girls get the encouragement early on. We just take the best students available to us – like anyone else. We're happy with the mix we have here. It's a natural mix you know, a result of the environment.' He looked at Louise's unrelenting face. 'Darwinian,' he said feebly.

'My committee would like to encourage more mature women students to join your courses,' Louise stated firmly. 'That is our function. We are proposing to feature you at our open day next week.'

The professor looked increasingly uncomfortable. His hair was becoming more and more independent in his distress, it stood up around his head and waved rather like the tentacles of a sea anemone seeking nutrients. 'Very kind,' he said. 'Very kind indeed. But we're fine as we are. Fine. Thank you. But I hear that Technology have tremendous difficulties in recruiting girls,' he added cunningly. 'Perhaps you should talk with them.'

Louise nodded. 'We will talk with them. But let's stay with you for a moment. Do you have any publicity material, any campaign boards, any displays you would like us to use?'

The professor tried to smile. 'Certainly, certainly. We have a travelling display we take out to schools, we could set that up at your open day. And we could man it too.'

159

Louise recoiled, quivering with dismay. He coughed, looked down, looked up to check her face again.

'Do you mean "staff" it?' Louise asked icily.

The poor fool still did not know what he had done to cause such offence. 'Yes,' he said simply. 'I'll send along a couple of our graduate students, good chaps, they'll put it up and be on hand to talk to anyone.' He paused. 'Is it *all* women?'

Louise nodded. 'We prefer it to be women only,' she said. 'I assume you have female graduate students or members of staff?'

'Well, of course we have one or two,' he said weakly. 'And most of our lab technicians are women, and *all* our secretaries and admin assistants are women.' He beamed at Louise encouragingly as if she would be thrilled to learn that every menial job in the department was done by a low-paid woman. 'All of our cleaners are women,' he went on, warming to the theme. 'We're not prejudiced against women, you see. Now I come to think of it, across the whole department we actually employ more women than men! I could ask one or two of them if they would attend.'

'Graduate students, women, display material. We'll allocate you a stand,' Louise said gravely. She ticked off the items on her pad and then handed him a leaflet. It was printed on defiant pink paper and headed OPEN DAY. The 'O' of open was drawn into the biological symbol meaning woman. The professor received it with care as if it might spontaneously combust.

'Thank you,' Louise said. She rose to leave.

'And this woman who is vandalising our noticeboards,' the professor ventured nervously. 'Absolutely nothing to do with your group?'

Louise shook her head. 'We are not vandals,' she said.

'The committee is a highly respected long-standing organis-ation. But perhaps we should ask: are your noticeboards offensive?'

The professor looked amazed. 'How can they be?' he asked. 'They're only pictures and posters. How can they be offensive?'

'Do they show women in poses and postures which indi-cate that women are sexual objects? Are they thus implying that women are sexual rather than intellectual and spiritual beings? Do they imply that all women always welcome and invite sexual overture and thus justify rape? Do they create a climate in which women feel themselves judged on their bodies, not on their abilities?'

It was clear that none of these concepts had ever been put to Professor Edgeley before. 'No, no,' he said hastily. 'Nothing like that. They're just a bit of fun. They just brighten the place up a bit. Give the lads a bit of a laugh . . .'

Louise looked at him witheringly until he trailed off into silence. She smoothed her tight-fitting skirt over her slim hips. 'Thank you for your time,' she said sweetly, and left.

Tuesday

LOUISE RANG MIRIAM on Tuesday afternoon before the Fresh Start committee meeting to warn her that Josephine Fields had been sighted in the Sci/Ind department, attacking noticeboards. Miriam, who had a sobbing woman with three small children in her office, was not very interested. 'Josie will do what she wants, I suppose,' she said. She handed the woman a tissue from the box which stood permanently on her desk. 'It can't be too bad. See you tonight.'

But Miriam was over-optimistic. It was very bad indeed. Josie Fields arrived late at the meeting accompanied by one thin grey-haired nervous woman, one buxom smiling student, and one purple-haired, ring-encrusted punk rocker in black leather. 'This is Sarah, Gilly, and Mo,' Josie introduced them. 'The sub-committee.'

'Sub-committee?' Naomi Petersen repeated at her slowest and most pedantic. 'I don't recall us establishing a sub-committee.' She turned a smile of conscious charm on to the three newcomers. 'It's very good to see you here,' she said. 'All the same.'

'We were going to set up a sub-committee of women working in Sci/Ind,' Josie said stubbornly. 'I already have. I've been over to the department several times this week and it's even worse than I thought. There are very few women students and the place is riddled with sexism and abuse. Sarah is a technician in the department, Gilly is a second-year student and Mo is a secretary. They've joined our campaign to re-educate the department. These are our proposals, I have made copies.' She thumped a depressing weight of papers on the table and spread them out in an uninviting fan.

'Hang on a minute,' Miriam said.

'Is this on the agenda at all?' Naomi asked. 'Or is it Any Other Business?'

'This is here and now. This is urgent,' Josie proclaimed. 'We can't possibly recruit women to the Sci/Ind department until they reform their working practices along the lines of our proposal. And I refuse to take part in any open day which attempts to recruit women into that environment.'

'Louise has met with Professor Edgeley,' Miriam said. 'And he is prepared to co-operate with us. He recognises the problem.'

'Edgeley!' Josie gave a scornful snort of laughter. Mo and Gilly laughed with her and said 'Edgeley!' to each other like a well-trained Greek chorus.

'The department is entirely run by the rugby team,' Josie said. 'All work, all postgraduate work and grants are dependent on your being able to play rugby for the university. The team coach is Dr Frost. I suppose you know nothing about this?'

Louise felt herself at a profound disadvantage. 'I know that I was very embarrassed when Professor Edgeley asked me if I had been vandalising the noticeboards!' she said sharply. 'I suppose that was you?'

'Me actually,' Mo said. She had a small gold chain running from her left nostril to her left ear. Louise found herself staring at it, unable to look away. Mo was wearing very white pancake make-up with very thick black lines around her eyes. Her purple hair stood up in sharp spikes. She had a thin leather jacket with a collar turned up around her studded ears, she had a tight black miniskirt worn over bicycling shorts, worn over purple tights. Louise forced herself to stop staring and found herself looking instead at Naomi Petersen. Naomi Petersen was looking at Mo as if she were an iced bun.

'That's very direct of you,' she said, her low voice dropping even lower. 'What made you do it?'

'Her idea,' Mo said, jerking her head towards Josie. Her voice had an authentic working-class south London twang which marked her at once as a girl who had been carefully reared in the nicer parts of Hove. She grinned at Josie, showing one carefully blackened tooth in a white smile. 'Very cool.'

'The women of the department have been continually offended by sexist and pornographic material,' Josie said smoothly.

'Well, not exactly offended,' the older woman said. 'It's not very nice, some of it. But you get used to it, and they don't mean any harm.'

'I make all the pin-up girls little paper bikinis,' Gilly, the blonde student, said with a giggle. 'Just for fun, you know. And sometimes I paint moustaches on them.'

'They've all done what they can,' Josie said. 'But they need our support.'

Miriam looked at the twelve-item agenda before her. 'Can we get through the usual business first?' she asked. 'Quite quickly? And then really get to work on this?'

'You mean ghettoise it into a problem to be dealt with separately?' Josie demanded, pouncing like a cat. 'No, I don't think we can.'

Miriam glanced around the table for support. Naomi Petersen was smiling steadily at Mo, who stared back at her through black-fringed eyes, unsmiling but fascinated. Louise was looking down at the table top in silent depression.

'Oh, very well,' Miriam said. She looked at the older woman, the lab assistant: Sarah. 'What changes would *you* like to see in the department?'

'Quota entry,' Josie interrupted helpfully. 'Fifty per cent women, twenty-five per cent of them mature students. No qualifications demanded, just proof of interest.'

Sarah cleared her throat. 'Then I could get in as a student,' she said. 'I've got no A levels, but I've always wanted to take my BSc.'

'Quota entry to postgraduate work,' Gilly said. She gave a guilty giggle. 'It's the only chance I'll get. Quota pass rates for women at all exams.'

'We want the place run as a commune,' Mo said. 'Equal power for secretaries, students and lecturers. No second-class citizens.'

Naomi Petersen, whose own department was run like an outpost of the Third Reich, rested her perfectly shaped chin on her elegant hand and breathed: 'How interesting.'

Josie shot her a brief suspicious look.

'I don't think we can do this,' Miriam said worriedly. 'Look, let's work on these long-term goals and suggestions after open day. I don't feel we can demand quotas. You can't really open university degree courses to people with no qualifications at all. There *has* to be a minimum educational standard. And open day is next weekend. Let's aim at recruiting more women into Science and Industry at our open day and have an on-going project aimed at the departments and looking at the whole notion of quota entry.'

'I think the time is ripe for radical action,' Josie announced. She tweaked one of the chains on Mo's jacket to get her attention away from Naomi Petersen, who was now sitting back in her chair and smiling at Mo under her long curled eyelashes. 'Radical. Isn't that right, Mo?'

'Radical,' Mo assented, but she did not look away from Naomi.

'It would be good to see some changes,' Sarah said. 'I wouldn't want the professor to be upset but if they would leave the place a little tidier it would make things much easier in the labs.'

'Quota pass rates,' Gilly insisted firmly. Science courses were examined yearly and anyone awarded less than thirty per cent was expelled in their second year. Gilly could see that her days in the bath with the rugby team were numbered. 'It should be a matter of principle,' she said. 'I expect the support of the sisterhood.'

'If they just rinsed the test-tubes and flasks as soon as they had used them then they wouldn't stain,' Sarah continued.

'We can't make demands like this,' Miriam said wearily. 'We'll jeopardise the whole open day if we start trying to interfere in a specific department's work. We can try to re-educate them and we can bring pressure to bear, but our main function is to recruit women students and get them into education.'

Josie abruptly lost her temper. 'All you think about is propping up the system!' she shouted at Miriam; but she was looking at Naomi Petersen, who had leaned forward to whisper something to Mo. Mo's black-rimmed eyes had widened at the suggestion. 'Either we are a radical group committed to major change or we are in support of the system! You can't be both!'

'Open day . . .' Miriam started.

'Bugger open day!' Josie shouted. She pushed her chair back. 'I'm resigning from this committee on the grounds that it is not politically correct.' She flashed a disdainful look at Louise, who had the minutes pad before her and a depressingly blank page. 'I want it minuted that this committee is not politically correct. I am here founding my own committee – Creative Anarchy Group for Equality – CAGE – and I am announcing our first meeting, next door, now.'

She marched towards the door. 'Josie!' Miriam implored. 'What about consensus among sisters, you know . . .'

'You don't want consensus, you want conservatism,' Josie said cruelly. 'Who's coming with me?'

Wendy Williams got to her feet and went to the door, the three women from Sci/Ind followed, and so did a couple of other women from the end of the table.

'I'll just be a moment,' Naomi said quietly to Miriam, and took Mo to one side into the corner of the room and spoke to her rapidly and softly. As the others watched, Mo stretched out the palm of her hand and Naomi took a silver ball-point pen and lightly wrote her telephone number on the delicate skin of Mo's wrist. The two women paused for a moment, looking at the spidery blue numbers and the underlying tracery of matching blue veins.

'I hope I don't poison you,' Naomi murmured.

'Come on, Mo!' Josie said sharply and marched out of the room and down the corridor. They could hear her opening doors, interrupting meetings all the way down, until a bang of a door announced that she had found an empty room. Louise and Miriam were left alone. Naomi strolled back to her place and sat down, looking at them with serene anticipation. There was a little silence.

'Correspondence,' Miriam said wearily.

'We can't,' Louise reminded her. 'We're inquorate. And it's open day next Saturday and nothing planned and nothing ready, no members on our committee and only you and me to do it.'

For a moment Miriam drooped. It had been a long and exhausting day. Then she pushed her hair back from her face and gave Louise her old familiar grin. 'Well then, let's go to the pub,' she said. 'There's nothing left to do at all but get pissed.'

Toby sat at home with Rose's large box on his desk before him. He had not been tempted to waylay Louise on her way to her women's meeting, nor to cook her and Miriam dinner. Indeed, he felt a deep sense of irritation and grievance with both women though he could not have explained why.

He was also lacking signally in desire. He thought sulkily that Rose Pankhurst was an old witch who had put a spell on him. Ever since he had seen her through Louise's kitchen window, grimacing at their embrace, he had felt not a glimmer of sexuality. Not even the bright-faced adoring undergraduates stimulated him to a frisson of interest. He felt cold. He felt boring. He felt old.

There had been something about Rose Pankhurst's bright button eyes that had put him off, put him off very deeply. Louise had been in his arms, he had felt her easy sudden response. Miriam had been packing upstairs, it was a stolen embrace, like any one that they had snatched over the years of deception. Sweetest of all because of the quick clandestine desire of it. He had pushed Louise's questing hand from the flies of his trousers because he wanted to enjoy desire, not to be racked by it. But he continued to caress her, enjoying

168

the speeding of her breath and the flush in her face. The picture of Louise aching with unassuagable desire was one of the most attractive sights of their love affair. He adored teasing her into arousal and then watching her struggling to hide it. So with one hand firmly restraining her from touching him, he had allowed his other hand to wander down her cheek, over her breast and down to the soft warmth of her crutch. And then he had seen Rose's bright critical beam and he had felt his erection vanish and his desire wilt.

She had looked at him as if he were some kind of ordinary cheating husband. She had looked at him with disdain as if he were some horrid travelling salesman who had enticed his secretary into the back seat of his company car. She had looked at him as if he were not a caring, sensual free-thinking new man. She had looked straight through him, as if he were one of an old tedious type and not worthy of her attention, not a new man at all.

Rage would have been better, Toby thought sulkily. Out-rage, shock, even exposure would have left him with the moral high ground of being able to expose Rose as a prying old fool who had seen a fraternal hug and leaped to smutty and incorrect conclusions. Miriam would have believed him, Louise would have backed him up. Rose would have looked foolish and he would have been generous, forgiving, and kind.

Instead Rose's sharp black eyes had scanned him, had seen his hand straying to the welcoming heat of Louise's crutch while his other hand restrained her from touching the swelling in his trousers. Sitting in his study, before the box of cuttings, Toby felt himself grow warm and knew he was actually blushing at the memory. It was the pushing of Louise's hand away which had unmanned him before Rose.

It was such a shy rejection, like an old-fashioned girl in the darkness of a cinema. It was the gesture of a tease. Rose had caught Toby out – not in adultery, which he could have brazened through – but in coyness. Rose had seen Toby protect his own feelings and risk Louise's discomfort. Rose had seen Toby behave selfishly, egoistically, nastily. Toby could not rid himself of that picture. Rose's view of Toby had entered into his image of himself like a rush of cold water. It turned him off like a tap.

He pulled the box towards him. He had employed a second-year undergraduate to sort the pieces of newsprint into distinct piles. She had bound them with elastic bands and labelled them in her careful schoolgirl script. Toby read the labels. 'Recipes – puddings. Recipes – savouries. Cartoons and sketches. Book reviews. Suffragette attacks. Housekeeping hints. Court cases. Countryside news. Public meetings. Travel notes.'

He had not told Alison the student of his particular interest. His innate discretion warned him to tell her nothing. He said merely that the papers had come into his possession and he wanted them collated as research material. He had hinted that this tedious exercise of reading and sorting was the very bones and basis of research which would undoubtedly help her in her degree, and would prepare her for postgraduate work. Alison, who would willingly have sorted a dozen boxes just for the privilege of sitting on the floor of his room, even when he was not there, had knelt before Toby's cardboard box and respectfully sorted his clippings into these asinine categories.

Toby flipped through the recipes at random. They were, had he but known it, Sylvia Pankhurst's own recipes from her Price Cost Restaurant which operated in the Old Ford Road, Bow, during the First World War, serving food at cost price to working people. Louise, or even Miriam, could have told him of some of Sylvia Pankhurst's social concerns. But Toby wanted to share this project with no-one. Accordingly he dropped into the wastepaper basket at the side of his desk all of the Price Cost Restaurant's published menus.

The housekeeping hints so categorised by Alison were in fact advice for working women trying to survive on soldiers' pay, written by Sylvia as part of her general attack on the poor conditions facing women during the war years. The travel notes were Sylvia's diary of her travels in America, and in revolutionary Russia (including her meeting with Lenin). Toby glanced at the first couple of pages and tossed them into the bin without troubling himself to read further. The illustrations so carefully smoothed out and collected by Alison were from the *Dreadnought* newspaper which Sylvia published herself in an attempt to give working people the true news of the war.

The cartoons and sketches were Sylvia's own attempts at William Morris-style drawings, invaluable to historians of the pre-Raphaelite movement – and of course to modern wallpaper companies. Toby merely glanced at them and tossed them in the bin. He had no interest in art, and he did not look carefully enough to see the little SP initials in the corner of each precious fragment. The section of countryside notes – which included some rare original poetry by Sylvia Pankhurst, and her book reviews of revolutionary and Marxist books from 1917–21 – went the same way. Toby was not generally interested in any book reviews except those which he wrote himself, or those which condemned the work of his colleagues and competitors.

When the wastepaper basket was filled with irreplaceable invaluable material, Toby felt that he had gone a long way to clearing aside the dross. Before him he had only the public meetings' cuttings, accounts of court cases and those clearly labelled suffragette cuttings. He started to read.

Toby had two principal disadvantages working against him as he embarked on this course of study. Firstly he knew nothing about the suffragette movement other than the most commonplace facts. He vaguely remembered the Cat and Mouse Act, and the force-feeding of suffragettes in prison from his A level history. He remembered the Pankhursts, mainly Emily, the mother, and two daughters, Sylvia and Christabel: Sylvia who worked in the East End of London and became radical (he did not know about her putting Lenin straight on how to run a revolution in the heady days of Moscow in 1920) and Christabel who ran the campaign from exile in Paris. He had never even heard of Adela Pankhurst, the third sister, who emigrated to Australia.

His other disadvantage was no less grave. He was trained as a sociologist, not an historian, and artefacts from the past held no interest for him. Toby's usual research took place on clean bright computer screens with pretty coloured graphs, or with newly published papers in freshly printed journals. He resented having to read from yellowing newsprint, and he disliked the dusty feeling of the clippings. They smelled rather strongly of dog's wee and they strained his eyes. However, he staunchly read every word and made careful notes of all the rhetorical uninteresting speeches and the hints of organisational in-fighting. When he had read every one, noted it, and its date and publication where available, he left a note for Miriam telling her he would be home later, and drove out to Louise's cottage to see Rose.

It was strange driving up to the door of the little house knowing it would be empty since Louise would still be at the Tuesday Fresh Start meeting. Toby had his own key and could have let himself in, but Rose's guilt-inducing glare still made him uncomfortable. Besides, he was working, not visiting. He left the box of diminished clippings in the back of the car and strolled down the garden path to the blue van.

The dog was not at his post at the doorstep. There was no smoke coming from the chimney. Rose was not at home. Toby was so surprised that he did not know what to do. He waited for a little while by the gate, he walked down to the bottom of the orchard and looked out, in case she was walking on the common and he could stroll down the path to meet her. He considered driving back down to the village in case she was walking home along the lane. But she was nowhere to be seen. He decided to overcome his sense of diffidence about entering Louise's house and wrote on one of his nice new index cards: 'I have come to see you. I am in the kitchen', and tucked it under a stone on the van steps. Then he went back to the house, let himself in, and made himself a mug of coffee with Louise's best filter coffee in her smart glass jug.

It was strange being in the house alone. There had been times when he and Louise had planned to meet and he had arrived early, and used his key to let himself in. But that was different from being in the house without Louise's specific invitation, even without her knowledge. Toby strolled around the kitchen, touching things. He went into her study and looked at the books on her desk – Lawrence, he saw, and Kate Millett. He smiled with relief. Nothing very new and exciting would come out of the Lawrence essay then, he thought; and felt affection for Louise, who could always be relied on to tread loyally these well-worn paths, and would never rival his superior intellectual ability.

She had a notepad by the telephone and she had written on it:

ring Sarah,
see Edgeley,
ring Miriam.

Underneath she had written:

Toby, oh Toby, oh Toby.

Toby smiled broadly. It was quite something to enter into an intelligent woman's heart and mind. He felt better than he had felt for days. This view of himself – a man to inspire a highly intelligent woman to doodle like a schoolgirl – restored him to himself. He was once again attractive to himself, a potent lover, a rogue.

He wandered through into the sitting room. He liked the tidiness of the place. There was a special rack for newspapers, whereas in his house the daily papers were jumbled on tables and behind sofas, until they had an enforced clear-up because someone was coming to dinner. Louise's frivolous high-heeled slippers were neatly side by side at the foot of the stairs. Toby smiled benignly at them. Some day this house, this woman, these slippers could be his. They were his for the taking even now.

He savoured that thought and digested it with sips of good coffee. At home they drank instant coffee and made filter coffee only after special dinners or at weekends. Louise's spinster state had prompted her to look after herself, to do herself proud. Toby was not to know that the very things he most liked about her house – the tidiness, the order, the coherent style, the treats – were all symptoms

174

of loneliness and solitude. He mistook them for style, whereas they were nothing more than the absence of a companion, an excess of solitary time, and one of many unavailing defences against solitude.

He thought he might wait until Louise came home. She and Miriam were unlikely to delay long after the end of the meeting. He might wait for her to return and then take her to bed. He might even take her out for a meal at the Olde House at Home afterwards. Thoughtfully, Toby calculated the likely cost of a meal at the pub, and then nodded. He would have to pay cash since Miriam dealt with their bank statements and credit-card bills and would notice a cheque or the name of the pub on the credit-card statement; but he had enough cash in his pocket for a meal and a bottle of wine. He smiled, he felt expansive and generous: planning a treat for Louise, promising himself a romp in her big white bed. His desire for her, which had been so cold and quiet for two days, rose up as he inspected her property, enjoyed her prosperity, and basked in her secret adoration of him.

(Toby, oh Toby, oh Toby.)

Suddenly there was a face at the sitting-room window like a wrinkled brown mask, as silent and as threatening as a shrunken head: Rose Pankhurst. She and Toby stared at each other in mutual dislike until Toby started out of his trance and threw open the front door to her.

'Thank you for coming to find me,' he said warmly. 'I just came up on the off chance that I might see you. Louise is at a meeting, but I knew she wouldn't mind if I dropped in.'

'Yes,' Rose said. She stepped out of a pair of wooden clogs and walked into the room. She was carrying a small tattered bag like a gas-mask case. She sniffed the air like a hound after truffles. 'Smells good.'

'Coffee?' Toby asked hospitably. 'I just made some! I'm sure Louise wouldn't mind us crashing into her kitchen. Won't you come through?'

He led the way to the kitchen. Rose walked slowly after him and sat at the pine table.

'She's done it very pretty,' Rose observed, looking around her.

'Have you not been inside the house before?' It did not strike Toby even now that perhaps he should not have invited Rose into Louise's house without her permission.

'Mmm,' Rose said non-committally, who had known ever since her arrival where the spare key was hidden, and had seen everything she wanted to see in the house, except the contents of the computer which continued to puzzle her.

Toby put a mug of coffee and Louise's tin of biscuits before her.

'I've had a chance to look at your newspaper cuttings,' he said. 'They were pretty jumbled up with all sorts of other things but I got them sorted. And I've read them. A fascinating record of an exciting period.'

Rose took a biscuit and ate it with concentration. Then she took another.

'Now I've got the background, so to speak, I wonder if I could look at your more personal stuff?' Toby asked. 'You've got me hooked,' he went on with a winning smile. 'What exciting days those must have been!'

Rose nodded and ate a third biscuit.

'So tell me,' Toby said. 'What is your earliest, earliest memory?'

Rose smiled. 'Why, here,' she said. Her face relaxed as if the warmth of that long-ago summer were gilding it even now. 'We lived here. My Mum and Dad and half a dozen of us. I was born here. D'you know, sometimes in dreams

I see a sandstone wall and a rose, a yellowy pink rose, nodding against it. I think that's the wall here. Where she's got her study. The rose is gone, but you can still see the hooks for some plant which climbed up, right up to the bedroom. I can remember a tapping in the summer evenings, when I was supposed to sleep, and a yellowy pink rose nodding in at the window.'

Toby nodded. 'You wouldn't mind if I taped this, would you?' he asked. 'You just go right on remembering.' Inwardly he congratulated himself at the skill with which he was handling her. Start her with the boring childhood bits, get her confidence, and then move on to the profitable, interesting material. Stealthily he took his little tape recorder from his pocket, pushed it across the table until it was right under Rose's wispy chin and pressed the 'Record' button. From where he was sitting he could see the spool going round and round and the red 'Record' light glowed. Rose took another biscuit and crunched into it. Small noisy crumbs showered down on the little grille of the microphone. Toby tried not to flinch.

'But when did your family get to London?' he asked.

Rose grew suddenly wary. 'Oh, there were troubles,' she said. 'But we ended up in the East End. Then both my mother and father were arrested for campaigning for the ILP. Sylvia Pankhurst had opened the school at Old Ford Road and I went there. She took a liking to me, and she took me in to live with her. I went with her on all the demonstrations, to all the meetings, on all the campaigns. I can still remember her speeches – I could tell you them now!'

'Yes, yes,' Toby said. After an afternoon of reading speeches he felt that he had heard quite enough. 'And you helped her with the attacks, didn't you?'

Rose nodded. 'Her, and the others. Empty or derelict buildings, they'd send me in the back, through a little window or up a drainpipe. I'd run through the building in the dark and open the front door to them. Then they'd come in and set a fire. Go out, shutting the door behind them. The police couldn't work it out!' She nodded triumphantly and took another biscuit.

'She had no children of her own?'

'Not then, no. She had a child by her lover, but that was later. In the early days it was just me and her, and the others of course: Nora and Zelie and Charlotte.'

Toby was twitching on his seat with excitement. 'Tell me about them. This is what I want to know! This is the interesting stuff! Which one was the cross dresser?'

Rose looked faintly surprised. 'A dresser? None of them were in service,' she said. 'Charlotte had five children of her own, Zelie was an American lady, Nora was an English lady – she was the one with the money.'

'But which one wore men's clothes?'

'Nora wore a collar and tie and sometimes a divided skirt and sometimes big baggy flannel trousers. They were something a bit new then. Fashionable in a way.'

Toby shoved the little cassette recorder more urgently under Rose's chin so as not to miss a single word. Rose crunched into a Hobnob and a shower of crumbs pattered on to the microphone like hailstones on a tin roof.

'She was manly,' Toby prompted.

'Bit of an eccentric,' Rose concurred. 'Nice enough girl. Very wealthy of course, it was her who financed the People's Restaurant, and the toy factory, and the garment factory. Sylvia wouldn't pay sweatshop wages, so they could never make a profit. They might call it a co-operative and they might make good things but they could never make a profit.

Nora propped it all up with her money. And when Sylvia went Marxist – why, *she* went Marxist too!' Rose chuckled, blowing crumbs like a little sandstorm across the table. 'In her lovely suits and her linen shirts!'

'She was Sylvia's friend?'

'Friend? She was her shadow!'

'They were close.'

'There was no-one closer to Sylvia, especially after the American went home.'

Toby wriggled in his chair with excitement. 'Did they live together?'

Rose nodded. She ate another biscuit. 'Inseparable,' she said in a fine spray of crumbs.

'Were they lovers?'

Rose looked thoughtfully at Toby. He could actually feel his heart racing. If this greedy and disgusting old woman gave him the right answer he was on his way to the University of California, international renown, tenure and as many conferences in exotic locations as he could be troubled to attend.

'Something's been worrying me,' Rose said.

'What?'

'That dressing gown you stole. My burial gown.'

Toby could have screamed with frustration. 'Yes,' he said, smiling broadly. 'I don't want you to worry about anything. Please don't worry. That's fine. I've forgotten all about it. Don't apologise now, especially when we're getting on so well here. And you're telling me about Nora and Sylvia. I just asked you if you thought they were lovers?' Toby nodded sympathetically. 'It would have been perfectly understandable if they had been. There's no slur attached to a love-affair like that at all. Nobody worries about something like that these days.' (Except the *Spectator*, he thought delightedly to himself, the *Telegraph*, *The Times* and every journal and university that is gleefully joining the backlash against the feminist movement.) 'D'you think they were? Lovers? Sylvia and Nora? D'you think so?'

'I think it's too long,' Rose said. 'I've tried it on and I want to hem it up a bit, but I can't get it level on myself. Would you help me with it?'

'Sure,' Toby agreed happily. 'Love to. Can we do it when we're finished here? After you've told me about Sylvia and Nora? Where did they meet, for instance?'

Rose pushed the empty tin of biscuits away and shook her head. 'I can't settle without knowing that my gown will be right,' she said. 'I could go any day now. I don't want to be lying in my coffin with half a yard to spare at the bottom. It won't look right.'

'All *right*,' Toby said through smiling teeth. 'Let's do it at once, shall we? Let's do it now! We'll go to your van and fetch it, shall we? And get it over with?' Despite himself, the suppressed anger seeped through his voice.

Rose shook her head. 'You don't really want to be bothered with it,' she said sadly. 'It's just an old woman fussing about nothing to you. All these memories of the past, and me getting ready to die. A lot of fuss about nothing to a handsome young man like you.'

'No, no,' Toby assured her hastily. 'You know I'm fascinated by your story, Miss Pankhurst. You know how much this means to me. And I *do* want you to be comfortable. You must forgive my – er – scholarly impatience. But I want to be your friend. I will help you with anything you like. After all, I got the gown for you, didn't I? Let's make sure it's right.'

'I brought it with me,' Rose said with sudden alacrity. She threw open the gas-mask case and inside was the red chiffon gown packed tight. She shook it out in a flurry of crimson and then threw it around her shoulders. 'See, it's too long,' she said.

She looked like a wizened little child in an adult's dress. The hem touched the floor and spread out all around her.

'I can pin it up,' Toby said cheerfully. He dropped down to his hands and knees before Rose's extremely dirty feet and folded up a wedge of the fabric. 'How short? This short?'

Rose shook her head unhappily. 'I want it pinned and cut and then tacked and then hemmed,' she said. 'I want to do it myself.'

Toby sat back on his heels like a patient dressmaker with a difficult client. 'Shall I pin it for you?'

Rose was struck with a sudden brainwave. '*You* put it on,' she said. 'And I'll cut it and tack it while you've got it on.'

'But I'm much taller than you,' Toby objected.

'I'll allow for that,' Rose said. 'As long as the hem is shorter and straight. I can allow for it.'

Toby hesitated. He had an odd reluctance to put on Captain Frome's wife's negligee. He glanced at the kitchen windows. The evening outside was cool apricot and gold. Anyone could walk by and glance in. 'I'll cut it for you,' he offered again. 'I'm very good at that sort of thing.'

Rose shrugged her way out of the gown. 'You wear it, I'll hem it,' she said firmly.

Toby passively received the armful of chiffon. 'But we'll talk about the Pankhursts when it's done?' he stipulated.

Rose nodded. 'We can talk all night. Pop it on,' she instructed.

Toby tried to pull the flimsy gown on over his shirt. The armholes were too small. 'I can't get it on,' he complained. 'We can't do it.'

'You'll have to take your shirt off,' Rose said.

Toby hesitated for a moment, he looked towards the windows again.

'I'll draw the curtains,' Rose said helpfully. 'And slip your trousers off at the same time. I can't see where your ankles are with them on.'

She bustled around the kitchen, drawing the curtains. A sudden intimate twilight fell on the room. Rose switched on the lights and nodded approvingly at him. In the yellow electric light she looked younger, she looked elated. 'Come on,' she said encouragingly.

Toby laid his trousers carefully on a chair and put his silk shirt around a chair-back. He slipped into the chiffon gown with his teeth gritted; the fabric was silky and sensuous against his bare skin, he folded his arms across his bare chest and tried to ignore the seductive tickle of chiffon on his thighs.

Rose stood back, not a glimmer of a smile on her face, all professional intensity. 'I can't kneel down,' she protested. 'Not at my age. You'll have to hop up on the table.'

Toby, wearing only dark blue socks, blue Y-fronts and a scarlet chiffon negligee, felt his manhood draining from him. 'All right,' he said weakly. Lifting the ruffled skirts he climbed meekly on to the kitchen table.

'Do it up,' Rose commanded. 'I can't see the fall of the skirt if it's undone.'

Toby fastened the provocative ribbon bows up the front and then tied the red silk ribbon at the waist. Rose stood at the edge of the table and contentedly folded and pinned. 'D'you think it would look better with an extra ruffle?' she asked. 'Instead of cutting the hem off, perhaps I should fold it up to make an extra ruffle of fabric?'

Toby did not hear the car stop in the drive and Louise's key in the lock. Rose did.

'I don't see that it matters,' he said sulkily.

'An extra ruffle would be nice,' Rose pointed out. 'Fancy. Now turn around.'

Toby turned a little way.

'Turn a bit more,' Rose directed, alert for the sound of Louise coming in. Toby turned again so that his back was towards the kitchen door.

'It suits you actually,' Rose said loudly over the noise of the front door opening. 'Red's your colour.'

Louise, seeing Toby's car in the drive, and Rose's clogs in the porch and hearing voices from the kitchen, walked briskly towards the kitchen door and irritably threw it open. There was Toby, standing on the kitchen table with his back to her. He was whitely naked except for a pair of blue briefs, his socks, and a grotesque ruched and trimmed red chiffon negligee.

'I *do* like red actually,' he said. 'But men are always trapped in such sombre colours. I wish we could wear whatever we wanted without people being so conventional . . .'

Louise let out a clear and piercing scream of horror and dropped her files and papers on the floor with a resounding crash.

Rose whipped the red negligee off Toby's bare goosefleshy shoulders and was gone in an instant, leaving the couple alone. She only paused on the front doorstep to whisper to Louise, who was pushing her out: 'It's Mrs Frome's gown,

183

you know. He stole it from the washing line the day we went shopping. I didn't know how to tell you.'

'Just go,' Louise said tightly. She was creamy white with shock. She thrust Rose from the front door and then collapsed into a chair in the sitting room. Toby came from the kitchen, buttoning his trousers. Louise, who had once adored watching him dress, turned her head away.

Toby forced himself to laugh, a thin echo of his confident assured chuckle. 'God! That must have looked funny!'

There was no answering gleam from Louise. The face she turned towards him was mutely accusing.

'It's Rose's gown,' he said. 'She set her heart on it. She says she wants to be buried in it! Absurd, isn't she? She was so determined to have it that she went over the wall into Captain Frome's garden to steal it! Outrageous! And now it's the wrong length and she wouldn't do any work until we pinned it up. She made me put it on so that she could hem it. She really is a character!'

'Captain Frome says a man stole it,' Louise said dully. 'His description would match you. And your car.'

Toby flushed a little. 'Well, that was the awful part,' he said too quickly. He checked himself, he knew he was sounding glib. 'I didn't tell you. She got stuck in the garden so *I* had to get up on the wall to help her out. When the Captain came out, she was already down on the road, out of sight. She committed the actual crime, of course, but he only saw me.' Toby laughed with affected easiness. 'Ha! I admit to being an accomplice; but I'm not the prime suspect!'

'Why didn't you tell me?' Louise demanded, her voice tragic. 'Does Miriam know?'

'Tell you what? Miriam know what? About Rose's little pilfering?'

Louise shook her head. 'No!' she cried in a sudden burst

184

of emotion. 'Of course not! About *you*, Toby. How long have you been dressing in women's clothes? Is it to do with Miriam and you? Or is it my fault?'

Toby tried to laugh again but his heart was not in it. 'This is ridiculous,' he said.

Louise threw a pained look at him and went through to the kitchen. The biscuit tin was empty, the table scattered with crumbs and Toby's notes. Louise took it all in with one sweeping, condemning glance, like a vice squad inspector at an orgy. She put the kettle on. Her hands were shaking as she took down a mug.

She made herself a cup of instant coffee in silence, and then she went to the larder and poured herself a large measure of brandy. She did not offer Toby a drink though he eyed the bottle and thought he could have done with one, a large one.

'Are you a cross dresser or a full transvestite?' she asked, speaking in a slow deliberate monotone. She was completely, unnaturally, controlled. Her face was still waxy with shock.

'I'm neither,' Toby said gently. 'Of course I am neither. Come on, Louise, you know me!'

'I *thought* I knew you,' she flashed out. 'It turns out I didn't know you at all. Does Miriam know? Is this some long-hidden secret?'

'Of course not!' Toby snapped. 'There's nothing for her to know. What you saw was an accident. It looked ridiculous but there's nothing to it. I was just wearing the gown for Rose. I was modelling it for her.'

Louise put her head in her hands. 'Stop it,' she said suddenly. 'I can stand anything but not you continuing to lie to me. Please, Toby, trust me with the truth. You're out of the closet now. I can take it, I think. But you *have* to be honest with me.'

'I am not out of the closet!' Toby raised his voice. 'I was never in the closet!'

When Louise looked up at him her dark eyes were filled with tears. 'I will try to understand,' she whispered. 'I really will try to understand, Toby. But you have to tell me the truth. You have to share this with me. Perhaps I can help you. Perhaps we can get through this together.'

Toby, maddened beyond the restraints of good manners, strode to the glass cupboard and marched back with a tumbler. He poured himself a slug of brandy without Louise's invitation and took a deep swig. 'Will you listen to me?' he demanded. 'What you saw this evening was an accident. I have never in my life worn women's clothing. I have never in my life *wanted* to wear women's clothing. I put on that damned gown to oblige Rose because I wanted her to tell me about Sylvia Pankhurst. If you had come in ten minutes earlier you would have heard me interviewing her. If you had come in ten minutes later you would have seen us back at work. What happened was a break in our work. Rose was anxious about the gown. I was prepared to help her.'

Louise fixed him with her wounded disbelieving stare.

'Listen!' Toby exclaimed, his voice rising with frustration. He pulled the cassette towards him and wound the tape back at random. He pressed the 'Play' button. They could hear a strange pattering sound – the crumbs of the Hobnob on the microphone – and then Toby's voice saying clearly, excitedly: 'Tell me about them. Which one was the cross dresser?'

'Oh God, no!' Louise exclaimed. She pushed her chair from the table and stood up. 'I think you'd better go, Toby,' she said quickly. 'I need to be on my own.'

'No, wait,' Toby said. 'I'll play you some more. That was out of context! It makes no sense out of context!'

186

'*Please* go!' Louise shrieked. She seized him by the arm and pushed him towards the front door, gathering his index cards and his pens and his cassette player. 'Take all this with you! I don't want any of it in my house! Just go, Toby! Go!'

'But I can explain if you would only listen!' he cried as she thrust him over the threshold into the cooling summer dusk.

'Can't you see?' Louise demanded in a throbbing voice. 'Are you so perverse that you cannot even *see* a woman? Can you not understand what you have done to me? This is the worst insult to my womanhood that I can imagine! That my lover should want to wear women's clothes! That you should dress up and preen – and before Rose of all people! That you should refuse to be honest with me! You fool! Can't you see that my heart is breaking?'

She slammed the front door in his face. Toby staggered to his car. He flung his research notes into the box on the back seat and leaned his head on his hands on the steering wheel.

He waited for long moments. When it became apparent that Louise would not see reason and come out of the house, apologise to him and let him in again; and when no kindly angels rewound time a convenient half hour, to let him live his life more successfully, he started the car quietly and drove home to his wife.

Rose Miles stepped out of the shadows of the oak tree by the front door and went quietly down the path to her caravan with the satisfied air of a woman who has seen a difficult job well done.

Louise went to bed, woozy from the brandy she had downed when faced with the terrible sight of the man she adored standing on a table, half-naked, modelling a red chiffon negligee. She could not sleep. Hour after hour she lay in the gentle darkness reviewing her life and her love-affair with Toby. Nine years she had waited for this man to come to her and fulfil the promises they had made each other. Nine years of waiting, nine years of cheating on her best friend, nine years of lonely times, or unsatisfactory alternatives, of pretending to herself that she did not very much mind. Nine years of teaching herself to enjoy her own company when in truth, she longed for his arms around her. Nine years of telling herself that this was maturity, that this was an adult open relationship. Nine wasted years of self-brainwash.

When the walls of her bedroom grew pale with the dawn Louise drew a long hot bath and filled it with the most expensive bath oil she possessed. It reminded her of making love with Toby. But then, everything reminded her of making love with Toby. She put a hot damp flannel on her forehead and closed her eyes in the scented steam.

She could not think what she should do for the best. Her long faithful love-affair with Toby was over. She could not even think of him without a sense of panic and horror. There had been something about his legs viewed through red chiffon that she thought would make it impossible for her ever to desire him again. They might learn to be friends – Louise restlessly shook her head. Only if Toby spoke openly and frankly about his sexuality could Louise trust him again with any sort of affection. But his behaviour after he had been caught red-handed – she flinched from the mention of red – his behaviour showed that all he wanted to do was to brazen it out, to lie and continue to lie. Hot heavy tears rolled out from Louise's closed eyes and were blotted up by the hot wet flannel. Toby was a liar and a deceiver. She must have known that already, since she had been his mistress and helped him to deceive his wife. But to discover that he was deceiving her too, and with the connivance of a grubby old squatter, was almost too painful to bear.

The sight of him in the arms of another woman would have been less hurtful. He had always been explicitly open about his other affairs, and though they caused Louise sharp twinges of jealousy they enormously enhanced his attraction to her. Toby male, potent, amorous, promiscuous, an object of desire for half the women of his department, and the husband of Miriam, was simply irresistible. Toby queening around on the kitchen table draped in red chiffon was a spectacle of horror.

The water was growing chilly when Louise finally emerged from the bath, wrapped herself in a thick towelling robe and sat at her bedroom window. The sun, a pale promising slice of lemon, was rising in the east. Louise watched it in surprise as the birds' song grew louder and more insistent. Then she pulled on a sweatshirt and pair of jeans and went downstairs and let herself out of the cottage, across the garden, and on to the common.

She walked aimlessly, following her own pale shadow. Small ferns uncurled at the edges of the sandy path. Last season's heather flowers were white and dry at her feet. The grass at the side of the path was speckled with the purple and pink of early summer flowers: the long-necked gypsy rose, the tiny faces of willowherb. An early lark was singing above her in a sky which was slowly turning blue. A light wind blew the smell of Rose's woodsmoke after her. Louise walked without thinking, walked to escape thinking, her eyes on the pale earth beneath her feet, unconscious of the sweet smell of new-mown hay coming from the fields on

189

her right, deaf to the rising clatter of Andrew Miles's hens in his farmyard just half a mile further on.

She did not see the farm, she did not see him. He looked across his fields, a pail of scraps for the hens still in his hand. He shaded his eyes and he recognised Louise, and he saw at once the droop of her shoulders and the downward bend of her head. He thought, for a moment, of how a hurt animal will run and run from the pain of injury, without knowing where it is going, and that he had never before seen her walking this far from her cottage. Then he tipped out the feed for the hens, put down the pail and started to trot determinedly towards her.

He was out of sight, hidden by a dip in the field, for a few minutes, but even when he was striding briskly across his field at right angles to her, she did not see him. The sheep, greedy for feed, followed him, bleating indignantly, but not even their noise penetrated Louise's distress. She had no idea that Andrew Miles was anywhere near her until he put a gentle hand on her shoulder and said quietly: 'Miss Case . . . Louise.'

She spun around with a gasp.

Andrew Miles was very still, the early morning sun behind him, gilding his thick comforting jumper and his halo of blonde hair. He had cast aside his cap and without it his face looked younger, tender. His dark blue eyes were very steady, very kind. He stood as if he had somehow grown from the land, his Wellington boots firmly rooted in the sandy soil, his heavy-duty jeans as creased as the bark of a tree.

Louise cried breathlessly, 'Andrew, oh, Andrew! ' and flung herself into his arms and buried her face into the tickly warmth of his jumper.

Andrew picked her up and carried her into a hollow of

ground, cosy with last year's bracken and heather, warmed by the morning sun, and kissed her face, her tragic mouth, her closed swollen eyelids, and her hot forehead. Her sweatshirt slid easily up to her shoulders, her jeans he had to struggle with. Louise, imprisoned in a warm and determined embrace, closed her eyes and let the events wash over her as if she were a fainting Victorian heroine. In this agreeable state of incorrectness she felt his hands gently, gently, caress her all over: knowledgeable hands, gamekeeper's hands. She gave herself up, eyes closed, yielding as any Lawrentian virgin to the warmth and the weight and the seductive easy kisses of Andrew Miles, who proceeded to touch her all over and then slide easily and comfortably into making thorough love to her.

Louise, finding herself underneath a man for the first time in nine years, gave herself up to the deliciously improper sensation of being overwhelmed, of yielding to male desire. Worse and worse, she found herself so out of control of events that she came: with a whimpering grateful orgasm, with no warning and no mannered preparation at all. And Andrew Miles did not verbally confirm her satisfaction at all; but sighed a deep restful sigh of delight and then lay, very heavily, on her.

They rested for a long time in silence, and then Louise became slowly aware of small twigs sticking into her and insects or perhaps small animals biting her. She stirred and at once Andrew shook his head like a waking labrador dog and rolled off her. 'Sorry,' he said pleasantly. 'Were you squashed?'

Louise said nothing. 'Squashed' was not the first verb she would have used for their activity which had left her weak with profound satisfaction and with every distress washed from her mind. She pulled down her sweatshirt, and sat up to find her knickers and jeans. Andrew without embarrassment but with great interest handed her the small scrap of lace which she used for knickers. 'Pretty,' he said approvingly, and then pulled up his own trousers and pants which were bunched around his knees. He had not even had the grace to undress properly. Louise, with an appalled sense that something very drastic had happened, looked away.

'I must get home,' she said abruptly. 'Good heavens, is that the time!' She glanced blindly at her bare wrist; she had not put on her watch. Andrew was sitting comfortably in the little hollow, watching her.

'Come back to the farm,' he said without moving. 'I'll make you some breakfast.'

'I couldn't possibly!' Louise said with false brightness. 'I'm sure you're terribly busy.'

'What's the matter?' he asked gently. 'Come here.' He held out an arm to her to tempt her back to lie beside him; but Louise stayed beyond his reach. She knelt and retied her shoelace.

'We must be crazy!' she said with a nervous laugh. She shot a swift look at him. His welcoming arm dropped to his bent knees. He was looking puzzled. 'I had better go,' she said straightening up and turning to leave.

Andrew got to his feet and took two swift strides and put his arms around her. 'You come home with me,' he said gently. 'I've got a saucepan of porridge on the stove, and you can have a coffee and a sit-down. It's early yet, it's only seven. You're not generally even awake by this time. You've got hours yet before you need to be anywhere. You can tell me all about it over breakfast.'

'There's nothing to tell!' Louise said abruptly. She had been tempted for a moment by porridge and the warm kitchen smelling of coffee. But the thought of telling him about Toby and the red chiffon negligee shook her back to the nightmare of reality. And now she had tumbled into the arms of the odd job man and her life was more complicated and even worse than last night – and it had been in ruins then. 'Nothing!' she said.

Andrew looked at her carefully. 'Come to the farm then and I'll drive you home,' he offered gently. 'You look tired out.'

Hot tears of self-pity stung Louise's eyes. 'All right,' she said ungraciously. She fell into step beside him and they walked in silence towards the farmhouse.

'Come in for a moment,' he said to her as they went through the gate from the home field into the yard. 'I'll make you some tea if that's all you could fancy. Some toast.'

Numbly, Louise shook her head and trudged towards the Land-Rover. Andrew opened the yard gate to the lane, swung into the driving seat and started the Land-Rover. Louise said nothing but stared blankly ahead through the filthy windscreen as they drove the three miles to her cottage. Andrew drew up outside her front door and switched off the engine.

'Is it that man?' he asked. 'Toby? Has he upset you?'

'I hope you don't think that just because we . . . that because I . . . that what happened makes any difference to anything,' Louise said in a sudden tense rush. 'It was just silly, that's all. Just one of those things.'

'Lou . . .' Andrew started kindly.

Louise flinched at once from his shortening her name. 'Don't,' she said. 'Don't call me Lou, I hate it.'

He looked ready to argue.

'Nothing's changed,' she continued quickly. 'What

193

happened was a mistake. It doesn't matter. And it doesn't mean anything.'

Andrew put his hand over hers. 'It does matter. It does mean something. And it wasn't a mistake.'

Louise drew away from his touch. 'I'm an independent woman,' she said thinly. 'I won't be blackmailed.'

He took his hand from her but his dark blue eyes never left her face. 'I know you're an independent woman,' he said simply. 'I think you're simply wonderful.'

Louise gasped as if he had insulted her and struggled for the door handle. It came off promptly in her hand. 'Dratted thing,' Andrew Miles observed. 'I keep meaning to fix it. I'll get it done today, don't you worry.'

He got out of the cab of the Land-Rover and walked around to Louise's door. She had no choice but to sit and wait while he opened the door for her with old-fashioned courtesy that the Women's Movement had long ago identified as an insult to free able-bodied women, who can perfectly well turn their own door handles.

Louise stepped down and went to her front door; Andrew followed her and waited while she opened it. 'I am sorry,' Louise said. 'I think there's some mistake. I should make it clear that I'm not interested in a serious relationship with you.' She tried to find words to take the warm affectionate look from his face. 'We are quite incompatible,' she explained. 'Quite incompatible.' Her voice shook a little on a suppressed sob. 'You could not find two more incompatible people. And in any case, I don't believe in the notion of romantic love at all.'

She succeeded better than she expected. The confident warmth was quite wiped from his face. He looked shocked. 'You were just using me,' he said.

'I . . .'

194

'I thought that you were upset and had come to find me,' he said. 'But you were just using me as some kind of diversion, to take your mind off things.'

It was so near the truth that Louise could only gasp uncomfortably. 'No . . .'

'Just because you are a highly educated woman and I am only a simple farmer,' Andrew went on, aggrieved, 'you thought you could pick me up and use me and then discard me.' He turned from her and walked towards the Land-Rover.

'I thought you cared for me,' he said. 'I feel wretched.' He got into the Land-Rover and slammed the door with an enormous creak and a shower of paint. The engine bellowed into life. He did not look at Louise again. She stood on her doorstep helplessly watching his severe profile as he backed carefully up the drive, reversed into the lane, and then crashed the gears into forward and drove up the hill towards his farm. Louise could not see that once he was safely in the lane he laughed aloud, a great joyous bellow of a laugh. 'You precious lovely!' he shouted above the roar of the overstrained engine. 'My little darling! I'll have you yet in spite of yourself, my darling little lollipop!'

'Oh God!' Louise said miserably. 'Oh God.'

Wednesday

LOUISE WENT INTO THE HOUSE, picked up her car keys, and rushed straight to her car in a haze of misery and confusion. Old heather flowers and bits of bracken were clinging to her sweatshirt, but she could not bear to go back up to her bedroom and change her clothes. She could think of nothing to do but to get to the university library and hide herself in the silence behind the book stacks on political science where, since the '70s enthusiasm for sociology, nobody ever went.

Rose, sitting equably in her doorway enjoying the early morning sunshine, observed Andrew bring Louise home and then Louise's rapid departure for university. She raised her eyebrows in mild interest. The dog looked up at her and she rested a hand on his head. 'Coming along,' she said with quiet satisfaction. 'Coming along fine.'

She raised herself to her feet and then stopped as a sharp pain suddenly stabbed into her side. She put her hand to it and felt, beneath the rich fabric of her gorgeous orange flowered blouse, a hard pebbly lump. She smiled wryly at the dog. 'And that's coming along too,' she said again. 'Coming along fine.'

Louise drove too fast through the village and then put

her foot down on the accelerator when she joined the 'A' road to the university. Her mind was a careful and complete blank. She was not going to be so foolish as to analyse her behaviour nor attempt to come to any sort of terms with the events of the last two days. She was not going to make the mistake of trying to examine how her world, previously so orderly, so correct, had suddenly collapsed about her. She felt as if her very survival depended on her mindless speeding towards the silence of the library where neither Andrew nor Toby would be likely to find her, and where the chances of melting into the arms of a passing stranger, and enjoying the best sexual experience of her entire life, were negligible.

Louise's preferred parking bay near the squat library building was overcrowded. She had to drive around. In the end she found a space beside the science block. Getting out of her car, she was aware of a rhythmic ripple of noise, a drum beat and the squeak of protest. Around the corner, towards the Science and Industry department, came a column of marching women.

It was Josie at the head of the demonstration, of course. Wendy was close behind her and behind the two of them were the disaffected administration and technical staff of the Science and Industry department including Sarah, Gilly, and Mo: Josie's new recruits to The Cause. What was noticeable about the band of women was not their numbers – though there were about twenty of them, which in those apathetic times amounted to a mob – but the fact that they were all naked to the waist. They were carrying placards which were unsatisfactorily pinned to bamboo garden canes and thus bent so that the viewer – though there were no viewers other than Louise – could only ever see half of the slogan. Josie's placard read:

Wom
Unit
Agai
Sex

Wendy's placard read:

Rea
Wom
No
Pi
Up

What immediately struck Louise was the enormous variety of the shapes of breast that were on display. Josie, who always looked so mannish and skinny in her dungarees, proved to have opulent lightly tanned breasts with perky nipples which were hardening in the cool morning air. Wendy, who was quiet and plump, had round rather flat breasts with nipples which looked sorrowfully down at her feet, as if they rather wished they had not come. Behind them, in jostling, warm, erotic pairs, were braces of breasts of every shape and size, from the neat fried egg to the shameless blancmange.

'Louise!' Josie called, her eyes and her breasts collectively swivelling to face her in a demanding stare. 'Come and join us! We're occupying the Science and Industry block and holding a radical open day!'

'Why are you undressed?' Louise asked.

Josie smiled. 'To challenge the sexism of the pin ups,' she said. 'See the placards!'

She waggled her bamboo cane and her placard blew open so that Louise could see all the letters. Now it read:

Women
Unite
Against
Sexism

while Wendy's poster read:

Real
Women
Not
Pin
Ups!!

'Oh God,' Louise said faintly.

'Join us!' Josie called.

'The thing is,' Louise said weakly, 'is that the Fresh Start committee has always agreed that consensus is the way forward. Consensus is the female natural style. I think you're in danger, Josie, of being very confrontational.'

Josie shook her head violently. Her earrings and her breasts resonated in sympathy and then came to rest. 'Consensus politics is a male myth,' she announced. 'It's not a female tradition at all! It's male brainwash to enforce female passivity. We're new women now, we're radical, we're active and we're angry!'

There was a murmur of support from the women behind her. Louise held her research notes tighter to her modestly baggy sweatshirt and remonstrated, 'But, Josie!'

She was too late. The women behind Josie had been opening the doors with the department's keys and now they swung open. With little seagull cries the half-naked women trotted into the building. A porter, who had been observing

199

the women from a nearby building, came with well-judged slowness towards them. 'Hey!' he shouted weakly.

One of the women spun around. 'And what d'you want?' she asked fiercely.

The porter, Mr William Collins, could not answer truly. If he had done so he would have been forced to say that what he wanted more than anything in the world was to be back home in bed with Mrs William Collins, who had never bared her breasts in twenty-three years of marriage. Instead he said feebly: 'You can't go in there!'

'We're in already!' a woman screamed from an upper window. It was the admin room. The demonstration was following the familiar pattern of occupying the administration room and destroying the files. As Louise watched, fistfuls of boring and superfluous student reports showered down around them.

Josie gleamed at her in triumph. 'Makes Fresh Start look like the Women's Institute doesn't it?' she demanded.

'Actually the Women's Institute is a powerful instrument for ordinary women's self-affirmation,' Louise answered automatically but Josie had not waited for her reply. Breasts bounding springily, she laughed triumphantly and jogged after her little army into the building. 'Now this is what I call access,' she shouted.

Louise reluctantly abandoned her plan for sanctuary in the library and went to her office. She was early, there was no-one in the building and little danger of running into Toby. She longed to be safely behind the volumes of the Political Science Society 1932–85, but she knew she had to telephone Miriam.

'Yes?'

'It's Louise.'

Miriam was in her office, glumly reading a circular from central government on new policy for battered wives' centres. It seemed to be saying that as the party of the family, the Conservative government could not be seen to support people who were trying to break up the family, i.e. women selfishly fleeing for their lives. The new policy was to close down the refuges. This would assist conciliation between victims and their raping and abusing partners by giving them simply nowhere else to go, and would save taxpayers' money. Either the enraged husbands would murder the women outright – thus saving the DHSS payments on them – or they would financially support them and beat them up. Either way the government would have done its part in gluing together the fragmentary and un-satisfactory institution of marriage which sought to join permanently one set of people with few rights and little confidence, and another set with too much confidence and big fists.

'Oh, hello,' Miriam said.

Louise drew a breath. She had to tell her best friend that their organisation was out of control and their members were occupying the Science and Industry block thus setting back, by many years, their work of encouraging adult women to see the university as an attractive and welcoming place, and simultaneously scuppering any chance of per-suading Science and Industry lecturers to regard mature women students as anything more than hyperactive men-struating hysterics. There was also the information that Miriam's husband was either a transvestite, or cross dresser, or both, and a confession – probably now overdue – that for more than nine years Louise and Miriam's husband had been engaged in a love-affair which had always been intended to result in the desertion of Miriam, and the end of her marriage.

'Don't tell me anything depressing,' Miriam commanded.

'That's a bit of a tricky one.'

'What's happened?'

Louise plunged in. 'Josie and her new group have occupied the Science and Industry building. They're all topless. They're throwing the files out of the window. They're holding an alternative open day.'

Miriam was silent for a moment. Then she let out a long weary sigh. 'OK,' she said. 'Thanks for telling me.'

'Miriam?'

'Yes?'

'Is that all you're going to say?'

'Did you expect me to break down and weep?'

'No, but . . .'

'Look, Louise, practically every single thing in my life at the moment seems to me to be falling about my ears. We'll cancel our open day. We'll give up on the Fresh Start committee. Josie can do it her way. The refuge is going to have to close down within three months. Toby is in deep depression and won't talk to me at all, and I can't say that I care two hoots either way.'

'Oh.'

'Is it the party this weekend? Is it still on?'

'Mr Miles's party? Why on earth should you care?'

'Shall we go to it?'

Louise, still shaken from her encounters in twenty-four hours with an improbably dressed Toby, an amorous neighbour, and twenty half-naked women, wailed, 'Miriam, how can you *think* of going to a party when everything is going so badly wrong?'

There was a little silence. 'Oh, I dunno,' Miriam said

equably. 'I can't think what else to do really. If everything's as bad as I think it is, we might as well go out and have a little bop.'

'They don't call them bops any more,' Louise snapped.

Miriam chuckled. 'Well, let's go and find out! Can I come over this weekend?'

'Oh, all right,' Louise said crossly. 'But I'm not going up to the farm. You'll have to go on your own.' From her window she could see the back of the Science and Industry block. A long white banner was being unrolled from one window to another. It read: 'Women Support Women! Naomi Petersen and Louise Case Represent Us! Open Science and Industry to Women! We Are Everywhere!'

'Oh my God,' Louise gasped.

'See you tomorrow, about midday?' Miriam asked.

'I have to go,' Louise stammered.

'And don't worry so much,' Miriam counselled. 'What's the worse thing that could happen?'

Louise shook her head numbly, reading again her own name blazoned on the outside of the occupied building. 'I think it just did,' she said.

She put down the telephone.

It rang almost immediately. It was the head of the Literature department, Professor Maurice Sinclair, a man watching his prediction that a feminist specialist would bring nothing but trouble come to a triumphant vindication. 'It's Maurice here,' he said quietly. 'Glad to catch you in so early. I've just had a telephone call from the head of Science and Industry. He seems to be under the rather disagreeable impression that you have organised an occupation of his building.'

'Oh,' Louise said faintly.

There was a pause. Maurice Sinclair was the most elegant man of the university. He wore the palest of pale grey suits, his long white hair was always beautifully cut. He never raised his voice in either anger or joy. He had never been seen to manifest either anger or joy in any way at all. His greatest disapproval was signalled by the raising of an eyebrow and a quiet murmur of 'well, well'. He hated and despised Suffix University and longed to be back at Cambridge where he had completed his MA at the feet of F.R. Leavis, all those years ago. The appointment of Louise to his department with responsibility for a feminist reading of the great texts, and a suggestion that she should teach books other than the Leavis dozen, even books written by women, even young women, even young black women, he had greeted with a raised eyebrow and three 'well's. Since then he had undermined her confidence and work in a million slight unobjectionable ways and had been waiting patiently for her finally to despair and leave of her own accord; or for the funding of her post to surprisingly expire.

'Would it be improper of me to ask you to cancel this little exercise?' he asked softly, his voice almost a whisper. 'It seems to be rather inconvenient for them over in Science and Industry. Apparently your young ladies have destroyed the student records and are currently engaged in wrecking the computers and related equipment. While I am sure we all sympathise with enthusiasm and the – ah – revolutionary heat of the moment, I understand that these electrical goods are rather expensive and inconvenient to replace.'

'I didn't organise it,' Louise said flatly. 'I can't stop them.'

'Ah,' he said with quiet pleasure. 'That *does* make things a little difficult. Since, apparently, they have named you and Dr Petersen in Sociology as their spokes-er-persons. Dr Petersen is apparently out of town so she can hardly be held responsible. It looks as if you have been left to – ah – carry this particular baby, if I can – in these urgent circumstances – stoop to employ a cliché; and if the word "baby" is not offensive to you.'

'Dr Petersen and I were on the Fresh Start committee but these women are a splinter group,' Louise said, trying to speak firmly against Professor Sinclair's die-away whisper. 'I have no control over their actions and I don't approve of them.'

'That *is* a relief,' he assured her swiftly. 'I was so afraid that you would be getting cold.'

'Cold?'

'I'm told you are all naked?'

'I am fully clothed,' Louise said stiffly. 'And I am not responsible for this demonstration.'

'A schism in the broad church,' Maurice Sinclair commented contentedly. 'I thought all you women worked together so much more successfully than us crudely competing males?'

'Not on this occasion,' Louise said through her teeth.

'This leaves us in a rather difficult position,' Maurice Sinclair continued smoothly. 'I have been asked by my colleague Professor Edgeley to persuade you to persuade *them* – I hope you are following me throughout all these clauses? – that they should leave the building in return for full support from the Science and Industry department for your open day? Or is it their open day now? Forgive a mere male's confusion.'

'We have cancelled,' Louise said. 'And I am not cognisant of their plans.'

(One of the more irritating things about Maurice Sinclair's pomposity was that it was infectious; Louise would never normally have used a word like 'cognisant'.)

'Do I take it, then, that you are refusing to speak with your erstwhile colleagues while they continue to destroy university property and of course, damage the academic reputation of the institution which, after all, remunerates you for working towards its greater glory?'

'I am not refusing . . .'

'Will you negotiate with them?'

Louise paused. 'I don't know that I'll do any good,' she said feebly.

'I shall tell Professor Edgeley that the monstrous regiment is meeting for a parley,' Maurice said happily. 'I am telephoning you from my home at present, but under these rather dramatic circumstances I think I had better come in to university. Perhaps you would do me the courtesy of coming to my office to report what progress you have made, Dr Case. I must confess that I cannot restrain myself from feeling slight anxiety.'

'I'll try,' Louise agreed miserably. 'I am feeling slight anxiety too.'

'Most unfortunate,' Professor Sinclair said contentedly.

Louise paused outside the front door of the Science and Industry building. Confused Science and Industry students were standing around in groups on the grass outside, worried that they would be late for lectures. They were a likeable lot of young men. Many of them wore round pebble glasses to compensate for eyestrain caused by staring too long at diagrams of subatomic particles instead of going out to play when they were little boys. Those destined for industry rather than applied science were broader and more burly. They stood at the back of the crowd and heckled when they glimpsed the women passing before the windows. The nakedness of the women seemed to have failed to make its legitimate political point and had produced instead a bawdy bacchanalian atmosphere. It was not helped by the tendency of the younger and prettier women, whose re-education had obviously been scanty and rushed, to come to the windows with their hands spread bra-wise over their breasts and taunt the young men in the courtyard below, casting aspersions on their potency, and the allegedly inferior dimensions of their genitalia.

The porter was morosely guarding the outside door with the air of a man shutting a stable after the horse has bolted. Inside the door was a barricade of heavy metal filing cabinets.

Louise stood at the back of the crowd and looked up at the windows, hoping to see Josie. The window of Professor Edgeley's study swung open and Josie rested her neat breasts over the windowsill.

'Have you come to join us?' she demanded.

'Not quite,' Louise called back.

At once all the young men turned to her and stared at her in open curiosity. 'She's no good, she's got her shirt on,' one said in disappointment. There was a long low whistle from somewhere.

'This is outrageous!' Louise cried angrily. She marched towards the building, the sea of young men parting before her, until she stood under Josie's window.

'I've had my head of department on the telephone,' Louise said as quietly as she could. 'If you come out now you can have your own open day and Science and Industry will co-operate.'

'We're having an open day now,' Josie said. 'The department is open to women in a way that it has never been before.'

Someone inside the building set light to a pin-up poster and dropped it flaming from the window to the ground. The young men, who had all done their Health and Safety training, conscientiously rushed forward and stamped out the flames. They looked around for the Health and Safety Accidents at Work log book to report the incident and seemed uneasy when they realised there was none.

'What do you hope to gain?' Louise asked. 'You must see that you are making enemies for The Cause.'

'Publicity,' Josie said airily. She waved towards the back of the crowd where a photographer from the local paper was taking photographs. 'Shock! A bit of constructive anarchy.'

'All the technicians and secretaries who have joined you are almost certain to lose their jobs,' Louise warned. 'And the students will face disciplinary action, and maybe they'll bring the police in, it's damage and trespass.'

Josie stopped smiling for the camera and looked down at Louise instead. 'You know your problem?' she demanded.

Louise shook her head.

'You're a worrier,' Josie announced grandly. 'You're all screwed up. Give a little, Louise! Relax! Smell the roses! Experience life!'

Louise looked away for a moment. She realised she was grinding her teeth and set her jaw carefully. 'Can I come in and talk to you?' she asked. 'I am afraid that I may be right to worry.'

Another flaming poster dropped to the ground. At the back of the crowd a television crew was unpacking its gear.

'You can come in only if you agree to join us fully,' Josie stipulated. 'And recognise the rightness of our cause and my position as Leader.'

'Leader!' Louise demanded, genuinely shocked.

'We are storm troopers of sexism,' Josie said, her breasts and earrings joggling with sincerity. A couple of women behind her nodded emphatically. 'Storm troopers of sexism! And I am the Mother of the movement.'

Louise stepped back and collided with the television reporter. The woman's hair was a bright unmoving blond helmet. Her face was a smooth unmarked mask of perfection. 'Are these your students?' she asked in a bright professional voice, hitting every word with equal emphasis. 'Did you order this action?'

'No!' Louise exclaimed irritably. 'I was vice-chairperson to a committee now disbanded from which this group split. They believe in direct action and we believe in persuasion. They believe in creative anarchy and we believe in consensus.'

'Yeah! Louise is right!' Josie agreed from on high. She nodded vigorously. 'Tell her all about it, Louise. Tell her about the creative anarchy and the direct action and don't forget I'm Leader.'

The large black eye of the camera turned balefully on Louise. She heard herself stammering, excusing, trying to explain. Showers of burning pin ups scattered around them, causing the cameraman to curse softly about light levels but making the reporter look as if she were bravely transmitting from the front line of a battle zone. She wished with all her heart that she had worn khaki this morning rather than peach.

Suddenly a roar went up from the crowd of students. A small SE 434 computer was held high from an open window by a rather beautiful bare-breasted girl. It was not a particularly valuable piece of machinery but it was the most modern and the most efficient the department possessed. Most important of all, it held on hard disc the most exquisite

Mickey Mouse program that anyone had ever seen.

Every computer department staffed principally by men and attended principally by male students knows about the Mickey Mouse program. As a secret initiation rite every competent student working on computer programming learns how to programme the computer to print out – in dots, dashes, percentage symbols and colons – the large black ears, the surprised eyes, the cute button nose, and then the whole cartoon body of Mickey. Why this should hold such a peculiar fascination for otherwise grown men is a mystery which only they could explain – if they had the analytical and linguistic skills which, demonstrably, they lack.

Every student in the department had spent hours with the SE 434 adding new and more exquisite detail: a little light-sparkle in Mickey's eyes, a flower in his gloved hand, a fluffy cloud behind his head. Thus, when they saw their colleague, their playmate, their toy, the SE 434 held aloft by some naked bimbo, a groan of deep dismay went up from the crowd.

They had watched their pin-up posters burn without regret, they had heard the sounds of breaking equipment, they had seen their files torn and scattered to the four winds, but the threat to the SE 434 and the Mickey Mouse programme was more than anyone could bear.

In a single concerted rush they dashed for the door, displacing in the first thrust Mr William Collins the porter, and then flinging themselves against the double doors which were anchored by the filing cabinets.

The women at the windows shrieked like banshees. The SE 434 was hastily put to one side and the women fled down the stairs to the front doors to defend the portals. It was obvious that the barricades would not hold. The doors were creaking and groaning, but under the battering of nearly a hundred determined men, they were slowly but surely shunting the filing cabinets to one side.

'Regroup! Regroup!' Josie screamed. 'Upstairs and barricade ourselves in the office!'

She was hardly heard above the shrill shrieks. The doors burst open but already the quicker women had the back doors unlocked and were running over the smooth lawns towards the car parks. With a hulloa! like foxhunters the Science and Industry students were after them.

It was a new experience for them all. Many of the women had never in their lives been actively pursued by a single man, let alone one hundred of them, and though they screamed in terror there was a girlish delight in the way they twinkled across the grass, out of reach, but never too quick. As for the young men, they had no idea what they were chasing the girls for; most of them had never even seen a live naked woman before this morning and would certainly not have known what to do if they had been so unfortunate as to actually catch one. But it was irrelevant.

They were responding to the old call from their childhood when the shout had gone up in the playground: 'Catch the girls!' They were responding to the old archaic stirring when the cry had gone up on the plains 'Urrrjhj wooooohm!' which meant, 'there are women and there is a farmstead where they have invented agriculture, pottery, weaving, the wheel and cooking, while all we can do is rush round and kill things. Let's go down there and bash it up.' With primal roars of joy the Science and Industry students chased the half-naked women, just quick enough to make them run, but not quick enough to catch them, while the women ran as fast as they possibly could – without courting the danger of actual escape. They screamed as they ran, high banshee-like wails. 'The engineers!' they cried. 'The scientists!'

It was like a passionate re-enactment of the arrival of technology among a group of Luddite spinsters. Impossible to say how long this mythological progress would have lasted had not a more imaginative young man suddenly shouted, 'Duck them! Duck them in the ponds!'

Responding at once to advice as to what to do with these elusive creatures, the men suddenly speeded up. The girls shrieked as they ran but they let themselves be caught. All of them, the fat ones and the thin ones, the pretty ones and the plain ones, those of every sort of sexual orientation and the simple virgins, were caught by the enraged Science and Industry students and thrust gently into the ornamental lily ponds which punctuate the smooth lawns of Suffix University.

Many of the women clung to their captors as they went in, and the men were dunked too. Almost all the men leaped in anyway from sheer *joie de vivre*, and also because a surprising number of couples had turned to each other in the slimy waters and were passionately kissing. Young men who had never before been close to a woman other than their Mum suddenly found themselves entwined with warm, sweaty, duckweedy women whose faces were flushed, whose mouths were warm and soft, and whose expressions were undeniably willing. And the women of the short-lived Creative Anarchy Group for Equality, fired by the success of direct action, warmed by a brisk run, aroused by pursuing men and the sound of their own screams, put their hands out under the discreet camouflage of the green water and got a good grip on the traditional powerful symbol of patriarchy and found it was, as it should be, obedient to their slightest touch.

*   *   *

There had never, in the whole history of the university, been a more successful demonstration. Most of the women demonstrators, hauled out of the ponds by men more decisive and assertive than any they had known before, melted into their arms. And the men, finding themselves with hot wet half-naked women in their arms, responded with a directness and an honesty which is rare at any time, and almost unheard of in these carefully enlightened days. The more chivalrous of them took off their own shirts, like members of a nicely mannered rugby team, and draped them round the women. The more direct simply swept their trophies away, back to their rooms and set about drying them in the swiftest and most enjoyable way possible: by energetic friction.

Louise, watching her career as a feminist activist disappear into the lily ponds, smiled vaguely at the television journalist and slid quietly away.

She did not go back to her office. She knew the place would be hideous with the ringing telephone and the imminent arrival of one of Maurice Sinclair's most glutinous memoranda which would say, in short, that she was fired. She would not go to the library, even the soothing volumes of unread political scientists could not help. She went back to her car and drove off the campus and headed instinctively for home.

It was lunchtime but Louise ate nothing. She sat in her study before her word processor with her face as blank as the screen. All that was showing was the title 'D.H. Lawrence: *The Virgin and the Gypsy*' and Louise's new introductory sentence:

'What can the woman of today learn from this story?'

After that there was simple silence. Louise could learn nothing from the story. She could learn nothing from Rose Miles. She could learn nothing from the fleeing half-naked demonstration of the Creative Anarchy Group for Equality. She could learn nothing from the memorable image of Toby on the kitchen table draped in crimson chiffon. She could learn nothing, most of all, from her encounter only that morning with Andrew Miles. Her conscious mind refused to accept that she had lain beneath him and known nothing but a wildly physical joy and a sense of release and wholeness that nine years with Toby had never provided.

Louise sighed, staring at the screen, willing the essay to write itself. Summer was coming on. Where only days ago she had looked for apple blossom and seen instead the ominous sight of Rose's van, the trees were now a riot of green. The leaves were iridescent and emerald, the little buds of the apples were already showing a promising rosy flush. The rust on the top of Rose's van was darker and deeper. The steps were bedded down in the grass and small meadow flowers, from Louise's Meadow Mix, had surprisingly germinated and were sprouting around the wheels. Rose's dog sat alert at the steps watching her as she went back and forth with her arms full of gloriously coloured clothes and boxes filled with yellowing pages.

She was having some kind of clean-out, Louise thought idly. She left her desk and went to the French window to see Rose more clearly. For some reason, Rose was stacking boxes all around the wheels and the axles of the van. Perhaps she was making ready to move on at last, Louise thought. And she found herself suddenly filled with regret and a sense of loss. She had become used to the eyesore of Rose's van. She had become used to Rose's irritating intrusive presence. She was used to the little light in the orchard and the friendly face of the big dog. She was used to having Rose as her neighbour.

She opened the French windows and went down the path to where Rose was working, stacking one box on another.

'What are you doing?' Louise asked.

Rose stretched up, a hand on her back where she privately felt a new little pebbly lump, on the right of her spine. 'Getting ready,' she said.

'To move on?'

Rose grinned. 'In a way,' she said.

'Are you sorting out your things?'

'Aye.'

Louise paused. 'Will you be giving Toby your papers before you go?' she asked.

'He can have them if he wants them,' Rose said. 'D'you think he's got the balls to come and fetch them?'

Louise hesitated. Part of her was deeply offended at Rose's language and her casual dismissal of Toby. Part of her rejoiced at it. *Did* Toby have the balls to confront the mistress he had lied to and betrayed for nine years? Did he have the balls to come back to Rose who had witnessed his humiliation? Louise knew he did not. 'He'll send Miriam,' Louise said after a moment's thought. 'She's coming tomorrow.'

Rose nodded and lowered herself to the step. 'Can't think why you bothered with him in the first place,' she said pleasantly.

Louise sat in the grass. The dog lolled down, stretched his paws, and settled himself for a chat. 'He was terribly attractive,' Louise explained. 'Miriam was mad over him. He'd come from Oxford, and he was the only unmarried lecturer in the whole department. He was very – you know – glamorous.'

Rose nodded. 'I was at Oxford,' she volunteered.

'Were you? What, camping there?'

'No, at the university. I did my MA and then I wrote a thesis on the WSPU.'

'The suffragettes?'

Rose nodded again, turning her face to the sun. 'Good times,' she said gently.

Louise leaned forward. 'Why did you choose to do the WSPU?'

'My parents were involved in the movement, and we *did* know Sylvia,' Rose said. She grinned her conspiratorial grin. '*That* much was true, anyway. It was a movement I was interested in. I collected and kept a lot of cuttings, a lot of letters. A lot of photographs.'

'The research material Toby wanted?'

Rose nodded. '*Didn't* he want it?' she demanded with wicked satisfaction. 'He'd have done anything for me. Made me feel young again.'

'He didn't know you'd already used it?' Louise asked. Talking to Rose gave her the strangest feeling of vertigo, as if the ground were crumbling away beneath her and dropping her lightly and sweetly into a void of unknown but infinite promise.

Rose chuckled richly. 'I published,' she said. 'I'd have thought a clever lad like him would have looked me up. I'm in all the bibliographies. I published a history of the WSPU and a biography of Sylvia, and a couple of histories of the Pankhurst sisters.'

'Under your name?'

'Rose Miles.'

'But Toby thinks your name is Rose Pankhurst?'

Rose smiled gently. 'Can I help that?' she asked rhetorically. 'He's a bit of a one for getting the wrong end of the stick.'

'So his plans for research won't come to anything,' Louise said slowly.

Rose shook her head. 'No,' she said lazily. 'How could they? He never cared for anything I said. He never really wanted to know. All he wanted was a step up for his career. Not to know anything. And all he wanted was gossip and dirt. Nothing about ideas, nothing about ideals. It's a funny thing, that – there he is, a man who has given his life to books and reading and ideas, but all he really cares about is his own career, and smutty gossip.'

They were quiet for a moment. Louise could not defend Toby. She did not want to defend Toby ever again. 'It's absolute chaos at university at the moment,' she remarked idly. It did not seem to matter here, sitting in the warm sunshine with a dog at her feet and Rose, friendly and amused, at her side. 'Everything I've tried to do to make changes has gone wrong.'

'You're too old,' Rose said simply.

'What! I'm twenty-nine!'

'You're too old to be a revolutionary unless you were on the barricades at twenty. It takes training. You've been a good girl all your life, a hard worker, conscientious. The baddest thing you ever did was sleep with your friend's husband and *that* was convenient for everyone. You need to make some changes in yourself first.'

'Working women have rights that I can fight for,' Louise protested.

'They should be fighting for themselves,' Rose said sourly. 'These little groups, this do-gooding. It's just patronage from women rather than from men. Girls need to find out for themselves what they want and then go and get it.'

Louise thought of Mo the punk secretary and her purple

217

hair entwined with weed as a burly student fished her out of the water like an exotic mermaid. 'Girls are full of false consciousness,' she protested. 'They don't know what they want.'

Rose shook her head. 'Who are you to say? You can call it false consciousness or you can call it not knowing your place. I've heard both in my lifetime. But deep down every woman knows what she wants. It's the bosses and teachers, and leaders like you, who try and tell people what they should want and don't understand. Maybe they want to be silly little tarts; maybe they want to be rocket scientists. If they want it badly enough they'll find a way.'

'Are you saying that women should not be helped to gain positions of power?' Louise demanded. She would have been indignant but for the sun on her eyelids.

'Of course not,' Rose said. 'No-one ever thanks you for what they get on a plate. And what's it worth as a gift? Little favours!'

'But society is set up to work against women,' Louise said. 'Girls don't get the chances that boys get. Women don't get promoted. Women still don't get paid the same for the same jobs.'

Rose nodded. 'It's a bitch, isn't it?' she asked comfortably. 'But you won't change anything by setting up committees and telling women what they should want. They've got to want it themselves. And half of them want to be parasites and sex bombs, remember.'

'Are you saying that women ought to be happy to stay at home and support men and be second-class citizens?' Louise demanded.

'You've got to build the doorways for women,' Rose said seriously. 'That's easy to do. You can see where there is injustice. We knew that when we were fighting for the vote.

218

You make the doorways and the women will go through them when they are ready.

'There are seasons,' Rose said simply. 'Sometimes the time is right for a girl to have fun, sometimes for her to work and struggle. Sometimes to stay home and love a man, sometimes to run away from him. A clever woman follows her own path. And no one path is the same as another.'

Louise was silent for a moment. 'I wonder what my path is now,' she mused.

Rose gave her a look which was brimful of mischief. 'If you don't know by now you're a bigger fool than I thought,' she said. 'I want some tea. Could I have some water?'

Louise got slowly to her feet. 'I'll make the tea. But you've eaten all the biscuits already.'

Louise worked on her essay all Wednesday evening. By the simple precaution of disconnecting her telephone and not checking the ansaphone she managed to avoid two languidly insulting calls from Maurice Sinclair and two short appeals, made potent by the brief anguish in their tone, from Toby. By midnight she had a screen full of text. She printed it out and then faxed it to Sarah's office so that it would be on her desk by Thursday morning. The first paragraphs read:

D.H. Lawrence the sexist: a reconsideration of *The Virgin and the Gypsy*.

There is much the modern feminist can dislike about Lawrence: his obsession with male power, his insistence on male sexuality and his view of women as the recipients rather than the givers of sensuality

219

and mystery. But it is wrong for us to deny the liberating power of his view of sexual relations.

Old-fashioned feminists may concentrate on Lawrence's phallocracy, but we of the Second Wave can overlook this prejudice of his – as much a part of his time as his snobbery and his concern with the condition of England and the Empire.

What he has to teach us, as modern feminists, is both more potent and more liberating than his flaws. Lawrence teaches us about sensuality, about the freedom a woman can feel with a man who adores her, about finding oneself through sexuality with a male partner. Lawrence indicates that all conventions – those of feminist puritanism, as well as those of the patriarchy – are equally wrong. Lawrence shows us that a sensual woman can be free whatever her environment. Her task is to find a man with whom she can express this.

And Lawrence's sexuality is fundamentally heterosexual. It is the difference between men and women – which has for so long puzzled and distressed us as feminists – that is the source of Lawrence's deepest delight. As lovers, as enemies, it is the opposing nature of men and women which makes Lawrence's view of the world come alive. And he shows us, as perhaps we need to be shown, that the difference is nothing to fear but is in fact the source of our energy as women – that we are *not* men, but something wonderfully different.

Thursday

'I DON'T THINK WE CAN USE THIS.' Sarah's voice on the telephone on Thursday morning sounded as shocked as if Louise had sent her a picture of herself astride a grossly enlarged spark plug. 'I don't follow the argument at all, Louise.'

Louise, drinking coffee at the kitchen table, felt instantly uneasy. Feminist criticism is a new science, as prickly and as difficult as any Comintern meeting as it moves invisibly and without warning from one phase to another. 'What's the matter?' Louise asked weakly. 'I know it's late, Sarah, I'm very sorry.'

'It's not that it's late,' Sarah said, aggrieved. 'It's that it is so ... so ...' She paused. Clearly there was no epithet bad enough for whatever Louise had done. 'It's so sexy,' she said with disdain.

'Sexy?'

'Yes! As far as I can tell, what you're saying is that Lawrence should be read as a man who understands women's sexuality. And that what women want, if they're free to choose, is a man who will arouse them and love them and sometimes dominate them and sometimes be dominated! And that as feminists we should be developing our sensuality with free men.'

'Yes.'

'Well, I can't use this, Louise, it's not the line we take at all.'

Louise said nothing for a moment. 'I think I may have been a little confused when I wrote it,' she apologised.

'I should think so,' Sarah said sternly. 'Louise, this doesn't read like you at all! It's one thing to redefine dress codes and insist on a woman's right to wear what she wishes, including erotic underwear. But you seem to be going a stage further and suggesting that women will only be free when they acknowledge their desire for men.'

'Yes.'

'Well, that's quite slavish!'

'Yes, but the way Lawrence puts it is that if you acknowledge that you really desire a man, and he acknowledges that he really desires you, then you are free and equal in your sensuality. And your practical day-to-day life is free and equal too. For instance, we don't see Constance Chatterley and Mellors together very much, but I think Lawrence suggests that they have an ideally equal and liberating life together because of their shared sexuality. And the ending of the novel indicates that they will go to a new world together – because they are equal pioneers.'

'So if a man is a wonderful lover, the best lover you've ever had, you should go and live with him, and nothing else matters?'

'Should I?' Louise asked unguardedly.

There was a short silence.

'Do you want to reconsider this essay for the next edition?' Sarah asked patiently.

'Yes . . . I think . . . actually . . . No.'

There was another silence.

'I don't think I really want to work on Lawrence for a

while,' Louise said feebly. 'He puts ideas in my head.'

'Ideas?'

'Yes. I think I'd rather stay on feminist theory or maybe review something for you, Sarah, if I may. I'd rather not read Lawrence right now. I'd rather stick to something which we know is right. Something we've thought through and got straight.'

'I need a couple of reviews doing.' There was a brief space as Sarah hunted on her crowded desk for the books. 'Here's one that might suit you: *Separatism – the way forward. How a community of twenty women lived without men, 1988–1990.*'

'That sounds ideal,' Louise agreed. 'I'll pick it up later today if you leave it in my pigeonhole. Thank you, Sarah.'

'You're welcome,' she said pleasantly. 'By Wednesday week, please.'

Louise put the telephone down with a sigh of relief.

There was a knock on the door. Captain Frome was on the doorstep.

'Neighbourhood watch,' he said by way of introduction. 'I'm afraid we're on amber again.'

'Amber?' Louise asked. For a moment she thought it might be some new hallucinogenic drug.

'Amber alert,' he explained.

'Oh, you'd better come in.'

He had a large manila folder under one arm and a collection of pamphlets in his other hand. He put them all down on the coffee table and sat on the sofa. 'First things first. Here's the new *Convoy Alert!!* pamphlet. They've regrouped and they're headed back in this direction. The police will cordon off the village here, and here.' He pointed to the little lanes marked on the map. 'There *is* a party planned somewhere in the neighbourhood. Our job is to make sure that none of the blighters get within ten miles of Wistley. Any news, any gossip and suspicions, and you telephone this number.' Captain Frome's finger pointed to the telephone number printed in large figures at the bottom of the pamphlet. 'Inside here are a few details about making your home secure and how to recognise a hippy. You should have no trouble with that!'

'I?'

'The university is full of them, isn't it? Keep your ear to the ground. Some of your students may be in touch. This is a subversive movement we are dealing with here. We don't know how far the tentacles of it may stretch. Satanism, drugs, communism. We're going to Keep Wistley Free of the Hippy Menace.'

Louise nodded wearily.

'Now. Something even more serious.' Captain Frome's large grey-moustached face took on an expression more suitable for a funeral mute than for a morning caller. 'I took the liberty of looking into your squatter.'

'Rose?'

'Rose Miles. Rose de Vere, Rambling Rose, she's had a number of names.'

Louise said nothing but she felt wary.

'I have some bad news for you,' he said. 'Tell me first, which lawyer did you use when you bought the cottage? Local man?'

'I inherited it,' Louise said. 'From my aunt. She bought it from Mr Miles's father.'

'We have to hope it was a straightforward mistake then, and not a put-up job.'

'What was?'

'The conveyancing. According to the deeds held at the

county archive office, this was once two cottages with two cottage gardens.'

'Yes?'

'Your aunt only bought the one. They had been converted into one property by 1950, but originally there were two owners of two separate houses: Mr Miles senior – Andrew Miles's grandfather – and Mr Stephen Miles, his younger brother. Your aunt occupied the whole property but she bought only from Mr Miles senior. The property was never declared as one house, the garden was never declared as one garden. In theory, Mr Stephen Miles the younger brother, or his heirs, still own half of this house and half of the garden.'

Louise stared blankly at Captain Frome. He opened the manila envelope and spread photocopies of ageing documents on her coffee table. 'Then the trail goes cold,' he went on. 'But local belief is that Mr Stephen Miles had a number of children, all now deceased except for one daughter – Rose. Mr Miles senior had a son who inherited the farm, and *his* son is Andrew Miles, our Mr Miles. This cottage was used as a gamekeeper's cottage and then a farm labourer's cottage and then finally sold as one unit to your aunt, and subsequently inherited by you.'

'I only own half?' Louise asked.

'And the other half is owned by Rose Miles,' Captain Frome concluded grimly. '*This* accounts for why she makes so free with her accusations of trespass. She probably knows perfectly well that she is the owner of your orchard, and indeed, half your house. She's probably just biding her time before she strikes.'

'Strikes?'

'Blackmail, Miss Case. Presumably she came to discover the lie of the land and shortly she will be threatening you with a claim against your property. I should imagine that she will settle for a cash payment to go away – her sort usually do. But until you settle this matter, she probably has a full legal right to your orchard and to half your house and, what is worse, she is the Achilles' heel of the Wistley Keep the Convoy Out!! campaign.'

Louise was stunned into complete silence for long minutes. 'This is a nightmare,' she eventually said.

'It is!' the Captain confirmed. 'We shall be made a laughing stock. Here we are campaigning for total control of all travellers and their forced moving on, and here we have, in the heart of the village, half a property and a site owned and legally registered to a vagrant. We can't even have her moved on. We can't prosecute her for trespass. She *owns* her site. She has a legal right to *rent* her site out to others if she wishes. She could have a dozen vans on that orchard tomorrow and we could do nothing to stop her.'

Louise closed her eyes briefly and then opened them again. 'Nothing?' she asked faintly.

Captain Frome leaned a little closer and his voice dropped low. 'If I were you, I would go down to her van with a legally prepared document, quite watertight, and I would offer her a couple of thousand pounds to disappear and never come back.'

'She's very stubborn,' Louise said. 'I can't imagine her disappearing. And I haven't got a thousand pounds.'

'Then you may have to be a little stubborn yourself,' Captain Frome suggested. 'No access to her property through your gate, for instance. No visitors allowed. No deliveries. No services. Don't supply her with any water. Report her to the relevant Health authorities. Report her to Social Services. You have a friend who is a social worker, don't you? Ask her to register the woman under the Mental

Health Act as someone who should be restrained for her own safety. I think we can find ways of making her life here too uncomfortable to tolerate. We can probably get her locked up. There's a section of the Mental Health Act we can call in. Sectioned,' he said with relish. 'We'll get her sectioned.'

It sounded as if he was preparing to slice her into sample fillets. Louise said nothing. She was thinking about invoking the full force of the property-owning patriarchal law against one mischievous old lady.

'I don't ask for thanks,' Captain Frome said.

'Thank you very much,' Louise said. 'You have been incredible officious.'

'Just doing my duty as a neighbour.' He beamed at her. 'I *am* after all the new chairman of the neighbourhood watch committee. Sir Henry Wilcox of Wistley House was the original chairman but there was a vote of no confidence in him at the last meeting and I took the chair.'

'Did you?'

'He had shown himself very casual in his response to the emergency. Very casual indeed. But it was a close-fought thing. The whole issue swung on one vote.' He leaned forward and tapped his finger against his rosy nose. 'Your vote, actually.'

'Mine?'

'You gave me your proxy vote, if you remember. It was your one vote which swung the decision in my favour. So I'm the new chairman of the neighbourhood watch committee, and chairman of the Keep the Convoy Out!! subcommittee.' Captain Frome glanced at his watch. 'Heigh ho! I had better go,' he said. 'Though it *is* rather that time of day.'

Louise said nothing. She had no idea that 'that time of

day' indicated that it was noon and an appropriate time for her to offer Captain Frome a glass of dry sherry or, better still, a whisky and water. She merely rose to her feet and Captain Frome, an English gentleman, had no choice but to rise too.

'I'll leave these documents with you, shall I?' he asked. 'You'll want to take them in to your lawyer. I suppose you could consider suing your aunt's lawyer for incompetence. That could be a useful and fruitful avenue.'

Louise looked with distaste at the documents spread on the coffee table. It seemed to her that in two brief days she had lost her lover, her academic credibility, her job, and had now discovered that she did not own half of her home.

'Don't thank me,' Captain Frome said again, raising his hat to her and striding energetically to his Rover. 'The new neighbourhood watch committee does not seek thanks. Just support. Just support.'

Louise nodded dully. 'Thank you,' she said like an obedient child and stood respectfully in the doorway until he had gone.

Rose appeared from behind the oak tree that grew before the front door.

'What are you doing?' Louise asked abruptly.

'Listening at the door,' Rose said helpfully. 'So the party's still on, is it?'

'What did you hear?'

'All of it,' Rose said reasonably. She felt rather affronted at the implication that she might have been listening but failed to do a thorough job. 'All of it, of course.'

'About the cottage?'

'Well, I knew that already.'

'You knew that you own the orchard?'

'I told him so when he came and tried to turn me off. I

228

accused him of trespass on my land. It shut him up good and proper. That's the trouble with these little tinpot colonels. They hate to see a woman win.'

'You knew that the conveyancing was never done on the second cottage?'

'And that I own half the house? Yes, I knew that. I've always known that.'

Louise sagged against the doorpost. 'I think we had better go to a lawyer and get this straightened out,' she said wearily.

'No real need,' Rose replied. 'I only ever stay here in May. I never wanted the house. And anyway, I'll be dead soon.'

'Oh yes,' Louise said bitterly. 'So you keep saying whenever it's convenient. But I suppose you think you can come here every May, forever. And even if you *do* die, then who is going to inherit and come rolling up the drive next May? Who are you going to leave it to that I have to put up with for the rest of my life?'

Rose looked at Louise with a patient smile. 'Think. You have a little think. You should have worked it out by now, clever girl like you. Who d'you think will inherit the west half of your house? The sitting room, the stairs,' she paused for greater emphasis, 'the bedroom?'

'No,' Louise said weakly. 'I can't believe that you mean . . .'

'Bonny Andrew,' Rose said lovingly. 'Andrew Miles. You and he will own this house together. It's as if it was meant to be.'

That afternoon Louise drove into university at speed, parked a long way from her usual place and scuttled into the department with her head down in the hopes of being unseen. Cravenly, she waited outside the department office until she heard the telephone ring and the secretary become involved in a personal and unauthorised gossip. Only then did she open the door a crack and slide into the room. Susan, the secretary, signalled wildly at Louise with her plucked eyebrows. She put a well-manicured hand over the telephone. 'Professor Sinclair wants to see you,' she hissed in a stage whisper. 'Urgently and at once!'

Louise nodded, snatched up her post and got herself out of the room before Susan could free herself from the conversation. In the corridor she found she was trembling with a heady mixture of nerves, and elation at having escaped Professor Sinclair, and with a fighting chance of evading Toby.

She had a jiffy bag containing, no doubt, *Separatism – the way forward. How a community of twenty women lived without men, 1988–1990*, and an envelope from Sarah containing her rejected Lawrence essay. She had a folder enclosing a dozen student essays, and half a dozen unconvincing excuses. There was also an official-looking envelope marked with the university's crest, and two plain envelopes with Toby's handwriting on them.

Louise pinned a notice on the department noticeboard. It read: 'Dr Louise Case has to cancel all meetings for the next two days. Normal classes will resume on Monday. Students working on the Feminist in Literature option are to read and compare *Tom Jones*, by Henry Fielding, and *Money*, by Martin Amis, by Thursday of next week.'

'That should keep them quiet,' she thought vindictively and pushed in the drawing pin with force.

Like a ghost she melted from the corridor and slipped down the stairs. Turning her head away from Toby's office window she scuttled back to her car, flung her booty into the back seat and started the engine. Feeling secure at last she reached behind and pulled out Toby's two envelopes. The first she opened contained a short note dated Wednesday morning:

This is ridiculous. The explanation of my appearance is perfectly simple. I was modelling the gown for Rose to take up the hem. She will confirm this. If you cling to any other belief you are being paranoid and I suggest you examine your own subconscious motivation. I demand that you behave like a rational woman. Toby.

The second envelope had a longer letter.

You came into university today (Wednesday) and did not see me, nor have you replied to my note of this morning, nor have you returned my telephone calls. I left two messages on your ansaphone. Are you ill?

If you are still upset because of that ridiculous scene at your cottage on Tuesday night I can only repeat my assurance that you have misunderstood what was taking place. Really, Louise, we have been intimate for years. Don't you think that if any of your suspicions were well-founded that you – with your sensitivity and perception – would have noticed something before? Or that Miriam would have complained?

I will not address this matter again. It is too ridiculous. Please telephone me at once and we can meet and get back to normal. I want you to know that this brief interruption to our relationship has made things much clearer for me. Miriam and I are slowly growing apart. I think you know what this means to you and me. I know what you have always planned and wanted – I think the time is now coming for us to be together. Toby.

Louise scrunched both letters into a ball and tossed it on the floor. She let in the clutch and drove carefully away. She felt as if she had come to an important turning point in her life. On the one hand was Toby, hers for the claiming at last. But on the other hand there was the dreadful inexpungible memory of him, half-naked in red chiffon with his white ankles peeping out below chiffon ruffles, and his bony knee sticking through a provocative beribboned front opening.

'Oh God, no,' Louise said in unassumed disgust. 'No. It's not possible.'

She drove without seeing the road, without seeing the hedges starry with speedwell, illuminated by shining clumps of ox-eye daisies. Under the hedges were buttery yellow clusters of late primroses, in the woods on either side of the road were deep lush pools of rotting bluebells. As Louise drove slowly up the lane to her cottage ecstatic birdsong ringed the little car as thrush, blackbird, robin and coaltit swore their desire in rippling oaths into the warm blue air. When Louise parked the car and went wearily to the front door, clutching her letters, she could smell pollen and nectar and the perfume of flowers laying themselves out to please passing bees. Everything on the common was green and fertile and ready for summer. Bracken and fern were unfolding their tiny tentacles, reaching for the sunshine. The trees were as wetly green as lettuce. The cottage was besieged by rhododendron, their dark shiny leaves a near-black foil to the prodigal trumpets of purple and white flowers. The wild golden azalea extending tongues of saffron perfumed the air with a heady intoxicating scent.

Louise, blinded with more than her usual myopia, saw nothing and heard nothing, smelled nothing and felt nothing. She fitted her key in the lock and walked into her cold tidy house. She dropped the letters on the kitchen table and opened the one marked with the university crest. It was from Maurice Sinclair expressing his sorrow that the department would be unable to renew her post after the end of the summer term.

She nodded without surprise and opened the jiffy bag. The book *Separatism – the way forward. How a community of twenty women lived without men, 1988–1990* no longer struck her as a bold and adventurous experiment in social engineering, but as a curious waste of the time and energy of good women who could have been doing something more interesting. She looked closely at the photograph on the cover. Twenty blank faces under short unflattering haircuts looked back at her. They did indeed look determined, right-thinking, and forceful. They did not look as if they were having a whole lot of fun. Louise sank into the kitchen chair. She was afraid she had lost her lover, her job, and her Cause.

Realising she had eaten neither breakfast nor lunch, Louise went wearily to the little freezer, depressed by lack of food but not hungry. It was packed with small square boxes of frozen meals which rejoiced in the fact that the portions inside were so small and so inadequate in calories that Louise could have eaten the entire contents of the freezer and gained no more than a quarter of a pound in weight. Each meal, priced ounce per ounce far beyond the finest fillet steak, came in a small frozen bag fitted neatly inside its box, which sported a picture of lush and exotic sauce and tasty meat on the front. Louise was not fooled. She had lived off these miserable simulacra before. She knew there was nothing more to them than a little knitted soya thread and an equal amount of chemical additives. She selected one at random, freed it from its box, stabbed it with efficient malice, microwaved it and then decanted it on to a cold plate. She opened a bottle of wine without relish and placed it, and a glass, on her tray. She went to the larder and took out a giant emergency-size block of fruit and nut chocolate. Thus armoured against desolation, she carried the whole tray up the stairs to her lonely bedroom and put herself to bed with a Virginia Woolf novel similarly brilliant on technique but short on calories.

Drunk with wine and gorged with chocolate by half past nine, Louise lay back against her pillows and fell into a sottish slumber. She was still drunk at eleven when she was awakened by the roar of Andrew Miles's unsuppressed Land-Rover charging the hill. Once again Andrew, fuelled by Theakston's Old Peculier and now also by passion, misjudged the corner, pulled the wheel around too late, and slid helplessly and happily on his bald tyres towards the hurdle which blocked the gap in the broken fence around the orchard. Once again, through shards of breaking wood his Land-Rover came to rest amid the trees which grew before his darling's cottage.

Louise leaped from her bed in her frumpish cotton pyjamas, smeared with chocolate and groggy with alcohol, and looked out from her bedroom window. Andrew Miles was slumped in the attitude of a man knocked unconscious by his windscreen, and impaled on his steering wheel thrust like a spear between his ribs.

Louise took it all in, in a single heart-stopping moment, and screamed his name. She fled downstairs, tore open the front door, crying 'Andrew! Oh! Andrew!' She ran on her bare feet, regardless of the sharp gravel, to the Land-Rover just as Andrew, miraculously recovering from his injuries, opened the driver's door with the familiar resounding creak and received her into his open arms.

Louise had not had a man who stayed the whole night in her bed ever before. In her undergraduate days she and her partners had separated, driven apart by the discomfort of the study bedrooms at the university. Toby always went home to the marital bed even if Miriam was away for the night. He said he could not sleep elsewhere, and that in any case in this way they preserved a mystery and an erotic strangeness to each other. Her occasional other lovers she always dismissed. She might have sex with other men but there was only ever one man she wanted to wake beside. She had thus never slept with a man who, after a prolonged session of lovemaking which was both tender, experimental and, in the end, ravenously animal, curled himself around her like a fat dormouse on an ear of corn and fell deeply asleep, breathing beer fumes warmly into her ear.

Any attempt to disengage herself did nothing but make him tighten his grip. When Louise put a hand gently on his chest and whispered, 'Andrew, could you move over a bit?' he at once obligingly wriggled closer and held her tighter still. At one in the morning, suffering from both insomnia and claustrophobia, Louise shook him gently and said, 'Andrew, I can't sleep.'

He woke at once and moved on top of her in the darkness, kissing her face and neck and breasts with gentle sleepy tenderness. 'OK,' he said agreeably.

'I didn't mean . . .' Louise started.

'I love you,' he said, and slid inside her. 'You are absolutely the most perfect woman in the world and I love you.'

Friday

LOUISE WOKE AT DAWN to kisses and more loving. Somewhere in the back of her mind she remembered telling Miriam that lovemaking four times in twenty-four hours was a ridiculous Lawrentian fiction. She giggled at the thought and Andrew Miles, always responsive to her desires, obligingly tickled her. The subsequent play – as wanton as kittens and as hysterical as schoolchildren – left them amorously entwined on the floor amid Andrew's clothes and Louise's supper tray.

Finally they separated. 'I have to go to the farm,' Andrew said. 'Pigs want feeding. Shall I bring back anything for breakfast?'

Louise blinked at his assumption that he would be returning for breakfast. 'I was going to work this morning,' she said firmly.

'So am I,' he said. 'But I suppose we'll have breakfast.'

Louise opened her mouth to argue and then checked herself. He wanted to come back for breakfast, and she wanted him in her house. For the first time in nine years she glimpsed the possibility of a life with a man who spent his time with her, who was not always obliged to be elsewhere, whose primary loyalty was not always to another woman.

'What do you eat for breakfast?' she asked cautiously. It

237

was like a whole new world slowly extending before her. She had a feeling that croissants and coffee were not enough for a man who made love all night and then got up at six to feed pigs.

'Bacon,' he said. 'Eggs, toast, tomatoes, mushrooms, fried bread. Cereal to start and toast and marmalade to finish. Lots and lots of tea. Nothing special.'

'I haven't got anything like that,' Louise confessed, rather dashed. 'I have a baguette in my freezer.'

Andrew, pulling on baggy corduroy trousers, chuckled. 'It sounds positively obscene. Come up to the farm with me, and let's *eat*.'

Louise suddenly found that she was hugely hungry. 'I'll have a shower and come up,' she said. 'Don't wait for me. I'll be up in half an hour.'

Andrew, shrugging himself into a tartan shirt which woefully clashed with the trousers, shook his head. 'No. I want you with me. I'm sick of you being here and me being up the hill. I want you with me all day and I want you in my bed tonight.'

Louise held the bedcovers up to her naked shoulders. 'I have things to do,' she said. 'I have a book to review and essays to mark. Just because we . . . just because you . . . just because . . . doesn't mean that we have to make any big commitment to each other. It doesn't mean anything.'

'God in heaven!' Andrew swore, abruptly sitting down on the corner of the bed. 'What do I have to do to stop you tarting around? I love you, I want to make love with you, probably as soon as I have had some breakfast. Moreover I want *you* to cook my breakfast while I feed the pigs. And then I want us to have *dinner* together. I want us to have *tea* together. I want to go down to the Holly Bush and get *drunk* together. And then tonight,' he raised his voice and

238

brought his fist down on to the bed with each word as a hammering emphasis, 'tonight I *want you in my bed*!'

Louise paused for no more than a moment. 'Oh, all right,' she said with what she feared was a simper. 'All right by me.'

A broad grin spread across Andrew's face and he gathered her naked warmth into his arms and dragged her out of bed and on to his lap.

'What about the pigs?' Louise asked as they rolled lazily back into the shambles of the duvet and the pillows.

'They'll understand,' Andrew said.

Louise sat in the warmth of the Land-Rover while Andrew picked up pieces of broken hurdle and fence post and stacked them tidily against the orchard fence. The grass in the orchard was starry with dew, each blade of grass drenched in a string of droplets. Andrew lifted a pile of small pieces of wood and trudged with them down through the orchard to Rose's van and threw them down at her doorstep. His big boots left bold dark tracks through the luminous grass. Louise found herself watching him in a way she had never watched any other man, appraising the broadness of his back and the strength of his shoulders; looking at him not only as a lover, but also as a potential husband who would care for her, a man who would father her children.

He was generous, she thought. He was thoughtful. He did not have to carry the kindling to Rose's door, he could have left it stacked in the orchard and Rose would have helped herself. Louise put her head on one side and watched Andrew make a second trip with another armful of wood. He was a good man, kindly. He would make a good husband, she thought. If he was so considerate of the comfort of an old lady he would be a pleasant man to live with. He would be patient with small children, he would make a good father.

Louise checked her own thoughts with a guilty start. Liberated feminist women do not assess men as husbands, they do not plan marriage the moment they climb out of bed. But then she shrugged. She had never felt like this about any man before. She had seen Toby through a haze of envy when she wished he had chosen her instead of Miriam. She had never analysed his behaviour and wondered if he were indeed the most desirable man she knew. She had accepted her old judgement, the judgement of a girl of twenty, that he was the man she wanted. She knew now, at twenty-nine, that he was not.

She looked at Andrew Miles with a clearer vision, thinking of her needs, of her future, and whether they could indeed make a relationship which would last for them both. She thought of the little Elizabethan manor farm and the fields around it, and the common stretching away from it and thought she would like to live there, as Rose had suggested, in the big farm bed with a baby on the way.

He came to the Land-Rover and opened the door. 'What are you thinking?' he asked as he started the engine and backed the vehicle carefully into the lane away from the wreckage of Louise's fence.

'I was thinking that you would make a nice husband,' Louise said with rare honesty, breaking every rule of appropriate social behaviour between new lovers, and every rule of politically correct behaviour for liberated women.

He turned his head and gave her a swift happy grin. 'Yes,' he said. 'I would. I will. I will make a wonderful husband to you. Let's get married at once.'

'I didn't mean that!' Louise protested immediately. 'I was thinking theoretically.'

'Oh, bollocks,' he said. 'Of course we should get married.'

Louise said nothing for a moment as he drove carefully up the lane and then turned in the gateway to his farm. He stopped the Land-Rover, switched off the engine and turned to look at her, resting his hand gently on her shoulder and then turning her face towards him. 'I'm not joking,' he said. 'And I'm not theorising. I want to marry you and bring you here as my wife. I want children in the farmhouse again and a girl or a boy to have the farm when I'm dead. You're the only woman I've ever wanted and I want you very much. Will you marry me, Louise?'

'It's so quick . . .'

'I've known you and I've been caring for you for nearly a year,' he said. 'Anything that's ever been a problem for you and I've been there. Septic tank, snow, gutters, chimneys. I've never stopped thinking about you and doing things for you. For nearly a year, Louise. That's long enough.'

'But I always paid you!' Louise exclaimed.

'Well, go on paying me!' he said irritably. 'But for God's sake let's get married and live in my house. You can pay me all you like.'

Louise giggled irresistibly and Andrew pulled her gently into his arms. 'Say yes,' he whispered into her hair.

'Yes,' she said.

Louise had thought that Andrew had been joking about spending the entire day with her but she found that he meant precisely and simply what he said. She therefore spent the morning with him beating the bounds of his fields, checking sheep, moving his small herd of cream-coloured Charolais cows from one field to another, fixing the stop

241

cock in a water trough, and starting to clear out a barn for the next instalment of the hay crop.

At noon they went into the house for dinner. Mrs Shaw had left a huge pan of home-made tomato soup, and there was home-baked bread in the bin and a substantial cheese board. They ate with fervent hunger in companionable silence, listening to the detailed weather forecast and the 'World at One' and then 'The Archers', from which Andrew extracted a high degree of scandalised enjoyment.

'What do we do now?' Louise asked as he switched off the radio. She felt wonderfully tired after a night of constant lovemaking and the long morning in the open air.

Andrew smiled. 'I think we should have a little lie down.'

He led the way up the winding wooden stairs to the bedroom. It faced south over the Wistley common. Diamonds of golden sunshine filtered through the leaded windows and spread like an aureate counterpane on the big brass bed. Andrew shucked off his breeches, socks, and pants, and hopped between the sheets, patting the pillows welcomingly. 'Come on,' he said. 'I won't bite.'

'You might,' Louise said, stripping off her own clothes with equal shamelessness.

'Not very hard,' he said.

Louise slid into bed beside him and felt at once a rush of what must be joy, absolute joy, at the firm smooth warmth of him, at the confident touch of his hands on her body as he drew her to him, at the clear windblown sunned smell of him, and at the easy unbidden rising of her desire.

'What about the pigs?' she asked as Andrew turned her firmly on her side and caressed her long slim back, and her shoulders, and traced her vertebrae with his tongue.

'Pigs?'

'You're always saying, "pigs want feeding". But I've not

242

seen your pigs. I've seen everything but pigs; and we've not fed them this morning.'

He gave a guilty little chuckle and buried his head against the smooth skin of her back, and nibbled at her neck. 'I've not got any pigs,' he confessed. 'But it's the sort of thing that you can say when you want to get out of something or leave somewhere. I didn't realise I said it so often as to be noticeable. I don't have pigs – or only as a manner of speech. I have metaphorical pigs. I have theoretical pigs.'

Louise giggled and turned around in his arms and pulled his smiling face down to her own. 'You absurd man!' she said lovingly. 'Metaphors are my department. Theoretical pigs are certainly my department.'

They slept until half past two and then Andrew crept downstairs and made a pot of strong lapsang souchong tea with slabs of rich fruit cake. 'Wakey wakey,' he called to Louise, putting the tray on the bed. 'I want to turn some hay. You can come and learn how to drive a tractor.'

'I've got to go home sometime,' Louise said. 'I need my night things and I should check my ansaphone. I've got to shop for tomorrow. Miriam's coming to stay with me tomorrow night.'

'She can stay here,' Andrew said. 'We'll go and fetch your things on the way to the Bush if you like this evening. Phone her and tell her to come here.'

'She might not want to stay with you,' Louise pointed out, assuming a voice of chilly reproof. 'She was looking forward to staying with me in a caring and secure women-only environment.'

He looked thoughtful for a moment; but then – 'Nah,' he said. 'Better food here. Better company, nicer house, cosier rooms, an all-night rave and theoretical pigs! What more could a woman ask?'

'I'll phone her,' Louise said.

He passed her the telephone from the bedside table, and went across the landing to the bathroom. Louise could hear him singing as he splashed the water into the basin and she realised that she had made him happy, and that this was connubial happiness, as she, full of sceptical disbelief, had read of only in novels. She was making him happy, and his happiness made her happy, which in turn . . . she shook her head in a state of mild wonderment. All these years of waiting and longing for Toby and she had never had any idea that loving a man could be so easy.

She dialled the number of the women's refuge but the line bleeped and did not ring. So she telephoned Miriam at home, ready to put down the receiver if Toby answered.

'Hello?' Miriam said in her most pessimistic voice.

'It's Louise,' Louise said.

'Oh, hi.'

'Are you still coming over tomorrow?'

'Could I come tonight?' Miriam asked. 'The shit has really hit the fan here. I'm leaving Toby. The refuge has been bankrupted and closed. I'm out of a job, I'm out of my marriage. I've finished here.'

'Oh God,' Louise said. 'What's happened between you and Toby?'

'He's been seeing another woman,' Miriam said bitterly. 'For nine years. Nearly all of our married life. He's never been completely committed to me.'

'How d'you know?' Louise whispered. Guilt invaded her and drowned her new joy.

'He told me,' Miriam said blankly. 'The silly bastard told me this morning. I'd always known he had the occasional fling. And I did too. It was something which we knew about, but something we never discussed. We're adults, Louise, I don't need to know every damn thing he does. But suddenly he spills the whole can of worms at my feet.'

'Why?'

'Because he took it into his stupid head that you were going to tell me that he is a transvestite. He wanted me to know that he's *not* a transvestite – which he'd be really ashamed of. So he tells me he *is* a liar and a committed adulterer. He seemed to think that being a cheat for all of his married life was better than wanting to dress up in frocks.'

'I wouldn't have said anything,' Louise protested weakly.

'I wouldn't have cared if you had!' Miriam exclaimed. 'Bloody hell, Louise, I see worse than that daily. We could have coped with that. He could have borrowed my Laura Ashleys – why should I worry? But what I can't stand is the thought of him lying and lying for all those years, and then telling me, with that soppy little-boy-naughty face of his as if he was proud of himself.'

'Come out now,' Louise said, summoning a desperate courage. 'I have to talk to you.'

'I'll come as soon as I can. I've been packing all morning. I've got another hour's work and then I'll come. I'll be out with you at about nine.'

'I'm not at my cottage,' Louise said cautiously. 'I'm up at the farm.'

There was a brief silence as Miriam gathered information, collated it, and came up with an accurate analysis. 'You lucky beggar. You've scored with the sexy farmer.'

Louise giggled a rich sensual chuckle. 'More or less,' she said. 'Will you come and stay here?'

'Won't I be dreadfully in the way?'

'No,' Louise said. 'Something like a thousand dope-heads and a hundred weekend ravers are arriving tomorrow morning. The neighbourhood watch will be here at any moment. And we're surrounded by animals. It's not as if we're romantically alone together for the weekend.'

'I'm on my way,' Miriam said. 'See you at nine.'

Louise and Andrew drove down to her cottage as the light faded from the sky and a small sliver of moon rose and hung like an elegant minimalist lantern over the common. Louise went into the cottage and threw a couple of pairs of jeans, some underwear, a couple of sweatshirts, and – after a moment's thought – her silk pyjamas and silk dressing gown into a small suitcase and carried it down to the Land-Rover. There was a brief altercation as Andrew demanded that she bring all her clothes, all her books, all her work papers and indeed her word processor, ansaphone, and printer. Louise refused to bring more than she needed for the weekend. 'Then we'll see,' she said.

Andrew, with a stubborn look which she was beginning to recognise, pointed out that if there was any nonsense on Monday morning he would be within his rights as Rose's heir to move into his half of the cottage, and that he would not hesitate to do so.

'I am not accustomed to being blackmailed,' Louise said sharply.

He scowled at her. 'And I'm not accustomed to being fannied about. I don't like this will-you won't-you stuff, Lou. You said you'd come for the weekend and I want you there with me. I don't want you sloping off every five minutes to come down here.'

Louise felt her temper flare in a way she had not per-

246

mitted since adolescence. 'I do not slope off,' she insisted. 'I will not be arrested and imprisoned by you. We're having a love-affair, a relationship between free and equal adults. We're not going to tie each other down.'

'Of course we're going to tie each other down!' Andrew roared. 'We're in love! We're lovers! Of course we're not free. We're responsible for each other's happiness. What d'you want? To live alone and I come by at the weekend and screw you when my wife isn't watching?'

'Don't shout at me!' Louise shouted.

'Why not?' he demanded, volume undiminished. 'You make me angry!'

'Well, you make me angry!' Louise bellowed back. To her surprise she found she was squared up to him, her fists clenched at her sides, her voice at full pitch. And she was not afraid of him, she was enjoying herself hugely.

'Thank God for that,' he said, his temper deserting him in a moment. 'At least it's not one of these cold-fish reasonable relationships where we each do anything and nobody really cares.'

Louise breathed deeply and felt the wave of adrenaline dying pleasantly away. 'No,' she said. 'It's obviously not one of them.'

She looked into his face. He was smiling at her, his face filled with intense affection.

'So,' he said. 'Did we reach an agreement?'

'I don't want to work this weekend anyway,' Louise decided, casting her mind back to the cause of the quarrel. 'I'll just bring the essays that need marking at once and a book I have to review. Will they serve as sufficient commitment for now?'

His sunny smile was as untroubled as a little cherub.

'Fine. You pack a box. I'll just pop down and see Rose is OK.'

Louise watched him walk down through the orchard and went inside to her study. The red light on her ansaphone winked urgently. She played the message. It was Toby, his voice urgent and whiney.

'Louise, I need to talk to you urgently. Please return this call *without fail*. I also need to talk to Miriam who has done a dreadful thing. Please make sure she calls me. This is *really* urgent. I am at the university all evening since I cannot go home until this is resolved. I am depending on you. You *must* telephone me at once.'

Louise glanced towards the orchard. Andrew's big boots stood neatly beside the step of the caravan. Rose's dog dozed beside them. Louise dialled Toby's departmental office. He picked up the phone on the second ring.

'Toby Summers.'

'It's me.'

'Louise, thank God! I've been waiting for hours for you to call.'

'I only just got in.'

'Is Miriam with you?'

'She's coming out now. She's on her way.'

'I think she's gone absolutely crazy,' Toby said. 'You must talk to her, Louise, and then I'll come out and see her.'

'She sounded very upset,' Louise said cautiously.

'She's gone mad,' Toby cried, forgetting the cardinal rule that madness and women can never be anything more than tangentially connected. 'She's barking. She's stolen my cash card and she's robbed me of an entire month's salary.'

'What?'

'Since last Tuesday and on every single subsequent day, she has taken the maximum of two hundred pounds out of my account,' said Toby, spite making his enunciation dauntingly precise. 'She's emptied my account. I had seven hundred and fifty pounds in there and it's all gone.'

'It's not possible,' Louise said certainly. Toby's and Miriam's sexual standards might be flexible but they had always shown rigorous rectitude over their independent bank accounts.

'I tell you it's gone!' Toby wailed. 'What did she say to you?'

'That the refuge was bankrupt, and that she was unhappy with you.'

Toby moaned. 'The refuge! Oh God, that bloody refuge! She's spent all my money on those hopeless women!'

'Toby!'

'I'm sorry, Louise. I'm sorry! I don't know what I'm saying! I'm dreadfully upset. Also, we had a quarrel. Did she tell you?'

'She said something.'

'I thought you might tell her about the negligee,' Toby said. 'I wanted to clarify things for her.'

'So you told her you'd had an affair for the past nine years.'

'I didn't say who with.'

'Oh, thank you,' Louise said with weighty irony.

'Look,' Toby said. 'We're in crisis. There's no getting away from it, Louise, and you and I have to stand together. We'll tell Miriam we're lovers. She'll agree to let me go, I know she will. You needn't tell her about the gown, it wouldn't make any sense to her. And she can give me my money back. She can have the house if she wants, she can buy me out of my share. I shan't need a place of my own, once I'm living with you. I should have done it years ago. I'll come out now. We'll start our life together now.'

249

'No,' Louise said quickly. 'That's not possible. I'm not even in my cottage. I'm staying up at the farm.'

'My mind's made up,' Toby announced with awful decisiveness. 'I'm coming out at once, Louise. I'll come up to the farm to meet you there.'

'I can't . . .' Louise started.

'You and I are going to be together and we'll get my money back from Miriam. We'll counsel her. We'll help her with this. She's obviously suffering some kind of crisis kleptomania. We owe it to her to help her. I'm on my way. We'll be together now, my darling . . .'

'No!' Louise shrieked, but the telephone clicked and Toby was already gone.

Louise walked slowly to the Land-Rover as Andrew stepped into his boots at Rose's door. Rose came out on the step and waved to Louise. Louise waved back. Even at that distance she could see Rose's triumphant beam. 'Everything all right then, dear?' Rose yelled.

'Yes, thank you,' Louise called back repressively.

'Farmhouse to your liking? Bed comfortable, is it?'

'Yes,' Louise said shortly and got into the Land-Rover and slammed the door. She could still hear Rose's rich wicked chuckle. Then Andrew stepped into the cab and started the engine. 'Everything all right?' he asked. 'You've got everything?'

'Everything,' Louise said. 'But there's a bit of a problem with Toby and Miriam.'

'I should think there was,' Andrew said in a tone of reproof. 'Carrying on as you've all been doing.'

Louise looked him straight in his dark blue eyes. 'That's quite enough of that,' she said firmly.

Andrew pulled his forelock and drove out into the lane. 'Yes'm,' he said subserviently. 'Beg pardon'm.'

'Miriam says she wants to leave him, she's coming out to the farm tonight. I said that would be all right.' Louise shot a quick look at him. 'You said it would be all right?'

He nodded. 'It is.'

'But now Toby says that she's been stealing money out of his bank account, and he's coming out to sort things out.'

'Coming out to the farm?' Andrew asked.

'Yes,' Louise said awkwardly. 'I'm sorry. I told him I was there and he just said he'd come out. He didn't give me a chance to say no.'

'We'd better go down to the Bush then,' Andrew suggested helpfully. 'And stay there till they've sorted themselves out. We could stay at the Bush all night. Give them the place to themselves. Keep out of trouble generally.'

'Oh, no! They're my friends. I have to be there.'

'Seems to me like you've been there a bit too much already.'

Louise laid one finger on his hand as it rested on the gear lever. 'I warned you,' she said. 'That's enough.'

He shot her one of his wicked grins. 'All right, I'm done. But shouldn't they just get on with it on their own? There's an awful lot of talking and talking and talking in your world. Maybe they'll just go to bed and make up.'

Louise shook her head. 'I don't think they'll do that,' she said. 'There's the missing money, and Toby told Miriam he had an affair.'

Andrew pulled up outside the Holly Bush and switched off the engine. Louise tried to open her door but the handle came off in her hand. 'He lives dangerously, that Toby,' Andrew said with respect. He walked around the Land-Rover and opened the door for Louise. 'Rose told me that he's been stealing women's underwear and dressing up in it.'

Louise closed her eyes briefly. 'Please, Andrew, don't ever ever mention that again. I can't bear to even think about it. Rose should not have said anything, least of all to you. It was a distressing and very private thing. She should have treated it in the strictest of confidence.'

'Put you off him, did it?' Andrew noted perceptively. 'Well, I can imagine it would.'

Louise slipped down from the cab seat, her face closed and her lips tight.

'Very disturbing,' Andrew sympathised. 'I can see it would be very disturbing – seeing your lover, all dressed up in flowery knickers!'

Louise walked past him saying nothing, pushed open the door of the pub and went in.

'Worse if it was one of them basque things. Stands to reason. It would put anyone off,' Andrew said irrepressibly as he followed her in. 'Or stockings and suspenders,' he speculated.

There was something like a muted roar of approval as he came in. 'Is it on then?' someone shouted from the end of the bar. 'The party? When are they all coming?'

'You'll never get them in on the roads,' someone else warned. 'There's police patrols all the way up to the A3. And they're putting up the roadblocks in the village again.'

The landlord nodded at Andrew and drew a pint of Theakston's Old Peculier and pushed it towards him. 'Will you have a little drink?' Andrew asked Louise, with wilful provocation. 'A nice sweet sherry, or a Babycham or something?'

'I'll have a pint,' Louise said icily. She hitched herself up on a bar stool and smiled at the landlord. 'A pint of that please.'

'It's Dr Case, isn't it?' he asked. 'Not often we have the pleasure of seeing you in here.'

Louise, who had only ever been into The Olde House at Home, nodded. 'I think I'll be in a bit more often now,' she said. 'And I'll pay for the drinks. How much?'

The landlord looked thoughtful. 'That's £173.30,' he said.

The bar exploded in laughter, Andrew with them. Then he slid his arm around Louise's waist and hugged her tight. 'That's my slate,' he said. 'It's probably my dad's slate too. Put it down on the slate, George, I'll pay you after shearing!'

'So are they coming?' A man pushed past a couple of other drinkers and tapped Andrew on the shoulder. 'Have you heard from them? Is it still on? Or are the roads too bad?'

'I heard yesterday,' Andrew told him. 'They say they'll get through the roadblocks. They say they're coming. They've paid me for the field and they've booked the caterers and they've hired the electrics they need. They're all set. I expect them tomorrow morning.'

There was a ripple of approval and promises called to be up at midday and help the organisers set up tents and a stage. Andrew nodded his thanks and picked up his glass and guided Louise to a seat in the corner.

'So everyone here wants the party?'

'I did tell you so, but Captain Frome thinks otherwise.'

'How will they get through the roadblocks and the police control points?'

Andrew shrugged and drank his beer. 'They'll drive round. There's lots of tracks across the common that they could use. They'll find a way if they want to enough.'

At quarter to nine Louise glanced at her watch. 'I'm sorry, but we have to go. Miriam said she'd be with us at nine.'

Andrew obligingly drained his pint glass. 'So now we go

back home and stick our nose in their private business,' he confirmed.

'Well, it's my business too.'

'Not any more it isn't. Your business is me, your work, and the farm,' Andrew said firmly. 'And in a little while our marriage and the babies.'

He waved goodbye to the landlord and the men at the bar and shook his head at the shouts of derision that his drinking days were over.

'Babies?' Louise asked when they were in the Land-Rover together.

'Well, of course,' Andrew said. 'Don't you think we'd make wonderful babies? Don't you think they'd have a fine childhood, growing up at the farm? Don't you want to have a child of mine?'

Louise hesitated for no more than a moment. 'Yes,' she said. 'Yes to all of it.'

The farmhouse kitchen was warm from the big cream Aga and rich with the smell of cooking meat. Mrs Shaw had left them a big steak pie. Andrew put potatoes on the boil while Louise opened a bottle of wine.

'Will he stay to eat?' Andrew asked, counting potatoes.

'Would you mind very much if he did?'

'He can if he wants,' Andrew said. 'But I'm not having any funny stuff.'

'Funny stuff?'

'Creeping about in the middle of the night and wearing frilly underwear,' Andrew said firmly. 'Any of the funny stuff he does.'

'Are you being deliberately irritating?'

'Yes,' Andrew said smugly.

There was a knock at the door. The collie from his basket in the scullery barked once. Louise opened the kitchen door and then the outer door. Miriam stood on the doorstep with a small overnight bag in her hand. The two women embraced and stepped back to look at each other.

'Oh, Miriam,' Louise said tenderly. Miriam looked worn but defiant, as if she had come to the end of a long hard task.

'No need to ask if *you're* happy,' Miriam said. 'You're glowing.'

Louise lowered her voice. 'I've never felt like this in my life before. We're going to get married. We're going to have babies. I'm going to live here. Oh!' she added as she remembered. 'I've lost my job. I'm out from the summer term.'

'Because of the Creative Anarchy Group for Equality?' Miriam guessed.

Louise nodded. 'Maurice Sinclair was just waiting to get me.'

'You could refuse to go, start a campaign.'

Louise shook her head. 'I'm sick of campaigns and anyway, I don't want to teach,' she confessed. 'I suddenly realised that I don't know enough to teach. I want to read a lot more and think and write before I start teaching again. And then I don't want to teach on any one particular side. I don't want a label. I don't want to be responsible for the feminist viewpoint or anything like that. I just want to read and think and get students to read and think.'

She led the way into the kitchen.

Andrew came from the stove and shook hands very solemnly with Miriam. 'Hello.' He took her bag from her. 'Shall I show you your room?'

'Thank you,' Miriam said. Andrew led the way up the

stairs and ushered Miriam into the room next door to his. It too looked over the common, and as he drew the curtains Miriam could see the stars in bright drifts in the black sky. 'Wonderful night,' she said. 'And so dark! It never gets dark like this in town. And so peaceful!'

'You'll hear owls,' he said. 'And maybe a bark almost like a scream: that's a vixen, nothing to worry about.'

They went downstairs. Louise had poured wine. She gave Miriam a glass. 'Toby's coming out,' she said. 'He insisted. He wants to talk to you.'

'Oh, no.' Miriam turned to Andrew. 'I'm so sorry to inflict all this on you.' She was embarrassed. 'Louise, you should have told me, I'd have stayed in town.'

'I don't mind,' Andrew said agreeably. 'I said to Louise that you could both come. Just as long as he doesn't do any of his . . .'

'Andrew!' Louise interrupted swiftly.

He gave her a warm slow wink. 'Ah,' he said. 'Forgot. Sorry.'

There was a rap at the door. 'That'll be him,' Louise said. She opened the door and let Toby into the room, blinking at the brightness from the dark outside and the warmth and the sudden good smells.

'Hello.' Andrew shook Toby's hand firmly. 'Louise and I are going to be married.'

'What?' Toby shot a swift anguished look at Louise.

'Yes,' Andrew said before anyone could say anything. 'Three weeks' time, at Chichester register office. I'm getting the banns posted on Monday. It *is* very sudden but we've wasted enough time already. Me with the pigs and her –' he broke off with all the tact of a charging Charolais bull. 'With nothing but her work,' he continued. 'We want a proper married life now. Don't we, Louise?'

256

Louise thought of a hundred things to say in the face of Toby's strangled outrage, his goggling eyes glaring into hers. But she could think of nothing better than a swift smile at Andrew. 'Er, yes,' she said.

'But this changes everything!' Toby exclaimed incredulously. 'You never said, Louise. I had no idea.'

'Why should you have?' Andrew asked. 'It's been very sudden for us. We're very happy, aren't we, Louise?'

'Yes,' Louise said monosyllabically.

Miriam gave a muffled snort of laughter and poured herself and Andrew another glass of wine. He shot a brief smile at her.

'There's something I have to tell you, Miriam,' Louise announced determinedly. 'Something private. Shall we go into the sitting room?'

Miriam looked suddenly grave. 'Oh, all right,' she said.

'What about me?' Toby demanded.

Miriam did not even turn her head. 'You can wait,' she said sharply. The two women walked out of the kitchen and Louise closed the sitting-room door behind them.

'There's no need,' Miriam said abruptly. 'You needn't confess. I guessed. It was obvious once I thought about it.'

Louise was too ashamed even to look at her. 'I'm very sorry,' she said. 'I'm sorrier than I can say. I never stopped liking you, loving you. But I couldn't say no. I was really in love with him, Miriam. Truly.'

'I know,' Miriam said. 'I'd be angry with you except that I remember what it was like at the beginning. We both fell in love with him at once, and we wouldn't have been in love with him half as much without the other one egging us on. We were very young, and he was stunning then.'

'I should have told you as soon as it happened. I didn't *plan* it, I didn't intend to deceive you.'

257

'I know you didn't plan it,' Miriam said. 'And to be honest I always sort of knew. I thought we were very grown-up and trendy. We all knew it was going on but we didn't need to spell it out or make a fuss. And it suited me, you know. I can see that now. I liked how it was when we all lived in the same house. Like a commune, very '70s. And I always sort of knew.'

Louise was scarlet-faced and near tears. 'I wouldn't blame you if you hated me.'

Miriam shrugged. 'If the marriage had been real and passionate I would have hated you,' she stated coolly. 'If I had been madly in love with him and *stayed* madly in love with him then I would never have forgiven you. But it wasn't like that, was it? Not even from the start. So you didn't take anything that I wanted badly.'

'I wanted him to leave you,' Louise admitted in a small voice. 'Especially after I moved out here.'

Miriam shrugged miserably. 'Not much sisterhood about, is there?'

Louise dipped her head.

There was a sharp knock on the door. 'I want to make a contribution,' Toby's voice said. 'I want to be part of this discussion.'

Louise and Miriam exchanged a look of instantaneous, shared irritation, turned without another word, and marched shoulder to shoulder back into the kitchen.

'I want to say something,' Toby insisted.

'Much better not,' Andrew advised softly from his place at the Aga where he was watching a saucepan. 'Keep mum and it'll all blow over and we can have our tea in a bit of peace.'

Toby shot him a brief annoyed look and addressed the women. 'You can't go off and talk about this as if I weren't here,' he said. 'These are my relationships you are discussing. I insist on being part of the discussion. I have a contribution to make.'

Andrew shook his head at the folly of the man. 'Contributed plenty already, I'd have thought.'

'I enjoyed the friendship there was between the three of us,' Toby persisted. 'It seemed indivisible to me. I never had any sense of it being wrong. We know from other cultures that many units are made up of a man and two women. I think we intuitively adopted a lifestyle which was honest and appropriate and right for all of us. Polygamy is an honourable tradition and one in which the women are close and supportive; it's a feminist tradition.'

'Oh, really!' Miriam said irritably.

'Oh, Toby!' Louise said reproachfully. She could remember only too well the perverse delight of guilt and fear of being caught.

Andrew drained the potatoes and reached into a drawer for a large wooden masher. He set the saucepan noisily on the table and started mashing with enormous amounts of butter, salt, pepper and creamy milk. Toby eyed these preparations with some disdain. They had not eaten real butter in his house for something like eight years, or full-fat milk, or even real salt.

'That's all in the past,' Toby said, swiftly overriding the women's protest. 'What we need to think about is the future. Louise can't go rushing into an unsuitable marriage on the rebound. Miriam, you can't go dashing off like this. We've been a unit, us three, for nearly ten years, we have to work this through together. There can be no partings without a full mutual consent. We have worked at loving each other. We have to work through our goodbyes.'

'But I don't want to work it through with you,' Louise

said in a strangled voice. 'I've changed. I've changed towards you. It's over, Toby.'

Miriam grinned cruelly. 'And neither do I.'

'I was ready for this change,' Toby swiftly changed tack. 'I knew my relationship with you was waning, Louise. I don't think it has been right for us for some time.' He ignored her gasp of shock and turned to Miriam. 'I think we've been through some kind of cycle,' he said gently and persuasively. 'A cycle of distance and other distractions. I think what we should do now is concentrate on each other, and work towards becoming more intimate. I want to give our relationship and our marriage another try, I want you to be the centre of my life.'

'No.'

'You're upset now,' Toby said understandingly. 'But I'll leave you on your own for this weekend. You think it over.' He smiled at her, his roguish charming smile. 'I've been fooling around, Miriam, I don't deny it. But we're right for each other. We were when we first met. We are still. You know we are.'

Miriam stared at the table and would not look at him.

'I'll go now,' Toby said. 'I want to give you your own space, Miriam. I want to give you a chance to think things through.' He prompted Louise with a nod. 'Talk it over with Louise, she knows how strong our marriage is, and she's made her own decision to move on into the future. She knows we need to be alone together now.' He glared balefully at her. 'Louise has made a choice which leaves us alone together for the first time ever. I am sure she recognises her responsibility for making sure this works for us, at last.'

Louise glanced away.

'I am counting on you, Louise,' Toby said ominously.

'You have been so central to my marriage with Miriam, all these years. I am counting on you now to make the ending of this cycle work for all of us. I know you would not simply walk out and leave your friends, your best friends, to pick up the pieces.' His glance flickered towards Andrew, who was intent on his mashed potatoes. 'Whatever your decision about your future life, you owe us your support.'

He stepped towards the door. Neither woman said anything. Miriam was struggling with a sense of duty and obligation. Louise was completely persuaded that it had all been her fault and that with her out of the way, Miriam and Toby would be free to love each other fully. Andrew Miles was watching him with respect bordering on awe, the potato masher poised in mid-air above the creamy peaks of potato.

'Oh! Just one thing,' Toby added with complete casualness at the door. 'I think there's been some kind of muddle about the bank accounts.'

Miriam turned her face to him with a look of utter innocence.

'My account's been debited,' Toby said. 'Did you take my money by accident?'

'No,' Miriam replied. 'Of course not.'

'It's been taken out on my cash card,' Toby said. 'And my cash card's gone from my desk at home. And nobody knows my pin number except you.'

Miriam rose to her feet, outraged. 'Are you accusing me of theft?'

'No! No!' Toby retreated quickly. 'Just some kind of muddle or some kind of emergency. I thought with the women's centre in trouble, or with you planning to leave you might have ... well, I assumed you had ... well, anyway, Miriam, the money's missing. I've got no more than a fiver to last me for the whole of next month.'

Miriam gave a cry of outrage and rummaged in her handbag and dragged out her wallet. She took all the notes inside and pushed them into Toby's hand. 'There's a hundred quid, give or take,' she cried, choking with rage. 'And that's the last you'll ever have from me. Of course I wouldn't touch your pathetic salary, I'd rather starve than live off you. And of course I won't be coming home to you. You're an adulterous cheat and a liar and I hope whoever has your credit card takes you for every penny you have.' She pushed him for emphasis in the chest and then finally spun him by the shoulders and thrust him out of the door and slammed it behind him.

'And don't come back!' she yelled. 'I don't want you! Louise doesn't want you!'

'Nor me,' Andrew said softly and helpfully. 'I don't want him either. Not even in a frock.'

Brownie the collie dog, unaccustomed to marital rows, jumped out of the basket and gave Toby an admonitory nip on the ankles to move him along. They heard his yelp of pain and fear and his feet scurrying to the outer door, and then they heard it bang, and he was gone.

Miriam leaned back against the door. 'Oh God, I'm sorry,' she said, suddenly deflated. 'Andrew, I am so sorry. You wanted a quiet weekend with Louise and here I am with all this mess.'

Andrew waved the potato masher agreeably at her. 'Don't worry,' he said pleasantly. 'I wanted to meet Louise's friends. And we don't get a lot of entertainment in the country.'

Saturday

LOUISE AND MIRIAM stayed up late talking. Andrew went to bed at eleven, apologising: 'I have to get up early for the pigs.' When Louise crept in beside him at two in the morning he greeted her at once with a sleepy hug and then wrapped his heavy limbs around her until he had her enmeshed in his body. Louise let him enfold her with a sense of complete bliss and slept with a smile on her face.

At five in the morning, wrapped in a thick woollen dressing gown over his nakedness, he woke her with a cup of tea. Louise, after only three hours' sleep, gazed groggily out of the window to where the sun was burning the white mist off the meadows and the pale backs of the Charolais cows were a white archipelago in a sea of cream.

'Whatever time is it?'

'Half eight,' he said comfortably. 'Here, have some tea.'

Louise took the proffered cup and drank it gratefully. 'I feel very sleepy,' she said.

'Why don't you go back to sleep?' he offered generously. 'I'll do the animals. No need for you to wake.'

Louise snuggled back against the pillows and held her arms out to him. 'Do all farmers' wives get spoiled like this?' she asked.

'All of them,' he assured her. 'It's well known. A scandal

in the agribusiness. Are you awake enough for a little, very gentle, cuddle?'

'Oh, yes,' Louise assured him. 'I'm quite awake enough for that.'

Andrew dropped the dressing gown to the floor and slid into the warm bed to kiss her collarbones with particular attention and then the long smooth line of her neck while Louise closed her eyes and let Andrew and the early morning sunlight play on her skin with equal warm tenderness.

It was only when he had left her and she heard him singing tunefully in the shower that she glanced at the bedside clock and saw that it said, not half past eight at all, but a quarter to six. Louise closed her eyes firmly without any sense of guilt and went back to sleep.

She woke for the second time when it was truly quarter to nine and she could smell frying bacon and hear a gentle clatter from the kitchen. Andrew padded up the wooden stairs in his woollen socks and put his head around the bedroom door. 'Breakfast in bed?' he asked. 'Or will milady get up now?'

'I had the strangest dream,' Louise said. 'I dreamed that you woke me up at the crack of dawn and tried to pretend that it was nearly nine.'

Andrew looked at her seriously. 'How odd,' he said. 'But where d'you want your bacon sandwich?'

'I'll come down,' Louise said.

The three of them, Andrew, Louise and Miriam, ate breakfast and drank tea. Andrew's telephone rang intermittently through the meal and he answered it between mouthfuls.

'I thought rural life was supposed to be so peaceful?' Miriam asked.

'This is the party organiser, Stephen Flood,' Andrew said.

'I'd better go down to the village and see if there's any way round the roadblocks. They've got the village cut off but there's a back lane which could be open. I'll take the mobile phone.'

'What time are they due?'

'The crew are due about eleven, and the lads are coming up from the village about midday. The guests will turn up as and when they can get through the police blocks, I suppose. Nothing starts until dusk, about eight anyway.'

'Do you call them guests?' Miriam wondered.

'They're invited, aren't they?' Andrew asked with simple logic. He pocketed his mobile phone, kissed Louise on the top of her head. 'If anyone turns up while I'm gone, call me and let me know. They can start setting up in the lower meadow, you know the one. And they can run power lines from the barn.'

'All right,' Louise said. 'But what if Captain Frome comes, or the police?'

Andrew smiled at her and stepped into his boots at the scullery door. 'Tell them they need to have a warrant to come on to my land,' he said. 'If they don't have a warrant they have to wait outside the yard gate.'

He grinned and went out. They heard him whistle to his dog and then the rattling roar of the Land-Rover engine. Miriam widened her eyes at Louise over the top of her cup of tea. 'He's awfully sure of himself,' she said. 'He's an awfully –' she paused ' – definite man. I suppose you *are* doing the right thing? It's not just rebound from Toby?'

Louise swelled a little with pure female pride. 'Yes, he is awfully sure of himself,' she said. 'And I don't see why not. It's *his* farm, he works it, there's no reason in the world he shouldn't be sure of himself.'

'He's just not much like the other men you've been

around with,' Miriam said cautiously. 'He's not exactly a New Man, is he?'

Louise shook her head. 'Thank God for that,' she said. 'I wouldn't want a macho idiot, of course not. But he is blissfully straightforward, Miriam. He says what he wants and he does what he wants and you know where you are with him, and he never thinks about whether he's looking good, or politically correct, or anything.'

'But what happens if he wants one thing and you want another?' Miriam asked. 'What happens then?'

Louise shrugged. 'We fight it out,' she said simply. 'I've had a taste of that already.'

Miriam's eyes widened. 'You don't think that he might be violent, do you?' she asked. 'If you think that at all, Louise, you must not get involved with him.'

Louise chuckled richly. 'I absolutely know that he'd never hurt me,' she said certainly. 'And I shall have to learn not to murder him.'

Andrew stopped at Louise's cottage on his way down the hill and walked through the orchard to Rose's van. The piles of newspaper and books had grown higher around the wheels, and swathes of bright fabric were now draped over the bonnet.

'What are you doing?' he asked.

'Tidying out,' Rose replied. She had a large box of photographs in her arms. She thrust them towards him. 'Here, you can have these. There's some old ones of the family. Your Mum, and your grandparents. They're labelled on the back. I don't want them any more.'

Andrew received them reluctantly. 'Are you ill?' he asked. Rose was so pale her skin had a yellowish tinge to it, and she looked thinner. She leaned against the doorframe as if she were too tired to stand upright.

'No,' she said. 'I'm old. There is a difference.'

'Why don't you come up to the farm?' Andrew asked. 'I could tow the van up, you could park it in the yard. You could eat with us, you could sleep in the spare room.'

She shook her head. Her hand at her side felt that the hard lump had grown a little bigger. She cupped it tenderly, hidden from sight beneath a violent green smock top. 'No,' she said. 'Houses don't suit me any more. You're a good lad, Andrew. You understand. I want to be here. I chose to be here. And I've got my own way.'

He nodded. 'Telephone me if you change your mind, or if you need help. You'll know how to get into the house, I suppose?'

She nodded. 'She keeps a spare key taped under the windowsill. But I've not taken anything.'

'Go in and phone me if you feel ill or if you want me.'

She gave him a little push. 'Get away with you,' she said. 'With your illness and your needs. I'm not ill and I don't need anything. All I want is a bit of peace and quiet and to get on with my own business.'

Andrew nodded. He turned and went to the pile of broken wood that had been the hurdle gate. He gathered two armfuls and threw them down at the van steps. Rose nodded, but would not thank him.

'You know where to find me,' Andrew said shortly. 'And you know I'd rather have you up at the farm.'

'I know.'

He leaned forward and put his arm around her in a sudden, surprising hug. He felt the thinness of her old bones, as delicate as a sparrow, and the lightness of her body. Rose relaxed in his embrace and when he let her go he saw she was smiling. 'So you're happy,' she stated.

'Yes.'

'She likes the farm, she likes the house?'

'She likes it all.'

'Will you marry?'

'As soon as we can. Three weeks.'

Rose nodded. 'I knew it was right,' she said. 'I'm glad I was here to see it.'

'And help it on the way a bit?' Andrew suggested.

'A bit.'

'I could have got rid of that Toby on my own,' Andrew said defensively. 'There was no need to do whatever you did to him.'

Rose shrugged. 'Just a bit of fun.' Her wrinkled old face puckered into a grin. 'Oh, a lot of fun.' She thrust her hand into a big patch pocket on her scarlet-and-black striped skirt. 'Here,' she said. 'You'd better give him this. It doesn't work any more.'

Into Andrew's hand she thrust Toby's cashpoint card. Andrew took it and looked at Rose.

'You stole this off him?'

'I borrowed it,' she said. 'I had some debts to settle. I wanted to straighten things out. Old debts that needed clearing.'

'How much money did you steal from him?'

'I didn't take any money from him,' she said. 'I took it from the bank, same as he did. All I took from him was the card. But it doesn't work any more.'

'It doesn't work any more because you were taking money out of his account with the bank and now you've taken all his money,' Andrew said crossly. 'And now *he* thinks his wife took it, and *she's* leaving him.'

Rose laughed, a thin guiltless cackle. 'He won't forget me, will he?' she demanded. 'You'd better give it him back, tell him it wasn't that wife of his. Lord! What fools men are!'

'That *is* one way of looking at it,' Andrew said. 'Is all the money gone?'

She nodded. 'I needed it all,' she said. 'He has my newspaper clippings box. It's not my fault if he doesn't know what to do with it. He's still getting it cheap.'

'He may not think so,' Andrew maintained. 'You've shamed him before his mistress and separated him from his wife and stolen all his money. He may think that he's paid a rather high price for collaborating with you on a book.'

Rose giggled. 'I suppose so.'

'I'll look in on you tomorrow,' Andrew said. 'Got enough firewood? Food? Water? I suppose you can always light your stove with ten-pound notes.'

'I'm all right.'

'Will you come up to the party?'

She shook her head. 'I'm busy,' she said. 'Tidying. Don't come tomorrow until midday. But come then.'

'All right,' Andrew said. 'I'll see you at midday tomorrow.'

'Don't be late,' she insisted.

Andrew shot her a suspicious look. 'Are you up to something?'

Rose shook her head. 'I'll have a little job for you that wants doing tomorrow,' she said. 'At midday prompt. That's all.' She leaned forward from the top step and patted his cheek with a gentle hand. 'You're a good lad, I've always had a soft spot for you,' she said tenderly. 'Goodbye.'

* * *

At midday on the dot, the first of the two vans lumbered up the track from the common, honked at the field gate and then pulled into Andrew's field and started unloading. Andrew, Miriam and Louise went down to watch. A couple of cars from Wistley village came up the lane and half a dozen people got out and set to work helping unload the big speakers from the vans and spooling out cables. After them came a lorry with scaffolding for a little stage, and planking, and great rolls of tarpaulin. From the track over the common came a lorry with stage lights and gantries and rigging.

The field was a dry flat meadow two fields distant from the house. Andrew had only just cut the hay and the grass was soft and dry underfoot. The organiser of the rave, in an exquisitely pale purple Armani suit with an earring in his left ear, greeted Andrew as an old friend, and slid an interesting-looking brown envelope containing a large cheque into his hand. A second cheque, as deposit against damages, followed the first. Andrew tucked them carefully in his shirt pocket and winked at Louise.

'This is Dr Louise Case and Ms Miriam Carpenter – Steve Flood.' He leaned towards Louise. 'Here's our honeymoon money,' he whispered.

Steve shook hands with a warm dry grip. 'Pleased to meeetcha,' he said. His accent was Buxton, Derbyshire, come Brixton, come Bronx, but his smile was authentic. 'We are going to *party*!' He turned to Andrew. 'Had much trouble locally?'

Andrew shook his head. 'Nothing to mention,' he said. 'Did you get through all right?'

'We followed the map you sent us. We pulled off the road last night and they thought we was camping up. They didn't bother to watch us through the night so we just went quietly round by the lanes and then up over the common.'

'You drove over the common?' Louise asked.

Steve nodded. 'It was bumpy but it was OK.'

Louise looked at Andrew. 'I thought it was only foot-paths. Pedestrians only.'

He smiled. 'There's a coffin path,' he said. 'A coffin path is one where a coffin has once been taken. That establishes the right of a road to be used for wheeled vehicles and a procession, a funeral procession, not more than once a year. Not a lot of people know that.'

'Because I doubt it's true,' Miriam said promptly.

Andrew's smile was particularly sweet. 'Twenty years ago we used to have harness racing on the common,' he said. 'The gypsies would come and race their trotting ponies. Fifty years ago they had a big horse-fair after every harvest, people would come from miles around and stay for a week. Two hundred years ago it was common land with common rights for the Wistley villagers and no-one owned it at all – it belonged to the village to use as we wished. I don't see how it can suddenly become private land where you're only allowed to walk on a footpath.'

'Power to the people,' Steve said absently, taking a thread off his Armani suit. 'Power to the people right now.'

Andrew chuckled suddenly and turned away. 'You can run those electric cables into my barn. There's a row of points up on the wall where I do the shearing. Is there anything else you need?'

Steve shook his immaculately cropped head. 'You're OK,' he said. 'We'll just get this rigged.' He took off the exquisite jacket and laid it reverently on the seat of the lorry and then strode off across the field to where the crew were laying out scaffolding poles and planking in orderly lines and bolting pieces together.

'I want to turn some hay,' Andrew said, squinting up at

271

the sky. 'Will you feed the hens and fetch the eggs, Louise?'

'And the pigs,' Louise reminded him.

He quickly caught her to him and kissed her. 'Don't ever forget the pigs.'

The stage and the lights grew and grew until by four o'clock there was a recognisable building, anchored firmly to the ground by wire hawsers and tent pegs. They started to stretch the tarpaulin over the lights and sound equipment. All the time there was a constant stream of traffic coming up the lane, and sometimes entering the farm from the little track which stretched out to the common. Steve Flood had set up two mini ticket offices at the two gates into the field. Louise and Andrew took the collie and with him yapping and snapping at the big animals' heels, moved the Charolais cows again so that a gate to the common could be safely left open. The first-comers selected the best sites, deafeningly close to the speakers, and the later vans and trucks and little commercial lorries set up in a wide circle around the stage.

Then the police arrived. Andrew went out to the yard gate to greet them, an inspector flanked by a couple of sergeants with two cars of uniformed officers behind him, and, Andrew imagined, a hundred other officers checking their riot gear at the police headquarters.

'What can I do for you, Inspector?' he asked pleasantly.

'I see you have some trouble here.'

Andrew glanced behind him to the sunlit yard where a small flock of hens and a couple of squat guinea fowl were scratching over the midden heap. 'Trouble? No.'

'I meant there.' The inspector gestured rather irritably to the field where the lighting gantries were experimenting with strobes and lasers and each piercing beam of light was greeted with an ironic cheer from the two hundred or so people who were sitting on the grass or setting up camp.

'No,' Andrew said. 'I have no trouble here. Do *you* have trouble here?'

'I take it you have permission from the relevant authorities? That your papers are in order? That you carry full insurance and that these vehicles are taxed and registered? I take it that there are no illegal drugs or forbidden substances being trafficked on these premises?'

Andrew blinked doltishly. 'I just rented them a field,' he said artlessly. 'They seemed all right to me. Is there any law which says you can't rent a field, have a little party?'

The inspector looked sharply at Andrew's blank bucolic expression. 'Mr Miles, you know perfectly well that you are within your rights to rent out your fields. But I assume that you don't wish to be host to trouble-makers and druggies and hippies. And yes, indeed there *are* laws, specific laws banning impromptu parties such as this one. Laws which I could invoke.'

'If you want to,' Andrew said doubtfully. 'Then you could move them on and they'd be milling all over the county instead of settling down nice and quiet in my hayfield. They're insured, they've paid me. They're just people wanting a good time. You're not going to come wading in and causing a lot of stress and tension?'

'There have been complaints about lorries driven across the common.'

'Well, how d'you expect them to get here when you've blocked off the roads?'

'And about thefts in Wistley.'

'Would that be Mrs Frome's nightdress?'

The inspector looked uncomfortable. 'Theft is theft,' he said shortly.

273

Andrew nodded. 'Well, you can't come in here without a warrant. And a couple of lorries on the common and a missing nightie isn't worth a warrant.'

'I think you're making a big mistake,' the inspector warned ominously.

'Ah, so what?' Andrew exclaimed with sudden impatience. 'I can't go on worrying about Captain Frome's wife's nightdress, and the neighbourhood watch wanting us to win the Best Kept Village award.'

'I hope they leave as quickly as they came, that's all,' the inspector warned. He was nettled that he had not known about the tracks across the common. His map showed dotted tracks of footpaths and a tracery of little bridleways. He had not realised that the lorry carrying the lighting gantry could quietly cruise up the sandy paths between the sprouting heather. 'If they're still here in a month's time you will be coming to us for help, you will be begging for help.'

'Maybe it depends whether the roads are clear,' Andrew said. 'If you block all the roads and move them on from all the sites then they might well want to stay. If they can't get out then they'll *have* to stay.'

The inspector nodded. 'Stay in touch, Mr Miles,' he said grudgingly. 'We'll be very near, and if I have any information that there is drug trading here then I certainly will have that warrant and my men will certainly move in.'

Andrew nodded and leaned on the gate, watching while the inspector went back to his car, reversed up the drive to the lane, and then drove away.

'Bother?' Steve asked, appearing at Andrew's elbow.

Andrew shook his head. 'No trouble as long as there are no drugs going round.'

Steve shrugged. 'Bound to be some, but I've got a good

crew on the gates. There'll be no big dealers here at any rate.'

Andrew nodded. 'I'll have my dinner then. D'you want some?'

'The catering truck will be along soon,' Steve said. 'I'll wait.'

In the end, Andrew was right; and Louise, Captain Frome and the unhappy inspector were all wrong. It was a big party, there were about two thousand people dancing under the brilliant lights, reeling from the noise of the massive speakers. At the back of the vans there was a little trading in forbidden substances but no big dealers had arrived. A couple of young men, driving an elegant Mercedes, were recognised by the crew on the gates and turned away. A wide range of vehicles were parked in the fields from yuppie BMWs to beat-up 2CV vans, and people were camping in anything from deluxe explorer tents to Indian blankets.

Louise and Andrew danced under the bright lights and admired the laser show playing against the darkening sky. Louise had someone read the tarot cards for her and was promised a major change in her life and an opportunity for growth. Andrew paid a crystal healer to cure his backache brought on by years of heaving bales of hay. The woman rubbed him all over with aromatic oils and then walked barefooted up his spine. She then sold him a remarkably expensive crystal to keep in his pocket. He came out of her trailer looking flushed and guilty. Louise accused him of enjoying his treatment far too much for a nearly married man. They ate hot dogs, squashy and sweet, from the catering truck and drank organic mixtures of lemonade and cochineal which they were assured would enhance the alpha rhythms of the brain. Andrew put his hand in his pocket and brought out a handful of small green tablets. 'D'you want to try one of these?'

Louise recoiled. 'Andrew, for God's sake what are they?'

In the darkness his grin was mischievous. 'Cattle feed pellets,' he said. 'I could be making my fortune if I weren't an honest man.'

Miriam danced alone, circling her own bobbing shadow, sometimes hand-linked with others, sometimes in her own space. Her hair, loosed from the ugly rubber band, flowed around her shoulders. Earlier in the day she had gone into one of the vans and had her hair plaited with ribbons and beads into half a dozen locks with little bells tied on the end, so that when she shook her head there was a faint tinkling noise. She had thrown off her jacket and her baggy shirt flowed loose over her jeans. She was barefoot, dancing barefoot in the grass, with a strange concentration.

Louise went up to her and touched her elbow. 'Miriam, are you all right?'

Miriam smiled at her and she was the old reckless irresponsible Miriam of their undergraduate days. 'I'm dancing it off,' she said.

'Dancing it off? What d'you mean?'

'I'm dancing off the boredom and the anxiety. I'm dancing off the responsibility and trying to get things right. I'm dancing off my dreary bloody husband and being politically correct. I'm going to be free.'

'Have you taken anything?' Louise asked like an anxious mother, thinking of cattle feed supplement and lemonade and cochineal.

'Yes,' Miriam said and smiled her wide larky grin. 'I've taken my life into my own hands. I'm going to be free.'

Sunday

THERE WAS NO POINT in going to bed to sleep, the drum beats and the bass pulsed too loud and too deep, and the laser lights stabbed the sky almost as far as the stars, paling the moon and puncturing the blackness. But Louise and Andrew went up to their bedroom at about four in the morning and made slow leisurely love and then dozed. When they awoke it was golden and morning and the party had wound down to a quieter reflective mood. The catering truck was serving bacon sandwiches and hot coffee; many people were sprawled out on the soft grass, warmed by the sun, dozing. Miriam was in the corner of the field, resting against the gate in a nest of blankets. Her eyes were closed, she was fast asleep and she looked more contented and serene than Louise had seen for years. The DJ on the little platform was nodding over the turntables and playing '60s hits. Louise smiled to hear The Flowerpot Men singing 'Let's go to San Francisco' out into the blue horizon of Wistley common. She realised that she did not want to go to San Francisco, nor back to the '60s. For the first time in her adult life she wished to be nowhere but here and now.

Andrew checked his watch. 'Morning chores,' he said. 'And I promised I'd go and see Rose at midday.'

'I'll come with you,' Louise said. 'I need some things from my cottage.'

He slid his arm around her waist. 'Inseparable, eh? Rather nice, isn't it?'

Louise leaned back into the firm warmth of his shoulder. 'Yes.'

Andrew fed the cows and checked the sheep while Louise stirred up a disgusting pailful of mix for the hens consisting of garbage and hot water. They recognised her now and came running, scolding and clucking, when she came out into the yard. Louise led the way to their coop and poured the mix into the long low troughs. She went outside and opened the little flap doors to the nesting boxes and put a cautious hand into the warm straw to bring out the eggs and put them into the pail. She jumped back in fright when she touched a hen, determinedly sitting, blind and deaf to the temptation of the feeding trough, obsessed with maternity. The hen stared at Louise with stubborn yellow-rimmed eyes. 'There, there,' Louise said uncertainly, reaching a hand towards her. The head turned like lightning and stabbed at her with open beak. Louise whipped her hand out of the way and glared at the hen, who glared back with quite as much resolve. The contest of wills lasted only a moment. 'Oh, hatch the damn things then,' Louise said.

She carried the pail carefully inside, and stacked the new eggs on the correct shelf in the scullery. Later in the day she would box them for Andrew to take to the shop. The cracked ones she dropped into the big enamel bowl for the dog's dinner. Brownie the collie watched her with alert eyes and grinned his broad grin as if to persuade her to give them to him at once.

Mrs Shaw was in the house hoovering. Louise went in, put the kettle on and sat to drink her coffee, looking out over the fields towards the common. She could see Andrew's tractor driving up and down the rows of cut hay, the tines of the rake turning the windrows so the hay dried in the warm wind. She smiled at the thought of him, high in the cab, with the upper-class modulated voice coming over his Walkman: 'Emma Woodhouse, handsome, clever, and rich, with a comfortable home and happy disposition, seemed to unite some of the best blessings of existence; and had lived nearly twenty-one years in the world with very little to distress or vex her . . .'

In the nearer fields the sheep and lambs seemed unperturbed by the men pulling down the stage and folding the billowing canvas. The lambs jumped about, playing in sudden races and then stopping on all four feet and leaping in the air. On the field of the rave, Steve's crew were pacing the perimeter with large black rubbish sacks picking up every scrap of litter. Louise watched them with what she realised was a proprietary air. She wanted no litter left on her fields. She wanted no damage to her farm.

The little tractor pulled in to the side of the field and Andrew jumped down from the cab and started walking towards the farm. Louise poured another cup of coffee and set out the biscuit tin. She heard the outer door open and close and Andrew shuck off his Wellington boots with a gentle word to his dog before he came in.

'Coffee?' she asked, pushing his mug towards his place.

He took it with a nod of thanks and a handful of biscuits. He ate the biscuits quickly and gulped down the coffee. 'Ready to go down to the cottage?' he asked.

Louise nodded.

'We'll take the tractor and the trailer down later and you can pick up all your things,' he said.

Louise smiled at him. 'You are the most persistent man

I know. I haven't decided what I want to do with the cottage yet. I won't decide any quicker for you insisting on having my furniture here.'

'But it's such nice furniture. I've had my eye on it from the start. It's all I ever wanted really.'

'Don't rush me,' Louise warned.

'But we are going to marry,' Andrew reminded her. 'I will go and post the banns tomorrow. You'll come into Chichester too and we can buy a ring. I'll take you somewhere posh for dinner if you like. And later we could have an engagement party.'

'It is awfully quick,' Louise said.

Andrew stopped teasing with disconcerting speed. 'If you're not sure you should tell me now. If you don't want me . . .' He let the sentence hang in the air.

Louise shook her head. 'I'm sure,' she said. 'I'm scared and I'm amazed at what I'm doing, and I'm full of doubt and anxiety about it. But I'm surer than I've ever been of anything that I want to live here with you.'

Andrew took up her hand from the table and kissed it. 'Good,' he said. 'Nothing comes with guarantees, but I'll quarrel more comfortably with you if I know we're married. I wouldn't be able to settle with you otherwise.'

'You want to be married so we can quarrel?'

He frowned as he tried to puzzle out what he meant. 'I want to know that you're here to stay,' he said eventually. 'I want to teach you about farming, I want you to teach me about books. I want us to be able to quarrel and know that it's not the end of everything. I want you to be able to march out of the house in a temper and yet me know that you'll come back. I want us to be . . . bespoke.'

'You're awfully old-fashioned,' Louise said happily.

'And then there's the children,' he went on.

'All right,' Louise said. 'I'm convinced.'

Andrew glanced at the clock. 'I have to go and see Rose, I promised I'd be on time.'

'What's she planning now? It's not like her to run a tight schedule.'

Andrew smiled. 'I wouldn't know. She's a law to herself.'

They went out into the yard and Louise held the gate open for the Land-Rover. Two weary policemen straightened up in their patrol car and fixed them with a suspicious stare. 'I hope they don't stop me,' Andrew said. 'There's a thousand things wrong with this van.'

He drove with elaborate care down the lane towards Louise's cottage. In the little wood on the right-hand side the foxgloves were showing purple tips on the proud spikes of green and the rhododendrons echoed the colour with their buds. Louise rested her hand on Andrew's shoulder and knew herself to be content.

He turned into the drive and switched the engine off. He walked around to Louise's side and freed her from the stuck door. They went together down the path to the little van. Rose's tidying out had continued in their absence. All around the van were heaped boxes of papers and bright material. There was a thin sharp smell of petrol. There was no smoke showing from the chimney, the dog was tied to the steps in his usual place, but he did not sit up at the sound of their footsteps. His feathery tail stirred in the grass and daisies but his head drooped and his ears stayed down.

Andrew stepped out of his Wellington boots at the foot of the steps and tapped on the door. There was no reply. He made a sudden exclamation and stepped back and pulled out from under the van a red can of diesel. Then, without a word to Louise, he put his shoulder to the door and pushed it inwards. The van rocked as Andrew fell inside. Louise waited on the bottom step, looking in.

Rose was lying on her back in her little bunk bed, gloriously arrayed at last in the scarlet chiffon negligee. Her eyes were closed, her hair washed and brushed gleamed white and smooth on the meticulously clean embroidered pillow slip. Her face was serene, her mouth slightly smiling. She looked like a virtuous old woman deeply asleep after a day of good deeds. Only the extreme whiteness of her skin and the blueness around her mouth and eyelids showed that she was dead. On her pillow was an envelope addressed to Andrew.

The caravan was immaculate. Everything that could burn had been taken outside and soaked in diesel. Everything else had been thrown away during Rose's great spring clean. Nothing was left inside the van at all except the little bunk bed, as small as a child's bed, and the pure white linen sheets which Rose had been saving for this occasion.

Andrew took up the envelope, then he stepped forward and kissed both her cold cheeks. It seemed impossible that Rose, so infuriating, so vital, should lie so still and her skin should be icy cold. 'Goodbye, Rose,' Andrew said softly. 'I'll do it as you wanted.'

He turned and came to the doorway. Louise stepped back to let him out and he shut the door gently behind him.

'Go up to the house,' he said quietly to Louise. 'I have things to do here.'

'Is she dead?'

'Yes.'

'Was she really ill, then?'

'Yes.'

Louise put her hand to her mouth. 'I thought she was pretending. I was horrible to her. I accused her of faking it.'

282

Andrew shook his head. 'She was an old rogue. Some-times she was pretending, sometimes she was telling the truth. Sometimes she didn't know herself where the lies began and truth ended. She didn't think you were horrible. She had you picked out as a wife for me. She told me to court you. She thought she'd done a good job bringing us together and she was pleased with herself when you came to me. If she'd wanted anything from you she'd have told you; and if you'd refused her she would have taken it anyway. You don't need to feel guilty.'

'I'll telephone for the doctor,' Louise offered. 'He'll have to come out to write the death certificate.'

Andrew shook his head. 'We'll do this as she wanted,' he said firmly. 'You go into the house and fetch the things you wanted or make yourself a cup of coffee or something. Leave me with her.'

Louise put a hand on his arm. 'I'm sorry. You loved her.'

'Yes,' Andrew said.

Louise went to the window of her study, where she had first seen Rose's van just eleven days ago. Andrew was standing outside the van, his cap stuffed in his pocket, reading Rose's letter. When he had read it through he folded it carefully and tucked it inside his jacket. He untied Rose's dog and led him on the string to the Land-Rover and ordered him to jump into the open back. The dog, tail between his legs and head down, did as he was told.

Andrew walked slowly back through the orchard to Rose's van, and took up the red can of diesel fuel. He went up the steps and into the van. Louise watched it rock as he moved around the inside, and then saw him come out, the fuel spilling in a smooth stream from the spout on to the

283

floor. Slowly he walked around the van, soaking the boxes with the clear liquid. Louise put a hand to her cheek. She still thought that the doctor should be called, and an ambulance, and perhaps the police in a case of sudden death. But she knew also that Rose had a right to order this final chapter of her life as she wished, that she had spent her whole life living as she pleased and that it would be wrong if Louise's conventional sense of good behaviour spoiled things for Rose at the very end. Besides, Andrew had given Rose a promise, and would accept no interference.

When the can was empty he stepped well back from the van and checked the overhead boughs of the apple trees and the prevailing light southerly wind. Then he went to the Land-Rover and fetched matches from the cab. Carefully and without haste he lit and tossed half a dozen matches into the nearest two boxes. They ignited with a soft explosive blast which shot flames up into the air, blistering the old blue paint of the van at once. Within moments the other boxes had caught and Louise could not see the van at all for the dancing bright flames and the heat haze which turned it all into a shimmering wall of fire.

A thick cloud of black smoke billowed and seeped through the branches of the apple trees. Louise could hear cracking noises as the metal expanded suddenly in the heat. Andrew stepped back from the fierceness of the blaze, shielding his eyes. There was a hot acrid smell of burning and then a sudden roar as something inside the van went up. The first blast of flames lasted only a few moments but then the van was solidly alight, burning steadily. As Louise watched, the roof which had been patched and repaired with filler and plasterboard collapsed inward in a shower of sparks and a bright plume of flame spurted upwards.

Louise thought of Rose in her hard-won red chiffon gown

going heroically into the afterlife like a Viking chieftain on a burning boat and she felt suddenly freed from anxiety and triumphant. The flames were like a beacon: they showed that a woman could be born into any society at any time and still carve out her own path. She could choose her life and her death. All that was needed was a remorseless individualist determination to run her own life and defy the conventions and the sly damaging punishments that the conventional world can devise. Louise found she was laughing with a wild delight at the thought of the intractable old lady and how the manner of her going – illegal, inconvenient, and joyfully dramatic – suited her life. She opened the study door and walked down the garden path to where Andrew was standing leaning against the gate. She put her hand on his and when he turned to her his eyes were wet; but he too was smiling.

'Quite a blaze,' he said. 'She would have been pleased.'

They stood hand in hand, watching the van burn. The first bright heat of the flames was dying away but the structure of the metal glowed bright red and the inside of the van was burning steadily and hot.

From the lane came the whine of sirens. Andrew sighed at the prospect of imminent trouble. 'She wrote a note to me,' he said. 'She wanted you to have Lloyd George.'

'Lloyd George?'

'The dog.'

'Oh. Did she burn all her papers?'

Andrew nodded. 'That was her right,' he said gently.

'I suppose so,' Louise said regretfully.

'It was her that stole Toby's money, you know.'

'What?'

'She pickpocketed his cash card and memorised the

number. She watched him tap it in when they were shopping. She *said* she didn't understand how it worked, that she was just taking it from the bank. But she took out all the money until it was empty.'

Louise could feel her laughter rising. 'Oh, she was dreadful! She was a wonderfully dreadful woman!'

'She had three hundred pounds of it left. She's sent it to Miriam.'

'To Miriam?'

'In her letter she says for Miriam to buy a mountain bike and go.'

A police car turned in to Louise's gate, followed by another.

'And she left her share of the cottage to the two of us on conditions,' Andrew said.

'I thought you were her heir?'

'She's very determined we should marry. I'll show you the letter tonight. The cottage is left to the two of us on condition we marry.'

Louise nodded. 'She was an awfully bossy old lady.'

Andrew smiled reflectively. 'She was,' he agreed. 'I'm glad to have known her.' He turned towards the police cars. 'This may take me some time. You sort your things out here and go back to the farm. You can make sure that the ravers get off all right. If there's no damage to the fences or gates or anything you can give them their deposit cheque back, it's in the right-hand drawer of the desk in the farm office. If anyone wants to stay on it's eight pounds a night and they can stay till next weekend, but that's all. If I'm in real trouble with the police, I'll phone you. My solicitor's telephone number is in the back of the diary on my desk. You'd better give him a ring anyway, and tell him what has happened.'

Louise clutched hold of Andrew's sleeve. 'Will they charge you with something?'

Andrew grinned and shrugged. 'Well, I'm not their favourite responsible citizen at the moment. But it's not a hanging offence.'

He gave Louise a quick kiss and a hug and then turned and walked up towards the police cars, pulling on his cap as he went. Behind him the fire burned dully as the last remnants of Rose's treasures went up in a defiant plume of grey smoke with her.

At the farm Miriam was eating lunch in the kitchen when Louise returned with a despondent dog on the end of a piece of string. 'Mrs Shaw left the most wonderful salad,' she said, then she stopped as she saw Louise's face. 'What's happened?'

'Rose is dead,' Louise replied. She sat down at the table. Lloyd George immediately sat under the table and rested his warm chin on her feet. 'She died overnight. She had asked Andrew to go down there at midday today. She knew she would be dead. She left him a letter telling him to burn her body and her van. She left me her dog. She left you three hundred pounds to buy a mountain bike.'

A slow smile spread across Miriam's astounded face. 'She was a wonderful woman,' she said. 'And I'll damn well do it too. It was her who put the idea of running away in my mind in the first place. She told me to change myself before I tried to change other people. I wonder where she got three hundred pounds from?'

'I don't know,' Louise said, suddenly cowardly. 'But it's yours now.'

'Where's Andrew?'

'The police took him off. I think it's all probably dreadfully illegal. He told me to phone his solicitor and tell him what's happening.'

'But the rave organisers are leaving, they need their cheque back and they wanted to see him.'

'I'll deal with them,' Louise said, unconscious of her quiet confidence. 'I'll just go and phone Andrew's lawyer. I don't want him clapped up in irons all day.'

Miriam blinked in surprise as this new, assertive Louise went through to the farm office, made herself comfortable at the desk, and telephoned Andrew's lawyer with a succinct account of Rose's death and funeral pyre. Then she went out into the field with Steve and checked the fences and the gates and the absence of any litter and damage, and returned him his cheque. 'I wanted to see the boss, to make a booking for next year, if he's agreeable,' Steve said.

Louise nodded. 'You can deal with me. We'd be happy to see you back here again. About the same time of year, when we've cut the hay crop. We'll call it a provisional booking, I'll confirm with you in writing later.'

'OK. Same money?'

Louise shook her head. 'There'll be a fifteen per cent surcharge next year,' she said firmly. 'If we're going to make it an annual event then it has to go up in price annually. The pigs need feeding, you know.'

Steve put out his hand. 'Done.'

'Twenty per cent deposit to pay when you confirm the booking,' Louise said.

Steve grinned at her. 'So you're the new business manager.'

Louise smiled. 'Yes,' she said simply.

Steve waved the big stage truck out of the farm gate and

into the lane, and then got behind the wheel of his BMW. 'See you next year,' he said. 'It was a great party.'

'We enjoyed it too!' Louise called. 'Next year.'

The little convoy turned out of the field into the lane followed by a couple of the ramshackle vans. No-one had stayed behind and only the stamped-down grass of the dancing area showed that they had been there at all. Louise looked across the hayfield to the field near the common where the Charolais cows were grazing, and to the fields next door where the sheep were safe. Andrew's tractor was where he had left it in the hayfield. Louise strolled down the meadow towards it. She felt like trying a spot of haymaking.

The police held Andrew long enough to irritate him but then released him without bringing any charges. Rose had explained her illness and her desire for a traditional Romany funeral in her letter. She had consulted the GP at Wistley's weekly clinic and when the police inspector telephoned, he confirmed that she had cancer. She had refused all treatment but had accepted a large prescription for painkillers. In her letter to Andrew she said that she had been saving all her painkillers in recent months and had washed them down with a truly excellent bottle of port late on Saturday night. The police objected very strongly to Andrew running his own private crematorium, but the inspector decided that the charge of setting fire to a van and to the body of an old lady was too bizarre for the magistrates' court to sort out. He warned Andrew that he must never never do it again and Andrew pointed out, rather ungraciously, that he was hardly likely to feel the need.

They released him at six o'clock that evening after taking two full statements in triplicate. Andrew telephoned Louise from the public call box outside the police station at Chichester.

'I was starting to wonder if you were OK.'

'I'm fine,' he said. 'Can you come down and pick me up?'

'I'll take you out to dinner,' Louise offered.

'Done,' he said. 'Bring a clean shirt for me if you want to go anywhere in the least respectable. I smell like a cow-punching arsonist.'

'Sexy beast,' Louise said and rang off.

She went upstairs to their bedroom and took a clean blue cotton shirt from the wardrobe and held it for a moment against her cheek, looking down the valley of Wistley common. The sun was setting and the common was golden in the muted light. On her left a little rind of moon was rising, a pale gold. The fields were quiet, the cows on the distant field gathered in the far corner. The hay had been turned, the last three windrows hopelessly zig-zag from Louise's unpractised steering. The sheep were lying down like little puffs of cotton wool in the twilight. The pigs were hypothetical as ever.

Louise looked at the landscape which over the next years would become as familiar and as dear as Andrew's face, and knew herself to be deeply happy.

Then she ran down the stairs and out to the yard to fetch Andrew home.

Autumn

D.H. LAWRENCE, *THE VIRGIN AND THE GYPSY*,
A RECONSIDERATION.

For too many years feminist criticism has focused on Lawrence's obsession with male sexuality and his neglect of heroines who too often are mere mirrors for the dominant male ego. These represent genuine difficulties, especially for the feminist reader, but if we allow Lawrence this bias, we see that he has much to teach us about male-female relationships, especially at this stage of our development.

The demand by feminists for the so-called 'New Man' who should equal the woman in his caring and emotional nature has produced serious consequences. One of these is the backlash from men who cannot or will not conform to this new stereotype of behaviour, men who are inadequate or psychologically unfit. But there are also men, of a different sort, who cannot conform to the weakness and femininity of the 'New Man'. These are men who prize their assertiveness, their right to protect and defend their family, who insist on their difference from women – not their sameness.

As feminists we should understand this. We have been insisting for years on the right to explore our femininity despite the stereotypical images of women in our patriarchal culture. Now men too are saying that the patriarchal culture imposes stereotypes on them and they have to explore their gender's history and their personal psychology to find their true nature. What this true nature is likely to be it is still too early to say. But it will be neither the macho image of maleness that twentieth-century western culture promotes, nor the weak effeminacy of the worst of the 'New Man'.

Men's view of themselves is in a powerful and exciting period of change and, just as we have demanded their support in our experiments with taking our power, we owe them a reciprocal support as they explore their own genuine power, which is quite different from the exploitive and abusive power offered them by patriarchy. There are a very few men [Louise wrote smugly] who by virtue of circumstance and personal psychology have managed to be relatively untouched by the cruelty of unequal relationships between the sexes and can thus give themselves in a relationship with passion and with honesty, with sensitivity and with pride. When a woman is lucky enough to be loved by a man such as this – as the Virgin of the story is loved by the Gypsy, as Constance Chatterley is by Mellors – she knows that she has the foundation of a relationship which is not only deeply exciting, but which shows her the way forward and away from the battle between the sexes. The battle was always sited on false positions, posturing about stereotypes of behaviour. The reality is the wonderful erotic and romantic differences between genuinely enlightened men and women.

Louise stopped typing and gazed out of the window. Her new study in the farmhouse spare bedroom looked south over her fields and towards the common. It was early autumn. Andrew was ploughing a field for winter wheat and seagulls flew up like a plume of silver white smoke from behind the plough. The common beyond the little red tractor was in shades of ochre, bronze, russet and sepia. The dryer higher patches of grass were a pale bleached yellow and where the autumn bracken lay thick, a foxy auburn colour predominated.

Louise sat back, resting her feet on Rose's mongrel dog Lloyd George, at his customary place under her desk. She re-read what she had written, unaware as usual that she had completely failed to comment on Lawrence but had successfully described her own emotional state.

She rested a hand on the swell of her belly and felt for the first time the extraordinary sensation of the baby moving inside her. At once the little shape she had seen on the hospital scanner, the little patter of heartbeats, meant something more: the start of a new life, an individual taking shape, an heir for the farm, a child for Andrew and Louise.

Lawrence, the patriarchy, the evolution of new sexual relationships all receded into the background. Louise sat very still, her eyes on the sweet slopes of the Sussex hills, a little smile on her face, waiting for their baby to move again.

THE END

A Respectable Trade

Philippa Gregory

'The great roar and sweep of history is successfully braided into the intimate daily detail of this compelling and intelligent book'　PENNY PERRICK, *The Times*

Bristol in 1787 is booming, a city where power beckons those who dare to take risks. Josiah Cole, a small dockside trader, is prepared to gamble everything to join the big players of the city. But he needs capital and a well-connected wife.

Marriage to Frances Scott is a mutually convenient solution. Trading her social contacts for Josiah's protection, Frances finds her life and fortune dependent upon the respectable trade of sugar, rum and slaves.

Into her new world comes Mehuru, once a priest in the ancient African kingdom of Yoruba. From opposite ends of the earth, despite the enmity of slavery, Mehuru and Frances confront each other and their need for love and liberty.

'Filled with authenticity.'　*Today*

ISBN 0 00 647337 7

Fallen Skies

Philippa Gregory

'It is both uncompromising and brave'
ELIZABETH BUCHAN, *Daily Telegraph*

Lily Valance wants to forget the war. She's determined to enjoy the world of the 1920s, with its music, singing, laughter and pleasure. When she meets Captain Stephen Winters, a decorated hero back from the Front, she's drawn to his wealth and status. In Lily, he sees his salvation – from the past, from the nightmares, from the guilt at surviving where so many were lost.

But it's a dream that cannot last. Lily has no intention of leaving her singing career. The hidden tensions behind the respectable facade of the Winters household come to a head. Stephen's nightmares merge ever closer with reality and the truth of what took place in the mud and darkness brings him and all who love him to a terrible reckoning . . .

'Superbly crafted . . . a fine book.'   *Daily Mail*

ISBN 0 00 647336 9